The Pearls of Yesterday

L S RYDDE

INCLUDAS
Publishing est. 2013.

ISBN 978-0-9861927-2-2 (Paperback Edition)

ISBN 978-1-949983-10-4 (Hardcover Edition)

ISBN 978-1-949983-09-8 (Ebook Edition)

Printed and bound in the United States of America

First Printing, 2022

10 9 8 7 6 5 4 3 2 1 | First Edition

Cover Illustration by Sadie Hutchings

An imprint of INCLUDAS Publishing.®
Eugene, OR
includas.com
Bringing disability diversity and inclusiveness into the book world.®

To my papa, who fought mountains and oceans to find me.

One

THE PRESSURE WILL NOT GET to me. I will not sulk in this rejection.

I sniffle and text him back.

I don't take it personally. I understand you're too busy. Have a good summer.

Time to erase his angelically round face and red hair from my memory.

My heartbeat speeds up. *Everything will work out, right?*

I exchange my phone for pink gloss and apply four layers to my lips. The scent reminds me of strawberry.

I sniffle again and hold back tears.

Being dumped sucks. Not that I was in a relationship. It was more like a two-week arrangement after my sister, Astrid, asked him to be my escort for the ball. Still, the feeling sinks me to the bottom of the ocean.

The phone vibrates on the glass makeup table.

Please say he made a mistake.

It doesn't. It's a group text from my besties, Diana Sevyani and Joey Bijan, saying they're entering my backyard.

I reply with one word.

Coming.

On Mondays, we have breakfast and gossip about the weekend. School ended the first week of June and we have some time before our families travel or take up humanitarian work. Living in a wealthy town isn't all about the millions of dollars, the lavish mansion parties, and stylish fashion shows. We are also expected to do good for the community or rather, for a social status thing. And everything here is about social status. Reporters lurk in every corner to capture the latest scandals even if they're not true.

I personally like the fake philanthropy as an excuse to tutor kids. It lets me spend time with those who have yet to be corrupted by the social status and wealth of this town. I love the innocence of kids. The best is when I tell them about mummies and Ancient Egypt. Their faces suddenly light up.

At the thought of telling Diana and Joey that my third escort quit, I apply an extra layer of lip gloss.

During the private dance lesson yesterday, I asked him one simple question: What makes a real first kiss true? After that, he kept giggling and checking the time. At least I didn't ask him if having a first kiss at the ball would be magical, like with the previous guy who also bailed.

Lesson learned: don't talk to guys about kissing the way I talk about it with the girls.

The one-who-I-refuse-to-remember-his-name seemed excited to be photographed, meet important city officials, and dance in a fancy suit. He once told me he'd do anything to impress the right people so they'd invest in his music speaker business idea. I started planning it for him and he kept saying "Yeah!" a million times.

The ball is our moment to get recognition and business

opportunities from city officials, investors, and past winner spectators. It's basically a big reunion for everyone to catch up. It's where parents force their children to impress the mightily powerful so they can have a wealthy future. Not that I have to be forced to impress anyone, but I do have ulterior motives.

Planning to kiss someone is a full-time job. I've had to figure out who it's going to be, where it's going to be, what the lighting will be, and who will wear what. Let's not forget about the right lip gloss.

I look at my reflection in the mirror. At my brown eyes ornamented with starbursts of yellow around the irises and my long eyelashes which curl up toward bushy, black brows framing my brown skin. Maybe if I looked different, boys would want to kiss me.

I sigh and my elbows slide on the glass table.

This must be a sign. No boy is ever going to give me that romantic first kiss. No matter how hard I try to get to know guys and do what they're interested in—woodwork, technology, video games, music—I never get past the high-five stage. I'm the last sixteen-year-old in my all-girls private school to have virgin lips. Even the new students coming in from middle school this fall have more experience than me—according to the Ashleys. They're the two besties with the same name and birth month, who are also debutantes like Diana and me.

Valerie, my morning nurse, crosses my bedroom from the bathroom. "If there isn't anything other than putting this away, Abby, I'll go."

My room is spacious. It's got a roll-in closet with sensory light features, a king-size bed with silk pillows, and remotes galore. Every door to the outside has a remote or automatic button. I use phone apps to control the doors, lights, curtains, and bed.

The shimmery white wallpaper decorates every corner and window. Both windows are symmetrically even to the distance between the wall, floor, and ceiling.

Even though everything in the house is designed for me to be independent, I have a morning and night nurse to assist me. Valerie takes the mornings and talks my ear off about all the new cake recipes she tests during her spare time. Zaney is the total opposite. She hardly says a word at night. She teaches high school in the daytime, so I can understand not wanting to chat it up with another teen after a full day of them. I'm not much of a talker when I'm tired anyway, so the quietness works for me.

Not including my nurses, our mansion has a staff of six—a chef, two drivers, a maid, a gardener, and an office assistant.

I fix my frizzy hair and reply, "There's nothing else. Thanks."

My smile widens to hide the fact I'm heartbroken. I hope it isn't one of those scary, check-my-teeth smiles. I try harder to make it look genuine.

Valerie sets my pajamas into the white dresser. It gets stuck and she pushes it harder. Papi was going to fix it last year, but he isn't around anymore. Everything seems to remind me of him. We picked everything out in this room. Mother's interior decorator moved and added some things, but I disregard that thought.

I glance at the emerald clock on my nightstand. It reads two minutes before 10:00 a.m.

Punctuality means you have class, as Mother would say. Papi would say that losing track of time means you're living.

Valerie swings her tan backpack over her shoulder. "See you tomorrow at seven," she says, loosening her bun and quick stepping out of my bedroom. Each morning, she helps me get ready. First, getting out of bed, taking a shower or bath—I love the freedom of being in water—and getting dressed. I can do simple things like brushing my teeth and applying mascara. She helps me with the big things like transfers, dressing, and hair drying.

I snag a planner and tell myself four days is more than enough time to find a guy who can be my escort. Technically, the ball isn't until next weekend, but this Friday is the first rehearsal. No sixteen-year-old in the history of Verdan has been escortless to the ball.

My chair's black rhodium joystick is smooth and frictionless. I spin around in the fifty-thousand-dollar, rose-gold and black motorized wheelchair, taking mental notes of the guys I could ask. I lean my head into the headrest and speed off.

If Papi were here, he'd find a way to ease my struggles. He never failed at fixing the broken things in my life.

But he's not here, so I have to figure this out on my own.

Two

THE JUNE RAYS shine down on the silver tables scattered in the backyard. They're surrounded by carnations and Greek statues. It's cool enough to enjoy tea yet hot enough to wear a sundress, which is my favorite combination in the summer.

I tightly grip my teacup.

What if this is fate telling me I will never have that special, real first kiss, and that I've been cursed with having bad luck kissing anyone? While I'm at it, I should accept that I will be dateless for the homecoming and prom dances as a senior this fall. I can't have Joey and Diana be my dates forever. Not to mention, Diana is probably going to take her new boyfriend, Gustavo, and Joey, her hot fling, Talia, to all the school dances.

Then there'll be me, rolling side to side, sighing at all the couples kissing.

Joey wipes her mouth with her hands—hands that look both classical and biker tough wrapped in fashionable fishnet gloves—and grabs her breakfast: pizza.

"I have news!" she says and bites into her food. "I'm getting the nipples pierced tomorrow and I'm letting them party. Plus a new tattoo. Anyone want one?"

Joey has two small tattoos in places her parents would never see—a skull on her right rib cage and a rose with thorns on her hip. She couldn't hide her new haircut last month, though. Her parents—owners of a luxury car business they moved from Persia—took away the car they'd given her. I would have been bummed, but she got a motorcycle from her ex-boyfriend last month before she dumped him for Talia. Joey loves her purple bob too much to change it. Not even for a fancy car. Luxury isn't really her style, anyway. She refused to do the debutante ball even if it meant not being taken seriously or professionally by this town. I still haven't figured out how she's able to make her own rules and decisions.

I met Joey in kindergarten. Our friendship started out with a spelling lesson and a question.

"I'm Valisha, but my nickname is Joey because I like to spell Joey. J-o-e-y. You wanna play with slime?"

Nothing has changed. Except that instead of experimenting with slime, we experiment with body parts. Or more so, she tells us facts about what happens during our periods, why our boobs change size, and that you use over a hundred postural muscles and over thirty facial muscles when you kiss someone. Basically a full face workout.

Diana smiles. "No tattoos for me, but my dress comes in two days. We should try on ours together, Abby. I know I keep asking every month, but I've imagined us trying on our wedding dresses together one day. This is kind of like it." We promised we'd share the ball together since middle school.

I narrow on the red carnation swaying in the breeze. *What if I can't find anyone for the ball?*

"Yo, Abby!" Joey waves her hand in front of my face. "What's with the unibrow look?"

I nod and come up with a close enough response without giving away I was half-paying attention. "Yeah, tell me about what other tattoos you like, and yes, Diana, my ballgown comes tomorrow." Every time she asked to see the design, I promised that I'd show her the final look when I got it perfectly hemmed and measured. She flaunted her twenty different ideas, but I wanted to have the final product before I showed anyone.

Diana giggles. Hers is a quick laugh, sounding like a kid who's farted but won't admit to it. "Are you thinking about a boy?"

The red-haired girl was the first in the group to kiss, hold hands, and fall in love. Multiple times. In seventh grade, we devised a scheme to ensure each of us had dates for the first school dance. After the dance, Joey and I broke off our "relation-ships." Diana gave her crush a kiss on the cheek, and then held hands for an entire month until he wanted to hold hands with the new girl who sported a long ponytail and black nail polish.

"Yeah, *boys.*" I cover my face because she knows me so well.

When someone stole a cookie from my lunch bag in middle school, she knew and gave me hers. She must have intuitive powers because she never fails to hand me a tampon when I need it the most. I swear her purse is a Mary Poppins bag.

Diana stills her twirling spoon in her tea. She's a routine type of person—oatmeal every morning, curled hair on the weekdays, chewing gum only after a dinner date.

Every single one of her outfits is flawless. She enjoys styling up the hand-me-downs from her older sister because they're in season by the time Diana gets them—a perk of living in a home of fashion designers. Her curly red hair falls over her pale bare shoulders, freckles galore.

"Spill the tea," says Joey.

I grab my planner from my lap and slide it onto the table.

I've planned my life for years. My favorite planners are those with full-month views before the days are spread out on each page. Ever since Mother handed me my first one for the first day of first grade, I've planned out every event, class, and party. Back then, I drew pictures of food for meals and pianos for lessons. I don't draw pictures in my planners anymore. On the contrary, I write too much.

"Well, another one quit," I say, the words dragging. "I need a new plan of action. I once read that you must manifest your dreams. Help me make a list of potential guys?" I refuse to accept there's not a single one out there for me.

The pages open to last year's charts I created for my first kiss. I may have touched lips with two guys I really liked—Bentley and Sam—but those were just warm-ups.

My pro and con lists proved the ball was the perfect kissing location. It's better than in a limo, in a pool, at a café, at a carnival, under a tree, under the lights, at a wedding, at a school dance, during a holiday, or at a fancy restaurant.

Because the ball is the best chance for a magical, true first kiss. There's dancing, smiling, cheering, and flowers. Lilies to be exact, and I love lilies.

I flip the page and read the most important element of a first kiss: attractive eyes. The ones that take my breath away with that deep-soul-staring gaze.

A white gown will adorn me and my mother's ancestral pearl necklace will finish the look. Then it'll happen. The guy's lips will meet mine and we'll float up to the clouds. Fireworks will explode in the background and confetti will rain down upon us.

Diana sits up. "There are a lot of other guys. What about Bentley? You really liked him at his birthday party."

Papi introduced me to Bentley at a fundraiser when we were kids. His family owns a wood-making business—tables, chairs, bookshelves . . . wands.

Bentley and I would hang out in the limo when Roosevelt and Mary weren't driving anyone. It's really fun continuing our tradition with chicken wings and apple pies, although now it's pens, notebooks, and wands. Last year we started planning for his business venture and the limo rides became regular meeting rides.

Sometimes he sketches out what his whimsical limo will look like. Anything from the galaxy to giant red stars. Sometimes he practices magic tricks or tells me about the history of playing cards.

I'm so happy he forgave me for our terrible first kiss experience.

For his thirteenth birthday party, I made him a fun heart-shaped bowl of peanuts with cute notes at the bottom. The girls at the party decided everyone should feed each other food and then kiss, all while being in a dark closet.

No one knew anything about anything in middle school. Bentley himself had no idea he was allergic to peanuts. When he leaned in to kiss me, his lips began to swell. Our mouths touched for a second before he muttered that he felt strange and puffy. At first, I thought my kiss ruined him, but after I called his mother from the neighbor's house, she told me he must be allergic.

Luckily, someone else's mother was a nurse and she saved his life.

This is exactly why it's safer to plan my first real romantic kiss.

Joey ruffles. "If at first you don't succeed, you move on. Go ask the hamburger business owner's son. Josh's freakin' cute as balls crawling on walls."

Diana giggles. "Abby needs someone who can dance and remember to stay put, not walk off like Josh does at Halloween parties. We may have dated for a month, but he's a big flake. Gustavo has a friend who works at the bakery and is really good on his feet. I think his name is Khalid."

Diana changes guys more times than Joey changes hairstyles. Diana's parents wanted her to focus on herself for a few months before going on another date, but she falls faster than I can write in my planner. Not that there's anything wrong with that, I just hate when her heartbreaks come even faster. Although she says Gustavo is different.

Diana loves to tell the story of how she would have lunch at the Magenta Diner on Fridays, with her younger sister, Layla, for some sister bonding time. Gustavo waited on her table and then asked her out with a note on her receipt. Her current love story may only be a month-long relationship, but she blushes each time she talks about their dessert dates on his lunch breaks.

"Gustavo can help dance guide your escort, whoever you choose," Diana adds. Face flushed, she fixes her red hair as if he's nearby. She straightens her posture and smooths her yellow polka-dot dress over her knees.

"Thanks, I'll put Khalid and Josh to my list," I say, feeling a little hopeful. "I'm so happy you're happy, Diana."

"My soul is so happy." She gazes at the clear blue sky. "It's like when chlorine and sodium combine to form salt. That kind of happy."

Gustavo is a science major, so it's no surprise she is taking on his interests.

To be in love seems beautiful. To have someone to touch your hand and *want* to touch your body because they want to and not because they have to. I don't even know what that's like. I've gotten so used to doctors, nurses, friends, and family touching me for the purposes of helping me that I'm sure I've become numb to someone's touch. That's why I really want someone's lips to hug mine in a way that says they never want to let go.

I sigh and watch two butterflies dance with each other, wishing my life was that free and lovely with someone. They float over the carnation fence and into the grapevine-decorated Giordani property. The fountain pours out a stream of water next to the carnations where it connects us to them.

A well-suited guy lunges through the backyard door. Hudson Giordani? He's an ant compared to the three-story mansion. Phone in hand, he skips three steps at a time as if he's in a hurry but not. His build is sculpted even in a suit. The smooth slacks shine even from yards away. The Giordanis are the top ten richest families in Verdan thanks to owning wineries in Italy, Spain, and France.

"Is there any chance Hudson would go with me, you think?" I ask. So what if I haven't talked to him for the last four years. "Looks like he's here for the summer?" It's his last summer before college. Most seniors do a Europe trip—the majority left right after their graduation parties. But Hudson never had one, at least according to his social media. Then again, he's not one to post more than twice a year.

Has he thought of me over the years?

A memory flashes in front of me from Hudson's eight birthday party.

My lips graze the teal frosting. "Nope." I put the fork down. "The cake is too sweet. You have pistachio ice cream?" I ask Hudson.

"Yeah!" He hops up from the picnic table and dashes into his home.

"I know it's a big project, but think about my daughter," Papi says to Mr. Giordani.

He shakes his head. "I can't renovate my entire mansion so that it's wheelchair accessible. Just have them play in our back-yard. The patio is enough. I'll put a ramp on the porch."

"What about when she's a teenager? I won't be able to lift a heavy power wheelchair like I can a manual one."

When the neighborhood kids see Hudson with a large cup, pistachio ice cream spilling over the sides, they gasp.

"For you, Your Highness." He hands me the dessert.

The other kids point and ask for ice cream as well.

"Hudson!" his father thunders. "That ice cream is for your mother."

Mr. Giordani snatches the cup from my hands.

"Let the kids have fun," Papi defends us.

"Yeah, let's have fun," Hudson says. He wheels me over to the bounce house. "Can you jump in your chair?"

I laugh. "I'll ask my papi."

I was heartbroken when Hudson dropped me like a flat note and ignored me after years of childhood friendship. His last words to me were "See ya rollin' around."

I cried to Theo, my longest friend, for months, wondering what I did wrong. Secretly though, I wish Hudson and I could reconnect one day.

"Hudson is like royalty," Diana says. "He's never accepted an invitation to the ball, no matter how many girls have asked him."

Joey snags a nearby pen. She holds up her wrist, turns it one way and then the other. Seconds later, she's drawn a rose with thorns. It looks pretty good. "Didn't you want Theo to be your escort last year? He'll do anything for you. Ask him."

Her biceps flex as she crosses her arms, the defined muscles screaming, *I work out more than your boyfriend.* Her brow furrows. She looks mad, but that's her curious face. "Theo's got those superhero arms that can swoop you right up and toss you around the world. A massive kiss with wind in your hair. Kissing a bestie feels safe, no?"

Before I could even consider kissing my best guy friend, I first have to build the courage to ask him. Because last year's plans to ask him left me traumatized.

Every nerve in my system shoots fire in multiple directions. My stomach sinks. I gulp down my tea—that only fuels the flush in my cheeks. The thought of asking Theo does something to me. The pressure on my chest exacerbates my breathing. Tears threaten to fall as I think about what happened ten months ago.

Diana rubs my shoulder. "We'll cheer you on for whoever you want to kiss at the ball."

I clutch the teacup so tight, my hands go numb. "Kissing Theo would be *super* weird." I repeat it louder so I can remind myself *not* to ask him. No matter how desperate I am. "Super weird." I haven't told the girls that I was the reason my papi died last summer. They just think there was an accident at the lake.

"What would be *super* weird?" a deep voice echoes from the side gate.

Theo.

Three

THEO JOGS past the columns and carnations with a black bag in his hand. Wood chips hang off his worn-out mesh shorts, his sneakers are caked with dirt. A T-shirt is stuffed in the waistband at his hip, swinging side to side like a tail. The Winthers family can afford stylish clothes—they have a nice house and they own the aquatic center—but Theo believes in saving and recycling.

Sweat drips over the olive skin of his chest and forehead. At six-foot-four, he towers over me. He's seventeen, going on twenty-seven. Shirtless Theo is a sight I haven't seen in years. Just last year, he was skinny as could be. He's sculpted with muscle now. As if his whole existence just went *boom*, making his glistening abs hard to ignore.

Canoe building and cabin rebuilding will probably do that.

I catch myself and work my gaze to his face. My cheeks warm. I try to see the small boy under a million layers of the hardworking man he's grown into.

Those brown eyes are piercing yet soft at the same time. They remind me of melting chocolate. His nose has a bump at the arch that's barely noticeable because it's the strong, symmetrical jawline that draws the eye.

He pushes his hair over his ears. The strands are long enough to have split ends.

Are the signs pointing to Theo? The butterflies in my stomach send my appetite away. Probably not the good kind, because I'm scared he'd reject me, too. Not to mention that we could never share a romantic kiss, right?

He drops onto the grass with a grunt, breathing heavy.

"Morning runs shouldn't be this hot."

"What happened to *you*?" Joey asks.

Theo falls to his back. "I wanted to drop something off for Abby before heading to the aquatic center for work. Then a damn tire popped." He does a crunch, sitting up effortlessly.

"You can ride my motorcycle," says Joey. "You'd look sexy on it. I can drive back with Diana when her sister picks her up." Diana has been driven by her oldest sister since she was four and refuses to learn to drive. She doesn't want to ruin her routines.

"You can borrow one of our cars," I offer. No one will notice since we have a few—an accessible limo, Mother's car, and a truck. Astrid drives her own gold convertible.

Theo shakes his head. "Imma jog down to the cabin and grab a spare tire."

Without pause he rises to his feet and tugs his shirt from his side. He draws it over his head, his torso flexing. Those muscles moving ever so . . .

Deflection. I need a deflection ASAP. "Wait, did you say you have something for me?" He's never given me gifts other than campfires and canoe rides. One time he glued together pine cones in the shape of a cake and we decorated it together for my fifth birthday.

"Yeah," he says and rests his hand on his hipbone, bag hanging on his pinky.

He lowers to a squat and hands me the item. "Open this when you're ready. It's a gift from your dad I found at the cabin."

The cabin that once belonged to Papi—he built it himself. It's half a mile off our property. Theo agreed to take care of the cabin after his passing. Mother didn't want it—she didn't want to keep Papi's dusty things.

Theo's been practicing renovating the roof and interior because he wants to one day manage his own cabin-building company. Not that Papi didn't keep it up, but everything wears out eventually. Theo prefers hands-on experience over education. I tutored him all last year so he could graduate high school on time and not worry about summer school. Since I was getting ahead in my studies, it was easy to help Theo with his. I mostly took AP classes and he caught up on general eds.

Papi taught Theo how to build his first canoe and tie his first knot when Theo was just four years old. I think he secretly wanted a son, and Theo filled that void. Papi taught me how to knot and design a canoe. After turning ten, though, I wanted to do girly things, following Astrid's life choices of makeup and dresses when she turned thirteen.

Theo's father and mine were best friends but fell apart when Mr. Winthers went through a divorce after cheating with his wife's best friend. Theo didn't understand why his dad spent a lot of time with someone else. That's when Papi stepped up and really took Theo under his wing.

I tear up, then suck it all in. "Okay." I sound like a snowman with a stuffed nose as I hug the bag. "Thanks."

My eyes shut and the air is sucked out of me. The last day with Papi is painful to remember. Death brushes my shoulders.

I'm reminded of last summer where I perfectly planned a picture session overlooking the lake at the edge of the dock only to end up almost drowning.

The sight of Papi's hand reaching for me and Theo laying me on the ground flashes before me. The pinch in my chest comes fast.

I shake the memory. Being the reason he's gone weighs too heavy to bear.

Theo squeezes my shoulder and I'm brought back to life. He's the definition of home.

His sympathetic eyes have me wishing we were kids again, when our biggest worry was not getting my pink manual chair stuck in the grass.

The hummingbirds fly by as I remember.

Laughing under our favorite oak tree, a rush of yellow-and-white butterflies flutter past us in a field.

"Theo! Theo! Theo!" I point to dozens of the insects and push my wheels forward, but the grass makes it too hard to move.

He catches one for me and skips back. "Got one!"

Papi laughs. "One day I'll build you two a butterfly pavilion."

Papi loves building things.

Theo and I grin at each other. "You can do that for Abby," Theo tells him. "I'd want twenty cabins in the woods. When I grow up, I'm going to make friends with bears and take them on mountain expeditions. The stars will guide me and Einstein will tell me about new universe discoveries."

I giggle. "You're going to make friends with bears?"

"Yep, yep, yep! We'll build cabins all over and see the world. I'll travel the rivers, too."

"Okay! Don't forget to pack the North Star."

I spread by arms out, watching Theo free the insect, and say,

"The butterfly fairy just told me we need to roll down the grassy hill!"

Theo was the first person whose shoulder I cried on when Papi passed away last year. He cried, too, but we never talked about what happened—we just sat in silence with each other. I couldn't put words together even if I wanted and Theo couldn't say anything more than a sigh. Our shared grief brought us closer together, and now I can't stop myself from sharing the slightest bad moment with Theo. I'm tempted to say the last escort quit just for his sympathy.

He stands. I watch him. Maybe he's the prince that's been in front of me this whole time.

"Now, what *weird* things are you all talking about?" His hands find a place on his hips.

The girls and I exchange glances. "Nothing," we mutter.

Theo takes a biscotti from the plate on the table and bites down on it; the whole town probably hears the crack. "If I have to tickle it out of you, I will," he says, squeezing my shoulder.

"We were talking about kissing you," Diana blurts out.

Theo steps back and stares at her. "Really? Diana, I had no idea you felt that way about me." He single steps over to her and plants a peck on her cheek. "That's all I can offer."

My own cheeks burn red. Then the heat travels down my neck and chest. All the tingles may be telling me to consider him as an option. His lips do look soft and sweet. His eyes sweeter.

No, I do not like Theo like that. It's only the feeling of desperation coming over me.

Because he's never shown any signs of liking me more than a friend. Then again, Theo's never had girlfriends and only dated a few girls. And that was over a year ago. He would throw one-sentence explanations of the girls he went backpacking and on camping weekend trips with, but he never shared specific details. Maybe that's for the best since I'm a bit jealous he kissed Diana's cheek. I never thought about him with someone else, let alone seeing him show affection to another girl in front of me. It's so unusual, I want to look away but can't.

"It's not her, duh. She's with someone," Joey says, popping a new piece of gum into her mouth.

Theo rubs his chin and circles around her. "If I knew I was your type this whole time, Joey," he says casually.

"I'm having fun with my girlfriend, Talia."

She pushes him close to me. So close, I can see his chest heaving.

We lock eyes, and I don't dare say it's me. A bead of sweat runs down the side of his face. It's as if he already knows why I'm speechless, because his cheeks turn red. I eye his lips and then his broad shoulders.

"Can I volunteer at your aquatic center to get more volunteer hours?" The words speed up and work faster. "You have an event this weekend, right? The summer splash event with the kids, right? I like to plan things out. Right? Right."

"Yep, this Saturday, nine in the morning. My sisters will be there, too," he says. The lake and aquatic center are Theo's second homes. Most days he's up at six in the morning for a sunrise swim.

I wonder if I'll ever touch the waves again. The way I can dip my head under and then jump up. I can float, wasting hours staring at the sky. Almost drowning last summer has kept me at bay, but I do miss the freedom in the water. Will the water give me peace as it caresses me all round?

Or will I have a panic attack and drown? Will I see Papi's face in the water?

Theo drops his arm over my headrest.

My face feels hot. *He's so close.*

"You're really good at your job," I say quick. "Bet you could be really good at being an escort for the ball as well, right?"

A bead of sweat rolls down my scoliosis-curved back.

He chuckles.

"You're funny. But seriously, who *will* escort you? Sorry about the two losers who quit." He whips his phone out. "There's this guy I met backpacking last year and he's here for the summer. Everyone wanted to dance with him at homecoming last year, according to his sister."

Theo scrolls down his phone screen, face scrunching.

My heartbeat pounds in my eardrums as I stare into Theo's rejection. I don't have the guts to say that a third one quit.

What if I had gone through and asked Theo months ago like I planned? Would have he rejected me?

Last summer chokes me up. All the words get stuck in my throat.

He's never asked me or hinted at wanting to be my escort. Guess it's one thing to talk about the ball as kids and pretend to dance, and another to actually go together.

Besides, he's into woods and forest stuff, not dance and fancy suits stuff. He's never even been to a single school dance.

Smile and say thanks.

"No need," I mutter with the little strength I have. "I was being funny. I actually have a list of guys."

Four

HOURS LATER, I'm no closer to fixing my no-guy-wants-to-be-my-escort-for-the-ball problems. I've thought about going next-door and asking Hudson, but I can only handle two rejections in a single day. But I am mentally drafting up the perfect ball invitation for Khalid, Josh, and Hudson to be delivered tomorrow.

The wind grazes my cheek as I round a hallway corner. The scent of salmon and mashed potatoes for dinner lingers in the halls. There's an echo from the copper waterfall in the foyer.

Large brass vases stand at every five feet with fresh carnations inside. There's one by the main door with purple carnations. They were probably used as funeral flowers because they were dark yet comforting. Or maybe purple isn't their natural color, and the flower has been genetically modified. I bet carnations trace back to ancient Egypt. Maybe Cleopatra wanted to have a fun color party, so she painted the carnations in unexpected dyes. Although, I don't even know if carnations are from Egypt, Spain, or Greece.

Between the vases are pieces of jewelry on the cream walls instead of framed photos.

Giving the elevator a quick glance, I bet it's still broken. I haven't used it in the last ten months. Not that I need to go to Astrid's gym or Mother's master bedroom, but more and more things have stayed broken.

There are moments where I think Astrid is singing in the shower like she used to when we were younger. Then I realize it's the laundry machine clunking away.

Papi used to fix everything, but now that he's no longer here, nothing gets fixed. The mansion was never so out of tune when Papi was alive. But maybe fixing all the broken things he used to fix would mean we're forgetting him, leaving him behind. Nothing is the same, yet everything is the same.

Mother has refused to let anyone fix anything, which is so odd, since she got rid of his things so fast. Although, she won't confirm destroying his belongings. She never talks about him, and over the last several months replaced his things with fancy jewelry pieces or artwork. Frankly, I never cared about pictures of Papi. Hardly noticed them. But when they mysteriously disappeared one by one, I noticed every blank space.

I can't find a single family photo, and instead stare at pieces of gems and jewels in random places. Maybe Mother didn't actually love her husband. Maybe it was all an act.

Mother was born and raised in Verdan. She never goes against the grain. Her biggest risk was going to Europe for a summer trip twenty years ago and bringing back a Spanish boyfriend—Papi. The town pressured him to change his surname from Verez to Panashe, which is Mother's last name, to keep with the name of Panashe Jewelry if he wanted to stay in the town and pass on the legacy to his future children. The mayor—who's the brother of Mrs. D'aureville, the debutante director—didn't appreciate changing up the town's business names and visions. Over the years, there have been slight modifications, but nothing that would transform the overall organization of the town.

When Papi married her, Mother's wealthy parents gave them the mansion and their jewelry empire. They then went to travel the world, mostly via cruises. We see them in December for the holidays but that's about it. Papi's parents live in Spain. He bought them a house with the first bonus he got from Mother. We rarely visited Spain even though Papi talked about doing so all the time.

"Abigail Maria Panashe"—Mother's green eyes, outlined with half-eyeliner as if she did her makeup in the dark or cried most of it off, laser in on me across the living room—"I know you know every powerful person will be in attendance at the ball. We have spent a year perfecting everything. But you are missing the most important element."

She marches toward me—posture perfect, white blouse spotless, pencil skirt precise. Her stare is like a lecture in a single glance. On repeat and in overdrive.

I try not to breathe too hard. The stress of being a CEO must be unbearable. Before Papi died, she rarely yelled at me.

I'm convinced she works twenty hours a day. When Papi passed away, she would go to the office four times a day, then six. Soon after, she replicated the downtown office into a room downstairs.

She manages the entire jewelry company and sets high goals for herself. My whole family is driven by planning. Come to think of it, most of the town runs on schedules and events.

"This is serious," she commands.

I nod once. Just once, because twice is excessive and three is sloppy.

Astrid's heels tap across the floor, champagne in one hand and phone in the other. It must be six o'clock on the dot. Astrid entered through the backyard, grabbed a drink, observed Chef Daisy preparing dinner, and is proceeding to judge me.

Nineteen but acting way too old for her age.

She's as diminutive as me—barely over five feet—though while we wear the same clothing size, our bodies are shaped differently. I'm curved in all the wrong places; she's curved in all the right ones. Or at least that's how I feel even though no one has ever shamed me for having uneven shoulders and hips due to my scoliosis.

Astrid has Mother's green eyes, the smoothest, glowing sun kissed skin, and her oh-so-shiny and non-frizzy brown, golden curls.

I wish I was as strong as Astrid.

Elijah Kippurs, Astrid's fiancé, strides from the kitchen in a well-polished suit, beer in hand. His favorite line in any situation is, "Make sure you offer a contract." Followed by, "My firm can protect you from all risks when things go wrong." Elijah only cares about the number of clients he can sign. He wouldn't give me a family discount if I asked, which I never would.

He's the dark and handsome type. A pre-law student who will join his family's law practice upon graduation from Verdan University—VU—in three years, the same university that Astrid attends as a business major. Both his parents used to be members of Congress, and to them, status is everything.

"Abigail, you're the only one without an escort," Mother says with disappointment. "Please explain why this keeps happening. Astrid finds noble gentlemen for you who act

interested. But after dance practice, they suddenly vanish."
Mother's words lash at me fast, furious, and hot. They sting.

The heat of the moment is so intense, I'm sweating. The fire crackling in the living room—it's a fake fire that doesn't warm the room up but is there to give an elegant glow—and the steaming dishes being served on the dinner table don't help.

There's an entire crowd of the staff bringing food, plus Mother, Elijah, Astrid, and Chef Daisy. I swallow hard.

My hands run through my long, black hair a few hundred times. Reality sets in.

The ground cracks beneath me. Little by little, the floor separates and I'm stranded on the edge, about to be eaten alive by the gaping chasm.

"Not being able to keep a single escort is concerning," Mother says. "If you don't get one before the rehearsal, the director will disqualify you. I've called in as many favors as I could think of." She pivots toward Elijah. "Is your brother, Harry, free this Friday?"

I gasp. Harry is old, bald, and as cocky at Elijah. He calls me Tanya and asks how middle school is going. Anyone but someone of the Kippurs family line, please. They are too self-centered and are all about doing favors in exchange for other favors. I do not want to have that hanging over my head.

Picking the escort is the fun part of the ball. The debs have already picked the cutest guys. If I show up with a weirdo, it will ruin my life. I won't recover from it when I start senior year in two months.

I sink into my seat. Papi was my biggest cheerleader, but he's not here to be my shield. I'd give anything for his protection now. Give anything to hear his voice and see him stride across the room. He'd stand up for me and say powerful words. The ones that silence everyone. I miss his embraces and hugs.

When he'd ask me if I was okay without me having to say a word. He just knew how to read my face and what I needed, even when I pushed him away the last couple of years.

Astrid leans in. "You *have to* win queen, Abby. If that means, Harry, you will take it with stride. Why do you think I signed up to help the debutante planning committee?" She won queen three years ago and uses every chance to remind me of her victory. Mother won queen too, so the pressure is on. Although I'd never admit I care more about my experience and dressing up than about some crown.

"We'll be invited to VIP parties and meet the elite," she adds. There's the truth. Astrid wants me to win so she can soak in my glory.

People said she was the most elegant, the classiest of all the debutantes. CEOs and even the governor congratulated Mother on raising a well-rounded and cultured woman. Their compliments came with thousands of dollars' worth of jewelry sales.

"I-I-I . . ." Yep, words, those things used to explain things, are stuck in my throat.

"You owe this to your family." Elijah's comment is more of a threat. "You fail this and you fail them. Prove to everyone you're not some broken girl after you forced your father to give up his life for yours."

Elijah is the type to be cruel to me any chance he gets. I caught him rummaging through business papers in Mother's office over the holidays. There was a look of shock in his eyes, and then he stormed out, saying he was looking for a receipt. I didn't believe him and told Astrid, who told me not to worry about it. Since then, Elijah has been more snappy than usual these last six months.

Astrid darts her eyes at him and takes a seat on his lap. "Elijah, don't," she whispers harshly. No matter how many times she does this, he never quits his behavior. I've become almost immune to it.

I sit up and defend all the work I've put into being a debutante.

"Regardless of my date, it won't deter me from being a good debutante." I just want to have the best night of my life with my besties, along with the perfect kiss. "I have a list of potential escorts, don't worry," I say, my voice shaken.

Anyone but Harry, please.

"We'll have Harry as a backup." Astrid sips her champagne. "I'm concerned Diana will get in the way. She was on the news yesterday for her volunteer work planning a fashion show for the fashion museum. Her volunteer hours are toppling yours. Plus, Mackenzie told me Diana asked to do the exact hairstyle as yours."

Duh! Diana and I talked about having matching hairstyles. It's what best friends do.

Mother rubs my shoulder. "I know you know that the only person who can save your future is yourself. You have to fight to the end, because that's when you succeed. Crying behind closed doors when you lose is not a life I want for you."

That's one way to turn my insides out.

"Okay," I mutter, and eye the empty space above the mantel. There used to be a wedding photo of my parents on there. It was full of joy, with Mother laughing in Papi's arms as he kissed her cheek. We all used to laugh.

"Your GPA tops everyone's, but you need to improve on your community service hours," says Mother. "If not, the winning then will come down to the congeniality votes. Think ahead and be prepared if that happens. Meaning, the more you help the other debs, the more likely they'll vote for your congeniality status. As long as you get at least seven debs to vote for you, you will secure a win."

A deb must top two out of the three categories in order to become queen—most volunteer hours, highest GPA, and more than half of the congeniality votes. All the debs vote on congeniality before the ball, and you can't vote for yourself.

Not that I care much about winning queen. Mother and Astrid do, so I nod to please them.

"I understand. I'll check in on Pyper's math homework and her plans for college."

Numbers were never her strength and even though we'd been in the same grade for years, I recently learned about her math troubles. She said it embarrassed her she's still stuck in algebra when everyone has moved onto geometry and calculus.

Astrid and Elijah chitchat like a cat fight, but the kind that is sharp one moment and cuddly the next—totally unpredictable. Their love began on her first day of first grade and his first day of third grade. Their first kiss was at Elijah's eighth grade graduation party, and their first school dance was when she got to high school. Astrid has been planning for a glamorous wedding ever since. So much so that the stress makes them scream at each other at least once a week about buying unnecessary things or being late to meetings.

Mother answers a call.

The pressure builds in my chest. I need to escape. I need fresh air to clear my mind.

Who am I kidding? It's not the fresh air that I need. It's Theo. He is the shoulder I cry on. I wish I could ask him to march up here and tell everyone I want to do the ball my way. That he'll be my escort—or at least officially ask him. Because maybe I do want to kiss my best friend.

Without pause, I head to my safe haven.

My wheels speed across the polished wooden floor until I thump over the kitchen threshold.

In a rush, I pass the Greek statues and silver tables. The carnations line the lit-up curved pathways. My parents planted them when they moved in.

The wind whisks by and I think about how we used to be a family.

Astrid and I would smell the flowers and Mother would weave flower crowns I called my *sombreros de flores*. Flowers were how Papi won her over when they dated. He told me he once filled an entire room with carnations for her. Then he showed her how to craft the perfect bouquet. They shared them with the entire community. Papi knew how to spread joy and bring everyone together. She loved his passion for life, but I think it was his work ethic that proved he would be a great husband. Now it's as if she's trying everything to erase him from our memories.

I spin around the corner, passing the last carnations, and whip by the green bushes.

As a kid, I'd zoom through the garden, down the small hill, past the trees, around the lake, and up the dirt path.

The scent of pine is stronger here and I love it. A few yards further and the air will become colder. I'll be able to hear the frogs croaking in the lake. The flittering fireflies around the lake's shores are my favorite.

My wheels track along the gravel, not too fast though, since I haven't signed up for riding dirt waves today. I won't risk jumping out of my seat. One time I went too fast over a speed bump and almost flew out. Really did not evaluate the speed and air velocity on that one.

A smile creeps across my face. The peace of being in the woods grows. The trees and pine scent remind me of Papi.

I speed up, spotting a faraway light emanating from the cabin.

A whoosh of wind crosses my face. Suddenly, a hand digs into my shoulder.

My squeal is paired with someone else's deep grunt. I come to a sudden stop, my heart jumping to my throat.

Whoa.

Five

THE TALL STRANGER pivots and catches himself on a tree, pausing to take a breath. He's dressed in knee-length black shorts and a sleeveless black hoodie that hides his face. "Sharp turn, huh?" he asks with a laugh. His voice is deep.

"Sorry," I mutter, trying to catch my breath.

The sun gets in my eyes, but I pretend I'm not blinded.

"You . . . okay?" He snickers loudly enough for me to hear.

I glance down at his clean white sneakers to stop my eyes from watering. Wind, sun, and extreme cold tend to stream tears down my face even though I'm not crying.

The jogging outfit and evening walk are out of sync for this neighborhood. Being dressed for hiking or going on a run is an unusual look in this town. If you want to exercise, a gym comes to you. Astrid had a trainer and a studio set up on the second floor when she ran cross-country in high school.

He must be a visitor.

I glance up again, squinting. My vision blurs. I squint harder.

"Yeah." I stretch out the word into a sentence. "Just . . .

headed to my friend, Theo." I quickly wipe an unexpected tear from the blinding sunrays.

"What's wrong?" he immediately asks.

It's nice a stranger cares enough to think something is wrong. If I explain I keep getting dumped, it'd be more comedic than concerning.

"Is it the ball?" he asks softly, sliding his hood down.

I pivot to the right and get a better look at him.

Not a stranger at all.

Hudson.

It's great to see his face. Great enough to warrant a shy smile yet keep me speechless.

"Heard all your escorts quit. Their loss anyway." His biceps are the size of watermelons. "Your mom told mine." That thick, luxurious semi-curly dirty-blond hair is a mess in the wrong places. It sticks up on the side like he just woke up.

He stuffs his hands into the pockets of his shorts. "You okay?" There's genuine concern in his voice.

The hottest guy in town is inches away from me.

If we went to the same school and had a section in the year-book for charming guys, he'd win ten times over. In addition to having the sexiest smile, hair, lips, and everything else, he's really athletic.

I didn't care to know who he was dating or not dating, *too* much. And no, I never had a *serious* crush on him. I only reminisced on old times during school dances, remembering how he'd race with me and give me lilies when we were in grade school.

We were . . . just friends. My heart no longer pounds the way it did then. Although, the shock of seeing him has me breathless. It must be the crash.

I stroke my locks. Staring is definitely the appropriate reaction.

"Sorry for almost hitting you and tangling you up like spaghetti," I say, suddenly embarrassed.

I should be furious, mad at him for ghosting me four years ago. Despite living next door, he never had time for me anymore. Other friends seemed to be more important when I was twelve and he was thirteen.

One day, he ignored me at a school fundraiser and continued ever since. I later saw pictures of him attending his first high school party. First high school dance. First high school everything. I was in eighth grade, and as a ninth grader, he seemed to only want to hang out with high schoolers.

Hudson had been shy and skinny, with his famous high-pitched voice. But by last year, he was lacrosse captain and dating the head cheerleader. Girls in my school used to talk about the lacrosse captain every time he was on a break with his ex. They sent him consoling messages and posted pictures with him on social media, including Diana at one time.

My ears would perk up hearing his mother talking to mine about him.

I should want to run his ass over, not sit here unblinkingly glued to his face.

The rejection still stings, but I refuse to talk about what happened. Or didn't, as the case may be. Although, it is nice to see him grown up and . . . buff.

He looks so much older, with this scruffy bed head style. The exact opposite of the classy Hudson with hair perfectly combed to the side. It's been so long that I haven't realized how much he's changed. Everything we once knew about each other has changed. Even his voice, which I didn't recognize at first.

He steps forward. "I got yarn, so that's pretty close to spaghetti."

I laugh a bit and loosen a smile.

My eyes wander. To the trees, my mansion, the fence that separates our properties.

"It's nice to see you," he says, a coy smile playing on his lips.

"Ahum." It's official: the reason guys run away from me is because I have zero flirting skills. Not that this is the moment to flirt with Hudson.

We don't speak for what feels like the longest minute.

He pulls a ball of yarn from his hoodie's front pocket. It's a bunched up, fuzzy mass of wrapped strands. Knitting needles protrude from his waistband. "Knitting can help you feel better." There's a comfort to his voice and broad shoulders.

"Yeah?"

I can't believe he still knits. He never talked about it when we were kids, but sometimes I'd hear someone saying Hudson knitted a hat for them. Once, he gave me a scarf.

I laugh again. Most people don't walk around in sweats carrying around yarn.

"At least the ladies at the senior center love it. They have dementia, so it never gets old teaching them." He pauses. "Too much information. I go there because they remind me of my nonna, who's in Italy."

I wonder if part of volunteering has anything to do with going after the granddaughters who visit the senior center. "That's nice you do that. I don't knit, but thank you."

His crooked smile grows. "You might like it." The way he licks his lips is sexy, and the way he chuckles is more so.

His lips must be experienced. They must know how to apply the right pressure and when to let go. His tongue must know how to work every corner of a mouth.

My jaw falls open. Hudson chuckles again. I hold my breath at the thought that he has superpowers and can read my mind about us kissing.

This is the side effect of planning my first romantic kiss so much.

The heat in my back rises.

"My dinner is getting cold," I mutter, retracing the path I came from. "So . . . you actually knit for real," I say as a statement and a question. "Professionally?"

Hudson struts next to me. "More like a hobby."

He whips out the knitting needles and twirls them like drumsticks. "I knit when I need to clear my head. I can't stand when everyone sees me doing something and judges without asking me about it." There's a heated tone to the last sentence. "I smashed bottles earlier today. We can go some day."

The proposition is so unusual, I keep quiet. This is the most Hudson has shared with me in years. I don't know how to talk to him anymore. Let alone how to hang out with him.

"Oh?" I ask, hoping he elaborates. If he talks, I won't have the urge to tell him about my day, like old times. Or worse, ask him to be my escort for the ball and fantasize about his lips on mine.

"I got into a fight with my parents. Fucking hate how they control me." He grunts, chucking something from his pocket toward the faraway side fence.

"My dad sees me in an NYU sweatshirt and decides to tell the press I accepted the lacrosse scholarship as if I'm going there to study business law." Not many locals go to a college other than VU because everyone has connections there. Unless it's Harvard or Yale, of course.

Hudson's decision, though, stirred up some drama in the town, especially since he doesn't even need a scholarship or

NYU when VU has their own lacrosse team. His father has a second Giordani office in Manhattan—a few hours away Verdan—so that's probably why he wants Hudson at NYU.

"Congrats," I say.

"I don't want to go to college." He swings his arm and tosses something else into the air.

"What?" How can he not want to go to college with such an opportunity? It's a life plan with a high probability of success. "You're so lucky to go live in Manhattan. To be free and on your own. Why aren't you excited?"

Hudson laughs. "You can take my spot if you want. I got offered a prestigious scholarship as a first-year athlete *without* my dad's help and that feels good. Lacrosse has been my one constant, but it's all I know. I want something else to be passionate about. I hate following a plan. I hate the fancy parties. They're a waste of time."

Pivoting, he walks backwards. "Lacrosse was great, but I don't want to be professional. I *just* finished high school. So what if my parents hate that I'm quitting without a life plan and are taking everything away from me. What I'm trying to do is *not* feel caged in. Signing that athletic scholarship next weekend means they'll control my life. And not only them. Now it'll be coaches and teammates too. Plus, the girls on the cheer team, who are dating half the team. I'm so tired of people telling me how they want *me* to live *my* life."

My heart sinks, because once upon a time, a ten-year-old Hudson talked everything NYU. "But what if . . ." At the sight of his cocked brow, I stay silent. *Let it go.* "Good luck. If you need anything, I'll try to help."

A moment of silence stretches between us. When I draw my eyes to his face, the corner of his mouth curls up. He shrugs and says quietly, "I'll be cheering you on at the ball. My family and yours bought a table together."

Deflection is everyone's superpower in this town.

His piercing hazel eyes are too familiar for me to want to pull away. *I miss talking to you.*

I nod once. "Thank you."

"If *you* need anything, I'm a window away," he says and winks.

This could be my chance to ask him to the ball. I toss my hair over my shoulder. "Well—"

"Abigail!" Mother hollers from the kitchen. "Dinner now. Where have you been? And what are you doing outside?"

Hudson throws me a quick wave and jogs away. "See ya rollin' around."

I race through the backyard, in disbelief Hudson actually had a full-on conversation with me.

When I face Mother, I take a pause and run through her question.

What was I doing outside? *Hudson. Ask him.*

"Just talking to Hudson," I say.

Tapping her phone, she peeks into the backyard. "Interesting. I need to meet with his mother." They've been besties for as long as I can remember.

I bite my lip, thinking of how to ask Hudson to be my escort.

Six

Dear Hudson,

It was nice to "run" into you. I hope you had fun jogging and knitting! Sorry your dad is making your life frustrating. Remember when we got in trouble for stuffing our faces with too many milkshake-decorated fries? When we'd eat them in the secret place under the old mailbox and you'd bring me my favorite flowers—lilies? A week later, your dad laughed about it. I'm sure he's just overreacting and will come around to what you want to do. Wish I knew what else is going on in your life. I'm without an escort for the ball, which you already know. Can I ask you to the ball? If you're too busy, I get it. Or if you don't want to do the whole dancing thing, that's fine too. I hope we can talk again soon. Maybe we can do milkshakes and fries. Anyway, thanks for reading this and let's make plans or something.

Sincerely, Abby

Seven

It's 8:30 a.m. and Valerie has transferred me out of my bed and helped me shower. My yawning won't quit. Even when I'm brushing my teeth. I didn't sleep all night. I was reciting Hudson's letter in my head like it was poetry, wondering if it was good enough.

Still with wet hair, I tell Valerie I'll be right back. She says she'll change my bed sheets in the meantime.

Letter in hand, I race through the halls until I'm outside, and head toward the Giordani backyard. A girl can dream. If in twelve hours I don't hear anything, I'll have Diana or Joey ask for me.

The morning air is cool and misty. A chill runs through me.

It's been a few years since I sneaked through the side fence that separates our properties.

The water that pours out of the fountain next to the carnations echoes behind me. Yards away and up a small hill looms the Giordanis' luxurious castle-inspired home, with arches and balconies overlooking their acres of grapevines.

Their backyard is filled with large statues featuring buff men, buxom women, and lots of grapes. Twelve marble steps circle the mansion, setting it high above the surroundings. Grape vines decorate the fence that rounds the lush green grass. The property has three pools. I pass the diamond-shaped infusion one. It looks lovely. But the hot tub, with the same diamond-within-a-diamond shape that mimics the pool, looks even more appealing. I slow as I pass by.

I miss swimming.

The dewy grass glisters along a wave of pathways. Some lead to rows of vineyards and others weave to tennis and basketball courts.

It's as if I'm on autopilot when I face the old bronze mailbox at the side of the mansion. Years ago, Hudson and I would share notes inside the rusted grapevine engravings.

I pull the round knob. The mailbox hinges squeak. There are no spider webs, but it gives off a mysterious vibe like once I place anything inside, it might shoot up to the North Pole.

I carefully slide the folded paper onto the metal plate and shut the mailbox and put the faded-red flap up. Turning around quickly, I rush back down the same path I took. The morning breeze bites me a bit harder.

The birds chirp loudly on my way back through my backyard. Today, there are five meetings on my schedule. The first is the arrival of my ballgown.

"You can trust me with this secret. I am a lawyer, after all." Elijah's voice echoes from the gate near the entrance. "And *I'll* talk to the board."

I roll my eyes. Finishing the first year of law school doesn't make anyone a "lawyer." Before law school, he'd brag how he took so many AP classes in high school that he got credits for a full year at VU.

"The girls can't know about this money, especially Abigail," Mother replies. "Let's wait until after the ball to tell her, if we have to."

I sigh. Mother must be paying Harry to be my escort. This is worse than I thought.

Sneaking into the kitchen, I head back to my bedroom. The halls await the flood of people to pass through them. Chef Daisy won't be in to whip up brunch for another thirty minutes. Mother's assistant, in an hour.

I wonder how much money Mother paid Harry.

My allowance is enough to cover a fun trip every month, not that I adventure out anywhere, but I have kept a savings account for several years. If I paid Elijah what Mother is paying him, I'd feel more in control. Or rather, pay him to cancel the arrangement. It's pathetic knowing someone is being financially motivated to spend time with me. Then again, everything here is built on favors and business deals. Guess that's why everyone is rich around here: they charge each other for something. Pyper's parents paid her cousin to be her homecoming date last year, and they're family.

A thin, tan folder lies on a table near Mother's office. A page sticks out from the edges. It could be a bank statement. Snooping around is not my thing, but I need answers.

Rolling closer, I open the folder and find a stack of contracts for the jewelry company.

Contracts are never a good sign. I flip through the ten-page document. On the signature page is . . .

The front door slams. That must be Mother.

I shut the pages and back away from the evidence. *Was that Elijah's name at the bottom?* Why would he need to sign a company contract?

Stilettoes clack against the floor. They get louder.

"Hello!"

That's not Mother.

My rose-gold-rimmed wheels squeak on the polished oak floor as I pivot.

A woman with black bangs and a lace teal dress stands before me. The stylist, Xochitl, holds up a white garment bag. Our main door has fingerprint recognition software, so only people who've registered with us can enter.

"The dress!" I practically shout and race over.

She holds my holiest of holy grails. This is it, the moment I've been waiting for since I was five years old. When I knew I needed a princess dress. A princess dress for a special ball.

I designed the gown with Papi as a kid, and last year we worked with a designer to make it flowy and a custom fit for my wheelchair. Two months ago, I tried on a sample dress and the designer took extra measurements to ensure it fit perfectly. Then she finalized the actual ballgown and stitched up any loose ends. All the pretend-to-be-a-princess and not-worry-about-anything-else hubbub is now real.

The dress will give me magical powers to do whatever I wish. If I want to turn a pumpkin into a wheelchair-accessible carriage, it will happen. Everyone will applaud everything I do. They'll laugh at my mummy jokes and smile at my first edition book collection.

I will go anywhere and not worry about people saying things like, "Poor girl, who's going to make your decisions now that your dad is gone?" or "Good job for getting into town; we are so proud of you for taking the brave journey in your wheelchair."

I imagine a crown on my head. The one from fourteenth-century Europe that's stored in the basement's antiques room.

Wearing a centuries-old crown would give me the power to

be heard and seen instead of pitied, the girl who needs rescuing. It will give me strength and a voice. No matter what it takes, they will treat me like royalty.

I will be the one to tell people what to do. Not the other way around.

Daydreams are fun. I sigh back into reality.

At least I get to wear a century-old pearl necklace. Papi let me clean it once. He explained how taking care of sacred things means you value their history and what they've been through. That's why I visit the antiques basement at least once a month to check on all the items.

In my spare time, I obsess over the history of antiques. The best finds are firsts, such as the first photograph ever taken in Verdan—in the 1870s—or the first Verdan diamond ring designed for an engagement—in the 1890s. Most kids play with new toys, but I played with old artifacts passed down from my grandparents.

"Thank you for delivering the dress," I say. "You can leave it on the dining table. I'll tell my mother you stopped by."

Xochitl sets it on the edge and says something about the buttons but I'm too busy taking a picture of the garment bag. The zipper is calling me to open it up. But with my besties.

The front door swings open. A chatty Astrid replaces the stylist. She's back from a morning yoga session with her decade-long friend, Mei-Ling. Phone to ear, Astrid chatters on, her voice echoing off of the ivory-painted halls.

"Elijah approves of the winter wonderland wedding."

Quick steps echo on the foyer's marble floor.

Astrid passes a ruby-encrusted grape statue—a gift from the Giordanis. Her tight, black leggings accentuate her sculpted legs. Even in yoga, she sparkles in a diamond bracelet and earrings, courtesy of the family business.

I sit up and smile, pointing to the garment bag.

She sounds extra chirpy, almost giddy. "Don't worry—my wonderland wedding will be different from yours. It's the perks of planning our weddings together. Just got home. Talk later. Bye, Mei-Ling."

"How's the planning going?" I ask.

Her peony perfume overpowers me. I flicker my hand and back away.

"A-hum." She dismisses me and focuses on her phone.

"The dress is here," I say, tempted to ask how much Mother paid Harry. But I can't bring myself to do it. If I ask her, she'll ask Elijah and he'll tell Mother, and then I'll have to face everyone knowing that I know this is all a business transaction.

There's not a bigger disappointing feeling.

"Great." Astrid types into her phone. "Elijah sent me a picture of our honeymoon trip to Austria, but I love Iceland," she whispers to herself.

"He could be doing that on purpose. He does enjoy pressing your buttons."

"Don't distract me." Her attitude as a nineteen-year-old is harsher than when she was fourteen. She massages between her nose and forehead. "I'm busy."

The comment stings, and I no longer want to share anything with her. If she wants curt responses, I'll give her one-word responses. "Okay."

This is how I began to dismiss Papi. I gave him one-word answers. I hate myself for it, yet I retreat to old patterns.

My gaze rises to the wall. The one where paintings of each of us—me, Astrid, Mother—hang in ten-foot frames above the dining table, each one spotless and dust-free. There used to be one of Papi next to Mother, but his things disappeared little by little. I'm scared to find out everything's rotting in a landfill.

As much as I want to talk about Papi, I'm glad no one's forced me to face the pain of asking me how I feel. After his passing, Mother and Astrid went on with their daily routines, and I soon followed suit.

My schedule is so tight, I can only think about the future. No time for the past. I love structure and staying busy. When I do have spare time, I search for treasures to add to the antiques room in the basement. Distraction is my favorite defense mechanism.

Because for the first few weeks after the funeral, I kept remembering how the door would snap open, a heavy exhale would follow, and Papi would fall into the foyer armchair and struggle to get his shoes off. He'd call my name and I'd come rolling in ready to tell him about my day at elementary school. We'd hug and he'd teach me a new Spanish word. Astrid and I used to speak Spanish, but then we started taking French lessons, piano lessons, and etiquette classes. We didn't have time for Spanish.

Now my only vocabulary involves *hola* and *sí*, and sometimes a sweet remembrance, like the name of a flower. I wish I had stuck with Papi's native language. I'd love to talk to my extended family in Spain.

"I'll just text Joey and Diana to help me with the dress," I say, typing away into my phone.

Astrid darts a stare at me. "Do not text Diana. She's your competition, not your friend. We can't afford any failures. Uninvite her."

"But we're doing the ball together."

Astrid narrows her brows. "I'm serious or else I will explode."

"Okay, okay." I only text Joey. The last thing I need is drama between Diana and Astrid. That could get to the debutante director, and I'd have to pick sides or something. Plus, I hate confrontation. The pressure of standing up for myself or others has me feeling like a deer in headlights.

Astrid heads to the kitchen, parading down the hall, her phone a leash tethering her to everything of importance in her universe.

I really want Diana here. This feels wrong. Excluding my best friend leaves a sour taste in my mouth. Maybe once Astrid eats, she'll be less cranky. I roll into the rose-gold kitchen.

The space is filled with a fully-stocked liquor cabinet and a quartz table. The spotless table—the primary focus of the room—has a polished sheen. White tulips in a vase add a touch of elegance.

Astrid pours a glass of champagne even though she's way underage. "And don't worry about the father-daughter dance at rehearsal. Mei-Ling's dad agreed to step in since Grandpa can't fly back and forth from Spain that much or stay long since Grandma is due for surgery soon. But Grandpa should be here for the actual ball, and if not, I'll have a plan B."

"Right," I whisper. My stomach turns as I think of how Papi won't be doing the father-daughter dance with me. I wish I didn't have to do that part. Not that I don't want to dance with Grandpa. It's the pain of remembering Papi dancing with me as a kid and now being reminded he'll never dance with me again.

The bubbles in the champagne glass subside. Mother used to drink in the morning, but she seems too busy to even do that, unless she has a secret wine cellar elsewhere. Seeing Astrid do it the last few weeks is rather strange. Is she so stressed that she needs a drink this early?

"Everything okay?" I ask, aware she won't actually give me an honest answer, if any answer at all.

Total silence.

I fiddle with my phone and stare at Diana's number. "Why can't I invite Diana, again?"

Astrid ignores my questions and proceeds to grab pre-cut strawberries and bananas from the fridge. "*I'll* help you with the dress. Diana is constantly taking other deb's appearance inspirations and they complain to me she's going to steal their designs. You have to win, not Diana. Her family's fashion empire is perfectly fine and *we* need every good exposure we can get if we want to keep living lavishly in this town. There will be dozens of reporters and press at the event."

Keep living lavishly? Are we in some kind of financial trouble? Suddenly I realize that Elijah and his family are too wealthy to want money. It's silly to consider Harry would ask for money to be my escort.

I really need to investigate. Elijah could be investing in the jewelry company and that's what the contracts are for.

"Did Elijah give Mother money?" I ask. "What for?"

Astrid turns the smoothie machine on. It roars for a good minute.

Deflection.

Several scenarios run through my head: Elijah wants to design a special gift for Astrid and own the rights to it; he may be setting up some kind of trust fund for when they get married; he plans to murder us all and take over the business.

The smoothie machine thundering stops and I gawk at my sister to the point that it's probably creepy.

"That was a one-time thing last month. Don't worry about it," she says. "Don't ever get mixed up with shady business."

I worry about it.

"Let's have you try on your dress in twenty-five minutes," Astrid says and makes her way up the stairs. One hand holds her phone, and the other, the smoothie.

"Sure. Need to blow dry my hair anyways."

I fiddle with my phone, staring at Diana's number again. Then I stare at Hudson's old number, wondering if it still works.

Eight

TWENTY-FIVE MINUTES LATER, Astrid jogs down the stairs. She slips her phone into her dark-purple satin shorts and grabs the garment bag. "I have to leave soon, so let's hurry."

The front door snaps open and Joey stomps dirt onto the floor. "I'm here and ready to get you naked." She flings her shoes off and fixes her fishnet top that matches her fishnet tights.

I flash her a wave. "Thanks for coming."

We head into the nearest bathroom. It's the biggest one in the house. Seven bathrooms may seem like a lot, but when we have parties, there are never enough.

The golden countertops are paired with white towels of every size. Five couches could fit in here, although there are only two in place today. On the first floor, there are four toilets tucked discreetly behind artistically painted doors, including mine—the black one—which rises three inches so I can transfer on my own. Anything that's lower or higher than my chair is impossible for me to navigate.

Joey unzips the garment bag in one swift motion. We stare

in awe at the gown. The fabric is smooth, the satin finish giving it an elegant touch. As Joey moves the ivory fabric under the bathroom chandelier, it glistens in the light. The lace details on the shoulder straps are too graceful, too delicate to even breathe on. The corset holds a curved shape to mold my body, with seams running down on the side. The skirt weighs down to my toes with a slight fluff to it.

Astrid turns it over. It's a rounded back between the straps where the lace settles at the top. The buttons on the corset are real pearls rather than actual buttons. The train arches under the kneecap so I can sit comfortably, but you can't tell that by looking at the floor-length front.

I run my fingers over the fabric. "It's perfect," I whisper, and inhale its relaxing lavender scent. Okay, that's the bathroom air freshener. "I have to try it on."

Astrid quickly and efficiently puts her shiny brown locks up into a bun. "No bra, right?"

"No bra," I say, slipping one arm from my summer dress. I do the same with the other and Astrid pulls the dress over my head. She folds it neatly on the shelf next to her.

Joey unclips my bra and flings it across the room. "Let the titties party!" she says.

As the girls glide the white dress over my head, I peek at myself in the mirror on the wall. I have spinal muscular atrophy, a form of muscular dystrophy. It affects my muscles and therefore my movements. The scoliosis is pronounced. I call my uneven shoulders "bent taco ribs" and my asymmetrical hips "art." My frame is smaller than average, but nothing hurts except for the pressure on my butt, which I can alleviate by leaning over my left armrest or reclining back.

MD is a progressive disease for which the doctors gave me gene therapy injections, but I don't do that anymore. Long-needle injections into the spine are no fun, even if they do help keep my body from failing. Currently, I take the drugs orally. The treatment slows down the progression, but I'll never be able to walk again. Is the treatment working? I don't feel any different, but sometimes my stomach gets queasy from it.

With every neuron that dies, I lose physical strength because fewer neurons mean they can't feed the muscles properly. There was a time I could walk; then I could only stand; now I'm only able to sit with the right support. People assume I'm completely paralyzed, but I feel the slightest prick and squeeze.

When I explain I have starving muscles, people seem amazed that I can move my toes, as if using a wheelchair means I'm not allowed to. And no, I'm not bound to my wheelchair —I don't swim with it or sleep in it—it's a chair that helps me move around. *I* control it, not the other way around.

I can move my legs and feet. I'm just not strong enough to walk anymore. Unless I'm in water—not that I walk standing fully up. It's seated walking because my body doesn't fully extend to a flat, vertical position.

Joey navigates the fabric and Astrid pulls it around my butt so the bottom half of me doesn't look like a fluffy marshmallow. Astrid buttons up the back. It fits my curves and disproportions perfectly. The backside is molded to sit above the front wheels and footrest symmetrically.

It's comfortable, silky, and flawless. It's what dreams are made of.

I feel pretty.

"I'm ready for the ball," I say, lifting my chin and holding my head high.

"You're going to be a sensation," says Astrid. "Everyone will respect you and part the seas for you."

I squeeze her hand. "Thanks." Moments like these remind me that she wants the best for me.

"Your pops would be so damn proud," adds Joey.

Wish he were here to see me in the gown. In the pearls.

"The pearl necklace." I rub two fingers across my neck and turn to Astrid. "You have it?" It's locked away in a safe in her room behind a glass container. Her room highlights her debutante crown and awards on a wall shelf. Everything is white—nightstand, desk, makeup table.

She skedaddles without answering me. The necklace will bring the entire look together. Passed down from my great-great-grandmother on my mother's side, the pearls are a family heirloom. Every debutante in my family has worn the necklace since the very first ball.

I toss my hair over my shoulder and pose with one hand on my hip.

"Rock it!" Joey cheers and snaps a few pictures.

Moments later, Astrid returns and lays out the pearl necklace in her hands for us to admire. Each pearl is identical in size and roundness—unless one checks very carefully. The silk thread is more yellowish than white, and the knots between the pearls aren't that noticeable. It closes with a gold clasp engraved with letters too small for me to make out.

"It's so beautiful," I whisper.

"I've left the glass container on your nightstand so you can keep it until the ball," Astrid says.

"Really?" I dart my eyes at her. "Thanks."

I will cherish the necklace every second. To think about all the glamourous events it has seen and the hands that have touched it. The pearls' past will live on forever. I promise to treat them with dignity and respect, appreciating their history.

Astrid's phone vibrates in her pocket and she goes to

answer it. "Calm down, Elijah." She marches down the hallway into the kitchen. "I am leaving . . . . Stop yelling . . . . I know this is important, but I'm a little late and . . . Our future together is important . . . . I'll be there in time for your speech to the board . . . . Glad Harry has agreed . . . . I'm grateful for everything you do."

A single loud knock on the front door startles me. I stop gawking at the necklace and lay it gently on a towel.

"I invited Diana," says Joey. "You forgot it wasn't a group text. She's upset because she thinks you didn't invite her on purpose."

My eyes draw to Joey's face. "What?" If Astrid sees Diana here, who knows what will happen. Astrid will be furious I didn't listen to her. Diana will be upset I left her out. "It wasn't on purpose, purpose."

My heartbeat pounds in my ears. I'm not one of those girls who can spin a comedic scene from awkward situations. "Help me take this off," I say. Confrontation is not my strong suit. I'm the type who prefers to run and hide. Facing Diana means a lot of hurtful words and truths. It's too much for me.

We never go a month without trying on classy outfits together. This is the first time I'm trying on a new dress without her.

My breathing turns shallow and quick. I've never been in quicksand before, but this might be as close as I can get without actually being swallowed up. People say to not fidget or panic, but moving slowly and deliberately will sink me further if I don't get the gown off ASAP!

The front door clicks open.

"This button is stuck," says Joey. "Imma just pull you out of it."

I cycle through every explanation to not hurt Diana's feelings. Nothing comes to mind. She is a fashion enthusiast. Clothes are her life. She is the first to throw us a fashion show and redesign our outfits.

Joey tugs the gown up, intending to pull it over my head. It's too constricting. The fabric tightens around my body.

Joey huffs and puffs. "You're stuck," she says, yanking on the armpit holes. "We could cut you out with my pocketknife."

"Try harder," I whisper.

The back of my throat closes up. *Think, think, think.* There has to be a mathematical equation where I can suck in air and lower myself to the side or twist my shoulders so we can slide the dress over me.

Astrid is still arguing on the phone with Elijah.

"Try to"—I'm out of breath—"pull the gown harder."

"Hello?" a manly voice says from the foyer.

What if it's Harry? This is the worst-case scenario. Elijah's older brother is about to see me either half-naked or completely twisted into a pretzel. He'll immediately laugh and call Elijah. Then he'll run away and never say a word to me. Not that I'd care, but future family gatherings would definitely be super awkward.

Don't panic.

As Joey pulls the fabric over my head, my arms bounce out into a scarecrow position. The neckline is over my nose. I inhale, trying to compress the boob area, and then it happens. I can't move.

Do not panic. Do not go into freak-out mode. That's how quicksand wins. I wonder how many fossils and artifacts are buried in the deep depths of quicksand pits.

"You're stuck," Joey says like a broken record.

The guest could be someone else. Like Diana, who brought

Gustavo for reinforcement. She, too, crumbles at confrontation.

Joey tugs up harder, her feet sliding on the floor.

The fabric squeezes my ribs. "Ouch!" Now I really can't move. Or breathe, for that matter. The lovely lavender scent is miles away, and my warm body and my frustration are pushing my body odor beyond the limits of my deodorant.

This is not forever. It too shall pass. King Solomon had the right idea, but this is not passing. In fact, now my head and neck are on fire. All of me is on fire.

My arms are up and out, held in position by a dress that I'm worried about ripping. My fluffy hair is like a bird's nest. My breath heats my face warmer by the second.

"Astrid, help!" I yell, probably using my last full breath. "I can't see or breathe." My arms are starting to ache.

I'm considering taking a chance and yelling for Diana. She's the fashion expert, and her mom has taught her many tricks to fix any garment. If anyone can quickly defuse a fashion disaster, Diana's purse and hands can. Everyone at school goes to her when nylons rip or buttons pop off.

Astrid's stilettos clack across the tile. They sound ten times louder and heavier than a moment ago.

"I'll lift her and you pull down. Up and over her head isn't going to work." The deep voice thunders in my ears.

That's not Astrid or Diana, or Harry or Gustavo.

Before I can figure out who is doing what, firm hands take mine and loop them behind a neck. A male neck. A warm and smooth neck—familiar. Oh no, please don't let it be . . .

But I have no choice. I lock my hands together and hold my breath. The heavy fabric rubs against my wrist and expensive leather-scented cologne competes with my sweat.

Fingertips drag down to my shoulders as my cheeks press

into his chest. I've had doctors, specialists, nurses, and every kind of medical professional touch my body, to the point where it doesn't feel like my body is my own anymore. But this touch has me feeling my body in every way. Down to the last hair on my neck and the goose bumps on my arms.

Because . . . *Hudson.*

He slides the fabric down my face.

"One, two, three."

The whisper burns my ear further, not just because his lips are right there, exuding heat into the side of my head. I'm flat-out against his body. His arms wrap around my back and he lifts me.

Joey yanks the gown down.

I gasp at the quick motion, hoping Hudson can't feel my boobs through layers of expensive clothes. Because I can certainly feel *his* fit body. His muscles flex and extend with his every move.

My cheek is still plastered against him. I focus on taking elegant breaths rather than gasping for air. Oxygen floods my airways. Okay, the fear did pass, and I've come back up to the surface. That's the important thing. I should remember that. Being able to breathe is what matters here. Everything else—me being partially naked; me being imprisoned in a dress; me being helpless—is irrelevant. Right?

When Hudson lowers me back into my seat, I see him glance at me and then at the mirror, face reddening. The two seconds feel infinitely longer.

He saw my nakedness twice, both in person and in the mirror's reflection. Every disproportional part that curves me. All naked and helpless. Vulnerable.

My eyes tear up even though Hudson has turned away. There are no clothes I can put on to make me feel unexposed.

His memory of my body will live on forever, and there's nothing I can do about feeling embarrassed.

"You chill?" Joey asks me, tossing a towel over me, including my face.

"A-hum." My neck and chest prickle with heat.

Can I dissolve into the floor? Then I can live in the basement with my collection of antiques until everyone else has shriveled up into dry skeletons. I'll be fine with my ancestors and ghosts. They've been around for centuries and must have embarrassing stories worse than this one.

The dryness in my throat takes over and leaves me speechless.

I give Hudson a quick glance before staring at my footrest. "Thanks," I mumble so quietly, I have to say it again. "And apologies for this."

The redness in my face is full on. I'm too out of breath to say anything else.

This is not how I thought we'd start our ball partnership, but it's way better than having Harry. Right?

"I'll wait in the living room," Hudson says. Without looking back, he strides out and rounds the corner into the living room, his footsteps echoing on the smooth marble.

My heart's aflutter.

Nine

"ARE YOU OKAY?" Joey asks, pulling my sweaty hair away from my face.

"Embarrassed, but still in one piece," I whisper. "I need clothes."

He saw me naked. I'm burning up. *My imperfect boobs and uneven hips.* I sweep the back of my hand over my forehead, eyeing the string of pearls that ended up on the counter.

Joey slips me into my sundress without a word. It's an effortless task for her. Joey and Diana have gotten me dressed and re-dressed over the last several years more times than I can count.

My cheeks blaze with heat. "Can you make sure the pearl necklace gets back in the glass container in my room?"

"You got it, boss." She gives me two thumbs up.

"Seriously, that necklace is worth a fortune. More importantly, it connects me to my ancestors. Every pearl in its place has a special meaning."

She nods and puts on an impish smile. "It's my precious." Her *Lord of the Rings* impression is so good it's scary.

"Thanks. I'll go see Hudson."

I take in three long breaths.

Hudson touched my curved body. Not in that sexy way where he can't keep his hands off me.

I don't dare glance at myself in the mirror. I already suspect every inch of me is beet red.

Barely getting into the living room, a bouquet of lilies appears in front of my face.

"Your favorite, if I remember correctly." His voice is less confident than before. "You okay? Sorry if I hurt you."

I take the flowers—for me? "Thanks." A smile sneaks onto my lips. He's accepted my invitation. So many girls asked him and failed, and he said yes to *me*.

Wow, that letter worked fast.

He read my note and wants to be here for me. I focus on that and only that.

My giddiness is on full blast. But I can't let him see it. I take a deep breath and call upon every etiquette lesson I've ever had. No celebrating until we plan out the next several days.

He stands tall, his posture confident and his chin high. There's a gleam to his eyes. Tailored black Gucci slacks drape over luxurious black Valentino Oxfords. He wears his black silk suit jacket like a model. Every part of him is polished—the buff shoulders, the leather belt looped around his waist, the slacks that hug his legs perfectly. He's clean-shaven and not a hair is out of place. No trace of scrubby sleeveless hoodie guy from yesterday.

I cross one arm over my chest to form a shield. *I was naked in front of him.* The feeling just won't leave me alone. He's not saying much. He's not attacking me, yet I feel under attack with his every glance. His larger-than-life presence has me dumbfounded.

I glance everywhere but his face. The crackling fireplace that's always fake-burning. Our black piano that always automatically plays classical music in the background. The silver pitcher that is always on the oak dining table.

Pushing his blond hair to the side, he reveals an expensive-looking watch on his wrist. "You look good," he says. A smirk teases the edge of his mouth as he catches a glimpse of himself in the hallway mirror behind me.

His coy and crooked smile flushes my cheeks.

I stop gawking at his mouth and work my way up to his soft, hazel eyes. "Thank you." I slowly move away. "You look elegant." I clear my throat and nod politely. "I love lilies." See, I *can* put a full sentence together.

He winks and licks the side of his mouth oh so smoothly. "It's nice to see you . . . again."

The front door clicks open. It sounds farther away than it actually is.

"I came over to ask, can I officially be your escort for the ball?" he says, his mouth moving in slow motion.

I fix an invisible hair behind my ear to give myself time to process his words—the realness of that question coming from *Hudson*.

His eyes staring into mine is too much. My chest thumps and I have to pinch myself to make sure this isn't a dream.

My inner twelve-year-old self is shy that the hottest guy in town wants to be *my* escort. I deny I do a guitar jam and jump up and down in my chair—figuratively speaking.

Joey, and somehow Diana next to her, whisper, swaying my attention to them. They stare at me.

Hudson lowers to one knee, and once again, that closeness overpowers me.

"Uh." I stare at the flowers. "That would be lovely." I pause and gather my thoughts. "Yes, I accept. I'll schedule Demontae for our dance lessons."

"Yeah, okay." He pauses, staring at me as if waiting for me to ask him to dance at this very moment. Shock overload. Of course I want to, but . . . Diana.

I null over my lip, trying to find the words to ease her frown.

Hudson rises and takes the cue that I need to talk to my besties. He waves and I slightly nod, hating to watch him go.

I work my eyes to a nail-biting Diana, giving her a sympathetic look.

She stares at her polished gray stilettos. "I'm happy you got Hudson."

"Thanks. I'm sorry . . . . I wanted to invite you to see my dress, but Astrid . . ."

We never hide secrets from each other. Whether it's an outfit, a new tea, or a celebrity crush. We've always been open books with each other.

"So Astrid rules your friendships?" Diana fixes me with a hard look. "Let's stop pretending. Every time I mentioned dressing up in our gowns, you kept saying it's not ready, but you've been designing it for months. It is because you secretly want to win queen and think I'll take that from you?"

"No. I want us to do the ball together. Don't be upset . . ." I stop mid-sentence and twirl my hair with a finger. "Astrid has been extra controlling lately."

The last thing I want to do is lose my best friend because the stress of the ball is getting to everyone.

"I'm so hurt that I want to split in half like an atom," she replies and abruptly turns. She marches toward the door with Joey following behind.

"Take a breath and chew some gum." Joey hands her a pack

from her back pocket. "Stop walking so damn fast. Where are you going?"

If I know Diana at all, tomorrow she will cool down and we can talk about our dresses. Hopefully.

When they exit, I swallow the lump in my throat.

I find my phone and text Theo the longest message of what just happened with Diana. He has this cure to soothe me. Anytime I feel broken or weak, he's the person I turn to. Sometimes without thinking.

Ever since Papi passed away, Theo has taken Papi's place as my protector. No matter if I stab my hand with a s'more's stick or get mean comments on social media, he's the first to come to my rescue. He's my safe place.

Following, I send Diana a text of a poodle in a polka-dot sweater. She thinks fluffy dogs in clothes are the most hilarious visuals ever. I add that I don't want the ball to get in the way of our friendship and that I'm sorry I was scared to stand up to Astrid.

"Everything will be fine," I say, turning toward the hallway ramp that loops toward the basement. Checking on the antiques gives me a peace of mind, otherwise I'll be upset about Diana the entire day. I don't want to do that.

"Yes, it will be," Hudson says, materializing from around a corner.

"Oh, hi." I fix my posture. I pause for an awkward moment. "Er, what's up?" I never say that. No one here says that.

"Where are you going? The basement?" He casually slips his hands into his pant pockets.

"Yeah, was thinking about it," I say, voicing my thoughts out loud.

With that, I turn down the hallway decorated with fruit

paintings against ivory wallpaper and heavy tan curtains on large windows.

Hudson follows.

I like that he follows. His warmth next to me is nice.

Ten

WE EXCHANGE a few glances until he asks me how I'm feeling. "Diana just *left*," I say a little heated. "It's somewhat frustrating she's choosing to be mad."

"I got the perfect cure for that." He spins around and walks backwards.

"It's not like I didn't invite her to be mean."

Talking to him is easier this time around. It's as if we're back to our old closeness.

"Her hurt might be coming from someplace else, like the reminder of not being invited to a party or some shit."

I spot the antique leaf-decorated engraved wooden door. "Yeah, maybe." She could be having an off day or upset about something else. I rest my emotions and focus on the next task at hand.

I turn the knob and push the door open with my footrest. Before we venture in, I warn Hudson, "It's a bit dusty."

"It is still haunted?" he asks behind me.

"With ghosts and everything."

Once upon a time, this had been our hideaway, the place where we played *I Spy with My Little Eye* when we were kids.

"I don't believe in ghosts," he says. "Or anything you can't actually materialize."

The comment passes as a stale rose oil scent hits me. Dust filters through the air when we enter. The hundred-year-old mirror lies across the wooden nightstand. I switch on the century-old chandelier with a modern touch added—replaceable lightbulbs. The only replaceable items in here.

It's a mini museum that contains all of my family history. There are items from the ancestors on my mother's side who migrated from France and Colombia. And some from Papi's family and ancestors from Spain and Brazil: woven baskets, bird pictures, golden bracelets, and small wooden toys.

The walls are packed with books, lamps, jewelry, miniature statues, coins, and every kind of brass and gold gadget. It's a rectangular room with a window at the top right corner just above the ground level. Candles in old-fashioned holders are mounted in the walls at regular intervals. Papi used to instruct the staff to never clean this room because he wanted it to be a sacred space. Secretly, I think he wanted to be the only one to care for everything because he did so with love.

Dozens of first-edition books line the one wall. The largest item is a twelve-foot painting of the first train in Verdan from the 1900s.

A collection of glimmering gems and rocks shine in glass enclosures on the dining table.

How the things we make and how we end up where we are is truly a fascinating study.

I can spend hours with old things, uncovering their past and mapping out their histories. The room is a treasure trove for me. Or an archeological site. No one comes down here except for me. Astrid complains it looks messy and disorganized, and Mother fusses over how every corner is dusty. Some places in the mansion are more occupied than others. I'm the only one who cares enough to spend time here because I know no one else cares to, and thus it makes it my own place.

Across the room, the surface of a small cabinet houses my personal collection. First gum wrapper, first movie ticket, first toothbrush, first handmade wooden doll by Papi. Priceless, but only to me. I started the collection at three years old when I got my first dolphin necklace. The dolphin was my first imaginary friend. There's a special magic to firsts. They deserve to be cherished.

I suddenly remember Hudson is watching me. "Just ignore that pile of junk," I say, and hurry to shield my old things. In my mind, my "fossils" are cool, but admitting out loud that I want my things to be preserved is not cool. It's one thing to collect antiques decades and centuries old, but my collection is private.

Hudson slowly rotates in a full circle and whistles. "This is nothing. You should see my yarn collection."

I laugh a little. "You're funny."

He waves off my skepticism. "I'm serious. But don't tell anyone. It's a secret."

Okay . . . . I never imagined he had a yarn *collection*. He's never shared anything about it. Though I wish I knew where I stuffed the funky, holey scarf he made me.

Hudson's enormous smile widens. "You like scarves?" He pulls out a purple-and-black tangle of yarn. "My grandma helped me make it."

I giggle and poke a finger through a hole. "This is not a scarf. Plus, it's summer. Why would I want a scarf?"

He shrugs and exhales deeply, as if disappointed. "Just

thought you might want to have something to keep you warm at night. My older brothers say it's how you tell a girl you want to have a slumber party with her."

I giggle again. "You're a boy! *I can only have slumber parties with girls. Don't you have boy slumber parties?"*

"Boys don't do that," says his older brother from behind us. His twelve-year-old body towers over us. "Hudson, knitting is not how you get girls. I told you, it's all in the flashy cars and nice hair." He slides his hand over the side of his head and folds his arms together with a smirk. Hudson does his best to imitate his brother, but his smirk ends in a jack-o'-lantern grin.

I laugh once more. "Boys are sooo weird. At least Theo likes to talk about slumber parties." Theo is my best friend.

Hudson's cheeks turn red, and he stomps away.

I snap back to the present, wishing once more I knew Hudson better. "When did you start knitting?"

"My nonna would knit. I liked experimenting with the yarns and needles." Hudson leans against a cabinet. "I loved hanging out with her more than knitting. She told me that knitted gifts are the greatest gifts, but when I made a scarf for someone, it didn't go well. Now I knit in secret and volunteer at the senior center to teach old folks. Nothing impressive to show off, but it's rewarding seeing Danielle or Angel learn to knit even if they forget how to the next day."

"That's selfless of you, and I loved the scarf you gave me." My stomach drops. I hope I wasn't the reason he doesn't openly knit. I'm sure if I really searched for the scarf in a storage box, I could find it. "You should post pictures on the socials."

Hudson deflects. "It's over-the-walls dusty here," he says, spinning around. "Definitely makes it special."

I stare at the thick layer of dust on the cabinets. Part of me wants to wipe away the dust, and the other wants to treasure its sense of antiquity. The history of the dust particles.

There's this eerie silence as if the ghosts and spirits are watching us.

"Is this a throne?" Hudson drops into the eight-foot seat decorated with crowns. "This must be worth millions."

"Yeah, it's from ancient Egypt. My grandparents got it on a trip." Half of these items probably can go for millions. One-of-a-kind antiques that are rare and unique enough to be in a museum. The town once had a museum, but the Kippurs bought it and turned it into a law firm.

Hudson waves the dust away and sneezes, knocking off more dust on himself from the throne. His shoulders dirty, his hair looking old and gray.

I grab a napkin from the purse hanging on my armrest and rush to him.

"Lean down," I say.

He abides, and we're so close I almost inhale the old particles. I swipe the napkin over the side of his shoulder and neck.

There's a mole on his neck paired with a few freckles around it. I don't stare too long because he's clearly watching me analyzing his smooth skin.

Suddenly he sneezes and I shriek, laughing. The dust settles around us and now *my* hair is old and gray looking.

"I really should clean up." It's embarrassing. Sometimes it's easy to let things fall into a rhythm and a cycle, but a fresh, spotless look can give old treasures a shine. While cleaning, I might even discover artifacts that have new stories to tell.

"We can leave," I add immediately. Not that I'm trying to impress him, but if I was, this wouldn't be the way to do it.

"No, I like it here." He hops up and examines the part of

the room near the throne. "You used to say that each object has a story. We shall remember that."

When I sneak a glance at Hudson, he gives one back, hands clasped behind his back. With dust smudges on his face and clothes, he's lost some of the polish from earlier. But I like him this way.

Now he's full-on looking in my direction. His smile grows. Those pearly whites could be a commercial all by themselves. If he didn't breathe, he'd look like a cardboard cutout. Dust smudges and all.

There's a subtle light to his face from the dimmed chandelier swinging from the ceiling. The frosted glass from the window gives him a hazy shine. Hudson gets more handsome the longer I study his strong jawline and almond-shaped hazel eyes. A rush of heat spreads across my cheeks.

He holds my eyes with a long stare. The intensity in his gaze does something strange to my insides.

When he steps closer, I back up an inch. Something other than Hudson needs to warrant my attention. I've realized that being alone with him gets my brain all jumbled up.

A gold picture frame hangs next to a framed 1920s newspaper clipping with a recap of the debutante ball. I rest my hand around my neck. "Look." I point. "That's my great-great-grandmother with the pearls. It's the very first debutante ball in Verdan."

Hudson strides over, pushes his face close to the clipping, and nods his approval. "They were damn fancy. We're so going to out-fancy them." He does a tap dance across the room, kicking up a haze of dust. When I giggle, he dances back to me, finishing with a bow.

He sneezes again and I laugh. "We can go."

I slowly roll out of the room, leaving him to shut the door

behind us. As we head back down the hall to the living room, I find myself telling him everything without pause.

"I have an intense schedule today. I have to tutor kids, take a business class, and help the Ashleys and Pyper with summer school." All the tutoring gives me community service hours, but it's honestly more rewarding to see someone's face when they finally "get it." Whether that be math, history, or French, making someone feel smart is the best feeling.

"This early in the morning?" He's too cocky for his own good.

"Yeah." As much as I wish Hudson and I could stay in the antiques room forever, I speed ahead. He jogs, telling me how one day he'll show me his yarn collection and how the needles work together with the yarn.

It all sounds exciting even though I'm not into string stuff.

In the foyer, the front door swings open. Mother enters with her client, Mr. Lee, and his daughter, Natasha. Her smile is as big as the sun. Today we have several French worksheets to complete.

"Mr. Lee wants to get a heart-designed sapphire necklace for his wife's birthday," I whisper to Hudson. "My mother is having me tutor Natasha for an hour as a favor. But I'd do it even if Mother wasn't getting something out of it. Tutoring kids is my favorite."

"If I help and you get done early, can I take that remaining time?" he asks.

"Sure," I say, loving the idea of more time with Hudson. It's as if he read my mind.

Mr. Lee stops and answers a vibrating phone. "Don't flip out." He huffs and paces. "If Sylvia gets pushed out of the company, I want to make sure I get her last design," he says to the caller, brushing past me.

I replay the comment in my head. *Mother is being pushed out?*

The eight-year-old twirls in her tutu and rainbow shirt. "*Bonjour!*" Natasha sings.

"Good job. You said that perfectly." I motion her to a desk in the study room. "Today, we're going to learn about how to order food."

My stomach drops, thinking about the possibility that Mother could be jobless. There's no way that can happen. I refuse to believe it. There must be an explanation, must be more context than the worst-case scenario playing in my head.

Natasha skips across the polished floor. "I wanna order watermelon cake for my dad. He *loves* anything watermelon." She giggles to herself and dances into her seat. "My dad and I love to go to the Magenta Diner." She spins in the chair and wiggles her legs. "And then my dad—"

"That's great," I say, a bit louder than I intended. I open the binder with shaking hands. "Let's get started with writing."

I push away the pang of jealousy at the privilege Natasha has to spend time with her father. I wish I could open the black bag Theo brought over, but at the same time, it's too hard. I had peeked into the tiny opening. Inside was some brown, worn-out piece of leather, part of a book? It could be an old edition or something we read together. Either way, I'm not sure when I'll be ready to uncover what's inside.

I can't handle the pain that comes with remembering what once was when I can't handle a little girl talking about her father. I can't even handle finding out Mother's company could be falling apart. But what I hate the most is how Papi's death took our normal life and turned it into the forbidden memory we can't talk about.

Maybe I actually want to talk about it. Not doing so is just as hard.

Natasha hums a song to herself, writing French words. *Un gateau de pastèque. S'il vous plaît.*

"Your writing is way better than mine," Hudson says, glued to her every pencil stroke. "You must be a straight-A student."

She nods and goes on talking to each letter like it's a tea party on the worksheet.

I sigh deeply and remind myself of what Papi taught me. That life's plans are more perfect than my own plans.

Yet . . . is Papi's death sinking the business? What if Mother is paying Elijah to do something illegal just to keep us afloat? What secrets is everyone hiding from me?

Hudson meets my pained gaze and winks. His presence makes everything bearable.

His attempt at pronouncing French words gets Natasha and me giggling. I want to say how nice it is to have him here, but I keep the thought to myself.

We end up spending longer than usual with the worksheets because Hudson keeps misteaching Natasha what the words mean.

Mother invites the Lees to stay for brunch. Mr. Lee seems pleased with his purchase and with my tutoring. Natasha shares her new French phrases with him. Mother smiles, looking almost relaxed.

Then again, image is everything and people are really good actors. I need to get out of here. If I stay, I might cry, and that would be worse than being naked in front of Hudson.

There's no handbook for how to react if someone loses a

job. "I'll eat later," I say and excuse myself. My room has a junk food drawer when I want some comfort food.

Hudson whispers in my ear. "You free *now?*"

"A little bit." I pause because it's best if he leaves. "But." I can't risk him seeing a side of me that he won't like. I can't risk doing anything to scare him off as my escort.

"Perfect. Let's go steal the limo." As if that statement isn't ridiculous enough, he heads to the front door.

Hudson has to be joking.

Mother and Mr. Lee are deep in conversation, barely noticing our departure. Natasha plays with her food, talking French phrases to the silverware.

I pick up speed, circling into the foyer and past the marble table.

Hudson presses a silver button and the main door opens. He glances back at me, throwing me a crooked smile that's full of trouble.

Eleven

OUTSIDE, the limo sits in the center of our circular driveway —a space large enough for five cars—lined with different shades of pink and yellow roses.

Hudson fiddles with the vase next to the column closest to the front door and steals the emergency key from underneath. Just like when we were younger. He rounds the shiny black hood of the limo and slips into the open window of the driver's seat. It's a high step but not too hard for him. First it's one leg, then his body, and finally the second leg. A bulky guy like that must have been a gymnast in a previous life because he can bend and twist like no normal person can.

He grins. "Your turn."

I shake my head. "Pretending to drive the limo when we were kids and actually driving are two different things. We'll get in trouble."

Completely ignoring me, Hudson presses several random buttons in the limo. Until . . .

There's a click and the side door opens, a ramp automatically uncoils. The interior lights illuminate the space and the leather seat that protrudes from the corner. It's spacious enough for six people or three wheelchairs. Everything is automatic—windows, lights, drinks, seat warmers. If I want something, I can activate it via voice command.

"I'm taking this babe for a spin whether or not you come." He peeks through the large window space separating the driver from the passengers. With a grunt, he tumbles through it and dances to the middle of the ramp.

This plan has no plan, which means anything can happen. I'm the type of person who prefers every detail figured out. Most people don't have to worry about stairs at a restaurant or high tables at events, but for me, not planning means showing up to some place that might send me back home.

I glance back. "This feels wrong. Not just this, but something is wrong with Mother. The company, I think. And this is no time to be silly." I wave a useless hand. "We can plan for something tomorrow."

As much as I'd like to spend time with him, my worries about Mother overpower what I want to do with Hudson. I can't shake the strange feeling off that things are unstable. She could be receiving terrible news and I'm completely absent. This could be the last time I see her, and I'm choosing to spend time with a boy. The déjà vu of last summer flashes before me, ripping me open—the terror of pushing Papi away when he wanted to have a cup of hot chocolate with him.

"This might be exactly what you need," Hudson says, bowing low as if to welcome me inside the limo.

"I don't know."

"Be spontaneous." His answer does nothing to ease my fears. "When was the last time you did something *unplanned*?"

I can't think of a time, but keeping to a schedule is productive and keeps everything in control.

When I look into his puppy dog eyes, I'm sucked in. "Fine. Only for ten minutes."

He gives me two thumbs up.

I immediately regret my decision yet roll inside anyway. "Don't forget to strap me in."

"Sure thing."

He lifts my entire body in a swift motion. I squeal, clenching onto his jacket as we head to the front passenger's seat.

He sets me down—through the door and not the window, thankfully.

"There." His arm reaches across my chest with a belt, and then across the other side of me with his belt.

He's being sarcastic on purpose.

"This is not what I meant." I huff and push the unnecessary strap off. It zips back to its spot as he buckles me into my seat belt. "You need to ask permission before you get me out of my chair. *Plan* to do it." I keep a straight face. "*Before* you lift me, Mr. Smart Guy."

Hudson chuckles, then immediately nods. "Sorry, my bad. It's not funny. I won't do it again."

I nod back, keeping to myself. I can sit up in a regular seat with the support of the armrests.

As if I'm not fully convinced of his apology, he takes my hand and kisses the top of it. "I apologize."

He captures me with a devious stare, deep enough to clear my mind of any worries. Only for a second though, because I pull my hand back. The guilt of sneaking out hits me hard.

Shutting my door, he leaves behind a gust of wind.

The window glass is so clear, I can see my reflection. There are a million buttons on the dashboard and a few on the sides of the doors. But I have a million more anxieties building up. I comb my fingers through my long ponytail as my lip-biting habit begins.

"Done and done," Hudson says after securing my wheelchair. He shuts all the doors before sliding into the driver's seat —through the window, of course.

As we pull out, I take in the view from the front seat. This is so out of my comfort zone. I've never sneaked out of the mansion, let alone stolen a limo.

I stare at the reflective streamers wrapped around the trees. Miles and miles of land stretch out with fences and gates protecting exquisite properties. We're fifteen minutes away from downtown. In the day, the streets are filled with shoppers and business meetings in restaurants. The buildings seem to wear suits or dresses as if to impress the fifty-story black-and-silver building at the center of the square. Everything is shiny and clean, never a cracked sidewalk or visible trashcan within a mile radius of downtown. At night, the nightclubs and music festivities play on the east side. On the west side, hotels stand next to each other like blocks with sparkling hats on top, hinting at castle vibes. Jazz and country songs play on the loudspeakers of the red clock.

I glance at Hudson. He's not stressed out at all. The wind whizzes through his hair. Mine springs up. I try to catch each strand and hold them down.

"Trust me, you'll have fun."

He says it as if "worried" is written across my forehead.

I let my hair fly free and rub my lips together. *Don't worry.*

The sunrays glow on his face as he speeds up on a yellow light. There are barely any cars around since we're not on the main road, but the rows of Japanese cherry blossom trees in full bloom take up my entire view. The sidewalks have wooden benches with occasional canopies covering larger benches that could seat five.

"What if something goes wrong?" I whisper. For all I know, we could get stuck on a dirt road with no phone service. My stomach churns.

"Then I'll make it right." He's too confident for his own good. "I can teach you how to drive. Wanna take the wheel?"

My eyes widen. "No, I can't. No."

He chuckles at my panic.

"I'm serious. We should turn around."

I gaze at the trees outside the window as we drive. They transform into a more structured, artificial look as we speed into the downtown area.

Hudson raps on the steering wheel. "I would, but we're more than halfway there. Don't you trust me?"

I want to trust him with my life, but . . . "To be honest, I don't know you." My fears bubble up at the worst time. It's not that I don't *know* him, it's that he grew up so much that I don't know anything about him. Like knitting at the senior center. Like not wanting to go to college. Like not traveling this summer. He once told me he wanted to see the world and that he liked this girl a year older than him. What happened to all of that? He's a completely different person now.

His brows lift. "Wow, so it's like that?"

I collect every stray strand of hair and turn my ponytail into a side bun. "And you don't know me," I add sadly. There's a lot I've been through. Papi's death last summer for one, and being at war with Elijah.

"Ouch," he says, putting a hand over his chest and squeezing his breast. "Now that one hurt."

We slow for a couple pushing a stroller across the street. The buzz of music strikes me when we pass a vegan restaurant.

"I'm serious." He doesn't have a clue who I am. Clearly has no clue I hate being spontaneous. We're not children anymore. Growing up changed us.

His lips dance as if wanting to say something. "You're right. We used to be friends and I hate that we fell out of touch. My brothers wanted to be cool and I wanted that too. I did everything they did. Older kids were cooler—you know every kid thinks that. I was the youngest and so small, trying hard to catch up. I wanted to chase girls when they did. I'm sorry I got sidetracked with dating and lost sight of you."

I avoid his eyes by looking at a motorcycle passing by. "Okay." I pause. "Dating people means having less time for others." The sinking feeling sucks, but I accept it.

We stay silent until Hudson continues, "The constant motion of dating over the years got old fast. They only care about having fun. My friends are all athletes, and they encourage it, the partying and having fun. I broke up with my girlfriend last week. She couldn't spare me a hundred bucks for gas when I realized my cards were all frozen." He shakes his head. "I need better people around me, like you, Abby. I can't rely on grandmas to buy my knitted pillows and cardigans forever."

My eyes work to his. The closeness knocks on my front door, pounding, thundering to open the whole house up. When I do, butterflies in my stomach come along and I can't think about anything other than how he looks at me with those soft yet dangerous hazel eyes of his. How his stare traces to my shoulder and back to my eyes, giving me a faint smile.

Before I can say anything, he explains, "All the parties were stupid. All the rich people my family wants to impress don't care about people personally, just their worth. I feel used and alone, Abby. I'm not kidding. *No one* knows me. I don't have a genuine connection with anyone. Not even my brothers. Especially not my brothers. I want authentic people who want me for me and not my money." He scratches his head. "I've never said that to anyone."

I soak in his words. His *admission*.

A ray of sunlight flickers across his eyes when he checks the rearview mirror.

"I appreciate your honesty," I say and immediately want to say more. I want to hear everything he's been through and tell him everything I've been through. "You can tell me anything."

"Four years. I wasted four years on girls who ended up using me when the most important one was next door to me." There's a quietness to his statement. Is he saying he wished he dated me? "My brothers are part owners of the family wineries, and everyone thought I'd follow them. They thought I'd be a somebody, too." He drums his fingers on the steering wheel. "Those girls didn't want *me*. They wanted a Giordani. When Hayden and Huff left for college, I was lost. My parents tried to help me, but I hate organized learning crap. Especially other people's plans."

I'm stuck on his comment about how the most important girl was next door to him. Unless he's talking about Astrid, which I doubt—unless he secretly wished he could have dated her? I scratch my head and tell myself not to jump to conclusions.

A guitarist is playing on the street corner. People in professional suits nod and smile when they pass him.

"We can start being there for each other now," I offer. "Happy graduation, by the way. Did you have a party? We can celebrate over lunch."

"Thanks." Hudson is quiet for a moment. Then he continues in a voice laced with anger. "My father's graduation present to me was cutting me off financially last week. He wants to give me a reality check of not falling in line. But I'll wait until my contract offer expires next weekend. Then *he'll* get the reality check that I want to pick my own apartment, not the one they want. I want to live my own damn life. He said it was a teaching moment, so I ignore him when I can. I'm home when he's not and go elsewhere when he is."

"You're totally cut off?" I ask, shocked. Guess you never know what someone is going through. "Like, no money at all?" What about food, gas, and clothes? "You have savings, right?"

The panic is back. I consider having to move out of the mansion if Mother gets fired. Can that even happen if my family owns the company?

"That's only available *if* I go to college."

He drags his stare to me and says calmer, "Seeing you is nice. I like it." His tear-filled eyes get to me.

"Thanks," I mutter, wishing I could fix this for him. "You're smart, handsome, talented." Compliments go a long way in this town. "You can find a job or start a business. I'll totally help. My savings aren't millions, but it's a start." My offer is genuine.

Being broke has never crossed my mind. What if Elijah is giving Mother money because we are financially struggling, and no one wants me to worry about finances? What if this whole millionaire town is secretly broke and it's all a façade?

My two thousand dollars a month allowance hasn't changed. But what if that money is fueled by Elijah? I shiver at the thought. "We can talk about how much life sucks."

"Nothing we can't handle." He sighs and it's clear he's reverting. Those hazels narrow further into oblivion.

I lock my gaze on the window and squint at the oak tree ahead. It's smack in the middle of the street behind the red clock—the epicenter of Verdan. The intersection connects five different roads. We turn left onto one of them.

When a full minute passes—the dashboard's digital clock flashes off the seconds—he breaks the silence.

"My future is set. I'm a charming player who studies girls and steals a limo to go break wine bottles," he says sarcastically. "We're all doomed."

I laugh. "Wow, I didn't know this was your way of trying to impress a girl."

"It's not. I was joking," he says. He's a Giordani, the King of Hickeys, with a driving-over-the-speed-limit charm.

I feel an unexpected blush creep across my cheeks. I knew *that*, that he was only joking. He's clearly not trying to impress me or show me he's here for me because he likes me. We're just old friends catching up. He's doing a nice deed by being my escort.

The fantasy of us, the possibility of him liking me, the dream of us kissing slowly fades to the back of my mind. Or rather, I push it to the back of my head with both hands, my six wheels, and a stack of planners.

Hudson turns the blinker on and switches lanes.

"Wanna do fast food?" I ask.

Deflection.

Because stuffing our faces with French fries, daring each other to count how many we can fit in our mouths, is less scary than being in a tight space together. "Fries and chocolate milk-shakes?" Since we're going off on a no plan, plan.

"Wine?" He steps on the gas, and we take off so fast, I lunge forward.

"We're underage," I say as if he's forgotten his age. It's one thing to sneak out and a totally different thing to drink alcohol.

"If we get caught, I'll get disqualified from the ball for being reckless and then some."

"Don't worry, we won't drink and drive," he says seriously and whips a hard right into a parking lot.

There are a few cars here, but people are entering and exiting the place like a rotating coffee stand.

When we pull up to a tall building—a quick count says it's twenty stories—I lean toward the passenger window and look up at its twisting spiral form pushing into the sky. It's one of the most distinctive buildings in town.

"Isn't this where your family works?" I ask, dumbfounded. The large golden GIORDANI sign on the top of the building gives it away. We snuck out to look at wine? When I imagined something spontaneous, this was not it.

"Let's break things."

He leaps out and stares at the shadowy spiral.

"Wait, Hudson." I squeal. "Wait . . . No . . . . What are you . . ." I rap my knuckles on the glass window.

Twelve

PEOPLE in flashy suits occupy the lobby's every inch. There's someone with a professional camera, a leather briefcase, a coffee mug, a newspaper . . . A hefty security guard stands by each of the four elevators. Breaking things has to be a joke. "Hudson —" I drop my voice low. "We can't do illegal stuff, even if this place belongs to your family." I glance back at the limo in the parking lot.

I'll be disqualified *and* thrown in jail.

Hudson struts to the first elevator and throws a fake knuckle punch with the guard. The guy cracks a smile for half a second. Hudson casually strolls along like he's done this a million times before. Even if he's got the cameras wired and the guards in his back pocket, I don't approve.

As he leans against an open elevator door, I catch up. He's loosened his grin, acting as if he's the luckiest man on the planet.

"You're my ride back. It's the only reason I'm following you, but I can't let you go wild with vandalism." I glance nervously back and forth. "Right?" This feels dangerous.

"We're really going to mess things up." He winks at me. It's the kind of wink that's half-devious and half-silly, capable of casting a spell over me and anyone else.

"I'll allow a two-second peek, and then we go," I say in a stern tone and roll into the glass-walled elevator. I back into a corner and glare at him. I frown so deeply, I give my forehead a headache. A *foreache*. "I mean it."

I study him, but he doesn't look guilty. His face is illuminated by the elevator lights. The freckles on his nose are more visible here than in the natural light.

"So, *where* are we going?"

"Nothing illegal planned here." He throws his hands up before swiping a gold key card and pressing the R button. "Just the roof. It's the best place to get your frustrations out and be smashingly artistic."

"This is going to get us into so much trouble," I say more to myself than him. Mother's disappointment and her anticipated yelling ring in my head, on top of everything else she has to deal with. "Why are we doing this again?"

The key card goes into his back pocket. He keeps his smirk from completely forming.

"Because you're frustrated."

"Me?" I practically squeal in shock. "I am *not* frustrated!" I stare him down long enough to get blood rushing to my ears. They're more than red with fire—they burn a hot blue flame. So hot, they combust. But he meets my gaze, unfazed. He's so infuriating!

When the doors ping open, he struts out and shrugs out of his jacket. His shoes casually rap against the concrete floor. Rooftop couches and umbrellas stretch out in front of me. The beds are covered in silk sheets with canopies over them.

Liquor cabinets and a refrigerator stand in the right corner. To my left is a large glass cube with dark stains dripping down the walls.

Interesting.

Hudson turns on his heel and tosses his jacket onto a chair. "Come break things." A deceitful smile crosses his face.

I circle to his side, barely missing the tips of his shoes. If only I can give a commanding "no." Instead I croak out, "Let's draw up some plan for this."

He chuckles and moves toward the glass cube.

The two-inch-thick glass wall is coated with an almost invisible metal layer. The closer I get, the more paint splatters I count on the walls. It looks more like a bloodstain in a glass box than anything deliberately artistic.

Hudson opens a white chest that's against the wall and pulls out white ponchos and eye protection gear. He slaps goggles on me and himself.

"You're almost ready."

I squeal and rearrange the plastic over my nose.

Does this mean there's no backing out?

"I am *not* frustrated!" I declare once again.

He laughs, covering me with a white poncho, and then doing the same to himself. The outfit is rather comfy. If we're "breaking" paints, then maybe that doesn't seem like a half-bad idea. This could be fun.

Once we enter through the opening, he shuts the glass door behind him.

The box of empty wine bottles in the corner doesn't have paint or brushes. I glance from corner to corner. There's nothing artistic in here. Pieces of broken glass twinkle under the fairy lights strung across the roof.

"Wait a minute," I mutter.

The smash of a bottle echoes around us. I shriek and cover my ears.

"At least give me a warning first!"

Hudson hands me a smaller bottle. "Fine. You try."

I rearrange my goggles. "Fine, I will!" I raise my arm slightly and chuck the glass at the wall. It hits with a thump and doesn't break.

"This isn't for me," I say in an irritated tone.

He steps next to my side. "I'll help you." Bottle in my hand, he holds my hand, and together we toss it with full force. The bottle shatters. Red wine sprays everywhere. A few drops even make it to my poncho.

"My brothers and I built this years ago to get our anger out when our parents fucked up," he explains.

Seriously?

I'm not sure how to react. We are still hurting company property even if this space was created for smashing company wine bottles. I'll do just one more and then call it quits.

He gets me another one, and this time I chuck it at a corner. The glass breaks in half.

"I can do better," I say, disappointed with the outcome.

He tosses two bottles with one hand. Total show-off.

I tighten my goggles and wheel around Hudson, grabbing a bottle from the ground. I focus on the spot of the glass wall I want to hit. It's above my knees and to the left. I'm right-handed, but my left hand is stronger. I bend my elbow and raise the bottle, ready to launch.

It slips and crashes behind me.

"Hey, that works too," Hudson says with a laugh. "Get angry." He hands me another bottle.

I shake my head. "I don't get angry."

"Abby." A smirk curls his lips. "I won't let you quit." He leans in to the point that I can make out individual golden specks in his eyes. Those beautiful eyes.

"You can do this," he says with conviction. Papi used to give me encouragement when I wanted to give up.

Trying one more time does feel good.

Pivoting, I grip the bottle tight. "Okay, I will."

"Now throw that anger."

I take in a deep breath.

Angry. I can be angry.

I chuck it at the wall. The glass barely makes a sound.

"What pisses you off?" He tosses a bottle up. I catch it on my lap. "Yell."

I inhale and wish my family didn't keep secrets from me. "No one tells me anything!"

The glass slips a bit in my hand as I swing it upward at the ceiling. Then it falls hard enough to break against the cement.

"No one tells me anything," I repeat quieter.

A silent scream belts through my head.

"I'm tired of watching my family drowning in stress." I've come to the realization that I need to step up and help. "It's time I take our image seriously. There's no reason the board should have to fire my mother, and Elijah will not have money favors hanging over her head."

Hudson rubs my shoulder to soothe my tension. "It'll all work out."

"How do you know? You're not a businessperson, are you?" I ask. Even if he doesn't work in the business, he might be around it enough to know something. "Do you know anything about checking financials? Like how well a business is doing or its debts?" I pause. "We're so going to lose our home."

How do company contracts work? Elijah could be loaning

Mother money and in exchange gets to take our mansion. The Kippurs do like to take other people's buildings. His family has visited more over the months, acting like they're at an open house, investigating every corner and closet.

"If you must know, the jewelry company's stocks did drop after your father died. My mother talks to yours about it all the time. Even if the board wants to replace your mom because she can't increase revenue or attend meetings, I doubt you'll have to move out of the mansion. Two of my friends' families lost their jobs but never had to leave their home. Your family has savings and other assets to fall back on." He pauses, searching my face. "At the end of the day, the company's success is not on you."

My head hangs low. His comforting words can't mask the truth: we're in a worse situation than I could imagine. Time to panic. I have a year of high school left and Astrid is getting married in December. I could move into Papi's cabin with Theo, although it'd be strictly on roommate terms. Astrid will be okay since she'll move in with Elijah. But what about Mother? She is used to a certain level of luxury. It would kill her to beg her parents for money, after all they've already given her. They gave her the company and the mansion so they could travel and not worry about anything.

Hudson leans over. "That's adult shit. Not your issues to solve. Until then, we smash bottles."

I nod. Okay, we smash bottles. I'll smash bottles now and plan how to restore our image later. We'll need a team of professionals and important people to vouch for us. Mr. Lee seems like a good start.

Surely other companies go into a dip. We must have savings. We can use my college fund. I'll apply for scholarships and get student loans. Everything will work out. It has to because I don't want Mother or Astrid to fail.

I snatch a bottle and center myself in the middle of the cubicle. I let it fly and it shatters with a satisfying crash.

The adrenaline builds, my frustration burns hot, and I take up another one. "Ah!" The glass hits above the mark from the previous one. I get angrier. "I hate Papi is not here to save us!"

I gasp at that unexpected statement and glance at Hudson. "Sorry. I don't want to be angry about his death." The words fade at the end.

"Ignoring the pain doesn't make the reality go away," he says. "I'm here for you."

My breathing accelerates, and I take another bottle, flinging it at the wall. "Papi should be here for the ball!" Saying those words out loud releases a tension, a sadness in me. Or exacerbates it. I can't tell. "It was me who should have drowned, not him!"

A beat pauses as I exhale. I ruminate on Papi's last breath.

My shoulders deflate as Hudson rubs them.

"I'm sorry about what happened," he whispers. "I'm grateful you're here."

Today is not the day I talk about Papi, but I do have one more thing to say. The biggest bottle catches my eye and I grab it from the box.

"I wish I knew why Diana was really upset with me!"

I spin the bottle sideways and aim at the floor.

The glass shatters, tiny pieces bouncing on the cement.

"It really smashed!" My squeal is louder than I intend.

Hudson side hugs me, and I share my gratitude. "Thanks. I guess, I *am* frustrated. Have been for a long time."

"You're welcome." He flips the box over and drops down on top of it. "It really is nice to see you, to talk to you, Abby."

"Same here." A weight has been lifted off my shoulders.

There's something comforting about being near Hudson.

Then I pivot. "I won't let you quit, either. Let's plan your career together. There are options other than lacrosse." Talking about his problems is way better than talking about mine. If I go unpacking *all* my problems, I might crumble to pieces. Doing so will definitely scare Hudson off.

"Have you *ever* had a planner?" I ask.

"I want to control my own plans, not have plans control me." He shrugs. "I prefer the trial-and-error type of planning. You know, like dating. You try and see if you like it, and if not, you move on. If you really want something, you don't need a plan for it."

I wonder if he uses words like that with everyone. Building up walls between other people and himself, so they focus on the wall and not on him.

So they can't see him at all.

"I appreciate what you're trying to do," he adds. "But life is complicated. It can't really be fixed with calendars." He focuses on the purple-red stains running down the surrounding glass. "I have no doubt your planning skills are off the charts, though."

We stay put to the point where his warm breath becomes comforting. I try to understand his rationalization. Those wise words of his. They've planted a brick wall in front of me, and I stare at them.

He watches me, unmoving and calm. His eyes trace my face from feature to feature—from my brows to my eyelashes, cheeks, eyes, nose, and then lips. The way he examines every detail keeps me silent.

"I hate how this town applauds my getting into NYU when I don't even want college. I told the coach I wasn't going to sign the athletic contract, but until the deadline passes next weekend, everyone will keep trying to push me to sign it. That's why I need my own freedom."

"Anything I can do?" I ask.

It's my turn to study his face. It's a good face. A great face. But I can't tell if he's seriously that unconcerned with his future.

This might be a bigger problem than I imagined. I'm pretty driven about my future—impress everyone at the ball, conquer senior year, and take on college as a business major.

And he's . . . well, he's in park. Or maybe neutral.

Most likely reverse.

"Just be next to me," he finally says.

I nod. "I can do that."

He pushes my hair from my neck and plays with a curl. His eyes focus on it as if it's the most important object in the world. His exhale caresses my face. No guy has ever played with my hair before—besides Papi. Hudson is so gentle.

Little by little he moves closer as if wanting to collide with me. Actual lips are about to touch mine. The sounds from the distant street vanish as his breath crashes into me. My heart rate achieves new galloping records when his lips are an inch away.

There's a flush to his cheeks, and he's ultra-cute when he tilts his head. Those hazel eyes, they're laced with a light golden outline in the sun.

There isn't a whole lot I can wrap around about Hudson's future. But if I had to guess, I'd say he's about to kiss me.

Inches from me, he gives me a crooked smile and it's impossible to push the fireworks away. I can taste the butterflies building up in my stomach and traveling to the roof of my mouth.

"What is this?" a harsh voice yells.

My glance flashes to Mr. Giordani slamming the glass door open.

Thirteen

HUDSON JUMPS TO HIS FEET, pulling his poncho off.

"Dad, relax."

I immediately remove mine and fold it before setting it down. I straighten my lopsided shoulders and follow Hudson out of the small space. This is Mr. Giordani's place of business and we broke his things. Okay, not *his* things, but the bottles are part of his business things. Even if it's no big deal, I broke things on his property.

"I don't care what you do, Hudson," Mr. Giordani replies. "I had to call Abigail's mother to inform her of this incident."

My heart beats fast. "We apologize," I croak out.

Mr. Giordani's polished black leather oxfords clack heavily on the cement. They overpower my voice. They stop and I look up into his glowering eyes. He's telling me I'm wasting his time without saying a word. A cigar scent lingers.

I back up an inch and grab Hudson's hand. He squeezes it, rubbing my thumb with his. My heart rate settles down.

"Dad, don't fuck up someone else's life." Hudson narrows his stare at his father, who's three inches taller than him. "Stop trying to control everything. Cut your losses and accept that you're losing your edge."

Mr. Giordani cocks a brow and dismisses his son with a single flick of the wrist.

"We'll go and I'll pay for any losses." My voice shakes and so do I. Getting in trouble literally crushes me.

"You should make better choices if you want to be taken seriously as a debutante," Mr. Giordani says to me with a stern voice. "You are representing not only the town, but also your family's legacy." His words have me metaphorically tumble backward and fall on my ass.

"Yes," I stammer, looking past him to the elevator. No way I can make a get-away. "You won't be disappointed." I'd say anything right about now.

Mr. Giordani's phone buzzes. He answers with a cold, "Did you do that favor for the magazine?" He pivots, still shooting lasers my way. "I *am* looking out for our son's future."

Backing away, I suck in a deep breath and pull Hudson toward our exit. When we're safely inside the elevator, I swivel my wheels back and forth.

"This is bad."

"It's not." Hudson lowers to his knees and raises my chin up. "I'll confess everything to your mother. You did nothing wrong. We were just preparing for the ball, yeah?"

I shake my head. "Lying is even worse. My mother will be so mad. She's going to yell until the roof comes off."

"If she yells, tell her to yell at me." His thumb rubs my cheek. "Got a red splat right there."

The corners of my mouth slightly curl up. The affection trumps over how scared I am to face Mother.

He stands up, holding my stare.

The doors ping and I take my time rolling into the lobby. Two, ten, thirty seconds pass. Then I see Mother step out of a black car and go to the limo where Hudson had parked it. Diagonally and taking up several spaces, I now notice.

"We'll see each other again," he whispers to me.

I take a deep breath and nod. "Speaking of that, we do need to figure out our dance lesson schedule with Demontae. When are you free this week? The first rehearsal *is* three days away."

Hudson shrugs. "We can wing it."

My stomach plunges. "Wing it?" Terrified and worried are written on my face to the extreme.

"I'll look at some dance videos from previous years," he adds. "Don't sweat it. You've been overpreparing all year. Think about having fun this Friday. It's just rehearsal."

"A-hum. Yeah, okay." Fun. I can have fun.

I twist the ends of a few loose hair strands and roll toward the main doors.

Mother has unlocked the limo and proceeds to operate the ramp as if expecting me any second. If she's taking charge of working the limo, that means she's *really* mad.

Roosevelt stands next to her. He's a middle-aged guy with a bald head and gray eyes. He always wears a black suit and a chauffeur's hat.

I go onwards, fearing losing Hudson. "If I get banned from seeing you and Harry takes your spot, we'll hang out again, right?" Mother has the power to do whatever with my life. She's so going to ground me. In one sentence, she can take Hudson away from my magical ball experience and I won't be able to do anything about it.

"You can't get rid of me that easily." Hudson chuckles and walks backwards so he's in my view. "And I won't let Harry take you from me."

That sounds good. Feels even better. I take this moment as a sign that everything is going to be okay. Hudson has that effect on me. A sign that the ball will be perfect with him. So perfect, we'll share our first kiss together. As much as it would have been beautiful to kiss him on the roof, I believe that when everything aligns—our clothes, perfumes, dance moves, people cheering, lights sparkling—the world will be ours with our kiss.

"Give me your phone," he says, circling me. I hand it over. "I'm putting in my number. I'll call myself *Needle*." He hands it back and draws his own from his back pocket. "You'll be *Yarn*."

His phone vibrates.

"Okay, Needle," I say.

"Okay, Yarn." He winks and stays next to me until we're outside. "I'll take the company car back home."

"Thanks for being part of my debutante plan. See you Friday." That day seems like such a long time away. Because the truth is, I want to be spontaneous and spend tomorrow and the next day with Hudson.

He gives me a single nod. "As you wish, gorgeous."

Mother waits inside the limo as if it's her office and I got summoned. Just like that, the happy thoughts about Hudson fade.

I take in a deep inhale and enter.

We don't make eye contact. Not even when Roosevelt straps my chair in.

She's poised and positioned like the entire world is watching her every move.

"I'm sorry if you're mad Hudson and I took the limo. We needed to get rid of some stress."

My explanation falls on a stone wall. Mother stares ahead.

Her colored blond hair is swept into an elegant bun that accentuates her cheekbones, long neck and perfect posture.

"We didn't hurt anyone," I add. "I'm sorry I didn't tell you I left."

She turns to me and creases her brows. "Being spontaneous to get attention is not classy, Abigail. We can't afford being embarrassed at the ball, or especially before it. We cannot afford to look bad in the press right now. There was a reporter in that lobby and you didn't even notice. Mr. Giordani had to squash the idea that you and Hudson were sneaking around to do irresponsible things."

I watch her sharp cheekbones. The purse on her lap doesn't move an inch. I miss the mother whose laughter was contagious. I miss when she asked how I was doing instead of yelling at me when I disappointed her.

The limo pulls out of the parking lot and I watch everything move. The world just moves on and the people just move on.

"Is it because every time you look at me, you see Papi?" I ask out of nowhere. Maybe she despises me. "Do you hate being reminded of his death? Why don't we *ever* talk about Papi? Or were you pretending to be happy with him? Just got pregnant with Astrid and marriage was the answer, so you kept pretending to act happy until you didn't have to anymore?" We never grieved. We locked our secrets away and it's ruining me. Us.

She flinches, ever so lightly. I know I'm being cruel, but I want her to be honest with me. If not about the company, then about her life. Closed doors tell me nothing.

"The past is in the past," she says coldly. "The future is what's most important."

A sliver of me feels sorry for the disaster she created for

herself. She will never be able to overcome and free herself from the past, no matter how hard she fights to erase Papi's memories. She's killing his spirit, taking my ability to mourn him.

"I don't want to be controlled by anyone." I take a page from Hudson's book. Immediately I regret it with Mother's tilt of the head. Here comes a lecture.

"I am cutting next month's allowance for your outrageous behavior." She pauses, waiting for me for retaliate. I don't, because I sense she needs the money more than I do. She continues with a sharper tone. "Winning queen is more important for you than anyone else. Our image is crucial this year because then people will see us as a powerful family, not one that is crumbling. The future of our jewelry empire relies on how resilient we are—that a widow does not need a man to run a company. Do you want people to see you as strong? Do you want the company, which you will own one day, to survive this?"

"Yes," I reply and then go silent. I retreat to old patterns. It's safer that way.

I honestly have no idea what is going on with my family. That was Papi's job—he knew about every little and big thing, every problem. This feels like it could be over my head.

I text Theo, asking when he's free.

Within seconds, his text pops up on the screen.

I'm free tomorrow. On Wednesdays I have a long break now. Meet then? Have something to tell you, too.

Fourteen

THE CABIN IS ONLY twenty minutes away from the mansion, but it's as if I'm in the depths of a wild forest. Rounding the corner at the head of the lake, the bushes whoosh by. The glistening ripples in the water catch my attention. When Papi got bad news, he used to stare beyond the calm waters in silence.

At the bottom of the path, I swerve to the right, led by the aroma of pine. The woods sing their own tune of swooshing and cracking in the far away distance.

I slow down at the sight of golden window frames. They were supposed to be rainbow glitter, but Papi said he could only befriend the gold unicorn, whom gave him some extra paint. Papi used to line the windowsills with vases overflowing with red carnations: *claveles*.

A heart is engraved in the bottom of the wooden door—a throwback to the language I used as a kid—different heart symbols symbolized different emotions. This one is small and circular and means an honest heart is the key to opening this door.

Theo's been fixing everything here. The roof is new. As well as the porch chairs and the fire pit a few feet away.

Beethoven blasts from a speaker on a stump. The one Papi would sit on and tell me stories. I wish I'd asked about every tale there was to tell. I wish I hugged him every day and not just on his birthday. I wish I told him I loved him the thousand times he told me.

But there are no undo buttons in life, no deletes, no photo edits. There are just the ramifications of decisions made.

I sigh heavily, in disbelief I'm thinking about Papi in these ways. Breaking bottles did something to me.

Theo steps through the cabin door, holding marshmallows on sticks with one hand. To the right sits a whole s'mores station set up next to a burning fire pit. We used to do that with Papi—always a special occasion.

"Hey," I say.

"Hey!" Theo crouches down and wraps me in a hug. The scent of burnt wood and cinnamon mixes with the smell of his water-dampened shirt. I accept the affection despite how the armrest pinches my side.

The squeeze is a little too tight; he's like the superhero who doesn't know his own strength. If he went to open a door, he might pull it right off the hinges. Not that that's ever happened, but every time he swoops at me and hugs me, I feel like a pretzel that's about to snap.

He releases me and maneuvers to the fire pit.

It's nice to see him smile, roasting the white sweets over the orange flames.

Theo's living in the cabin for the summer as his way of giving himself the "college experience" even though he's not in college. He's the independent type who has been wanting to live in the woods since he was a kid. On the weekends, he visits his family—his mother recently remarried and his younger twin sisters love when Theo teaches them how to repair boats.

On an inhale, I'm about to share what happened with Hudson and his father and the bottle smashing and stealing the limo and Mother and our finances. But being in this moment with Theo is already making me feel better.

I exhale and instead ask, "Need help?"

Theo rips open a box of graham crackers and a bar of chocolate, all with one hand while managing the marshmallows on the sticks with the other.

"I'm making *fancy* s'mores." Once the s'more is oozing together, he pokes licorice feet and arms into it. "They like dancing." He wiggles the edible doll through the air on a complex trajectory back and forth.

"I love it." I laugh. "But isn't it too early for campfires, classical music, and s'mores?"

His extra-large, black work shirt sways side to side as he slides another marshmallow off the stick and squishes it between white chocolate and graham crackers. "You know, Einstein would say 'I love to travel but hate to arrive.'"

Theo likes to speak in Einstein code. I pretend to understand with a single nod.

When he hands me the treat, I bite hard and the cracker crunches.

"Tasty as always. Thanks." Chocolatey sweetness droops over the sides. I lick it before any can escape to the ground and proceed to stuff my entire mouth. My cheeks fatten like a chipmunk's.

"You like?" Theo asks and downs a full s'more in one bite, yet still being able to talk. "I assume you do because you never said otherwise."

"Of course," I mumble.

Theo jumps up and straightens his shoulders. "Dance with me." His spin trips him up and he squeals like a little girl but catches himself, straightening out his shirt. "We're good. I'm just getting the bad moves out of my system."

He spins again and crashes into a pine tree. "That one was on purpose." His pushup is paired with a half-wink that travels from one eye to the other.

I giggle and roll next to him. "If you say so."

Theo presses to his feet and stands tall, hands folded behind his back. "I've been practicing."

"Falling?"

"Ha-ha."

The Blue Danube, Op. 314 plays from the stump. I follow through with a spin of my own. I've mastered the art of going in circles without getting dizzy. Many dance instructors teach that you should pick a single spot to keep your eye on with every turn. I don't need to do it often now that I'm experienced; my circles are poised compared to when I was a kid.

More importantly, I've nailed not driving my wheelchair into a wall or a tree while doing circles. I've had over a decade to perfect the debutante dance, so crashing into anything would render my participation in such an exquisite event problematic.

The twigs under my wheels snap as I half spin into Theo. The tips of his lashes glow gold in the rays of the sun.

He takes my hand in his—it's twice the size of mine. The warmth rushes into my palms as soon as I weave my cold, skinny fingers between his. We don't hold hands a lot, but when we do, it's comforting.

We twist to the right and left, managing not crashing into anything.

The first time I held Theo's hand was at my pretend wedding when we were kids. I smile, escaping into the memory.

"I dare you to marry Abby," Astrid says in front of her friends.

The Elijah, Theo, and Mei-Ling laugh. But not ten-year-old Sam, a kid from Astrid's class.

"Okay." He accepts the challenge.

"What's gonna be my dress?" I ask.

Astrid grabs the first white thing she spots—Mother's purse—and hangs it over my head. "There. Now roll down the hall and kiss."

"Kiss?" asks Theo, looking at Sam and me.

"I don't want to do that," says Sam.

Elijah huffs. "Then you lose the dare. It's a verbal contract and there are witnesses."

Astrid adds in, "You know, a true love's first kiss can make you fly."

"O-kay," I agree. "I want to fly, but first let's eat candy so it's a sweet kiss."

We stuff our faces with treats until our cheeks can't handle it. We lean forward, eyes wide open. Our lips touch for a second. I focus on the sticky, wet sugar taste in my mouth.

Suddenly Mother yells, "What is going on in here? Girls, you know that sugar before dinner is wrong. We have an eating schedule."

"It was all my idea," Theo says and takes my hand. It's a bit sticky and dirty, but I like the weight of it in mine.

Mother looks at Theo and points at the door. "Then you get out! We have an image to uphold."

I sigh. "You're right, Mother. We apologize and will play tag outside."

Since that day, I've wanted to find a boy who will kiss me so good, it'd make me fly.

"You're amazing at dancing," I say.

I turn to the side and smile at Theo. My best friend who I appreciate more than ever. He keeps me on my toes, even when he decides I should practice my dancing.

I enjoy us for a little longer.

But then I unexpectedly wipe a sweaty hand over my thigh. This is new. Am I nervous to dance with Theo?

Maybe it's his palms that are damp? Is *he* nervous?

Theo's expression is stony. There's a hint of distress creasing his brow. I call it his deep-thinking face. It crinkles his nose and makes his lips pout in a funny way. Enough to make me wonder if he's holding in a fart or concentrating on an Einstein equation.

"I suck," he says.

"You're great. I'm honestly impressed you haven't farted." It's an inside joke. Whenever Theo stayed silent after a task, he'd let out a silent but deadly fart.

His brow furrows deeper. "I'm sorry I didn't get the hint that you wanted me to be your escort the other day. Of course that's what you meant, and I blew you off." He squeezes my hand. "I'll be your escort ten times over."

A vibration rattles through the side of my chair. I squeal and look down at the shoe that kicked my wheel.

"Shit, sorry." Theo steps back and drops onto the old stump. He cracks his knuckles. "We should start over. And over and over again until it's perfect for you."

"You're already perfect. Don't change who you are." I pause and replay his statement. "*You* want to be my escort?" I'd wanted that for a long time, but hearing him say it requires my brain a bit more confirmation.

"I want you to have the best ball, but I suck." He jumps up fast enough to blow air through my curls. He paces back and forth, fast-talking. "Playing around about going to the ball together is different from the real thing. There has to be a manual on being an escort. Let me read up on it."

I've already got an escort. Those words are too hard to spit out.

"There is a debutante rule book, but . . ." I clasp my hands together on my lap. "Theo, you don't have to force yourself to do this." I start with a good anchor. I want him to see that this is not for him, because Hudson has me covered. But Hudson and Theo are not the best of friends. I'd hate for Theo to think he's not as good enough for me as Hudson is.

Theo nods. "I want to. This is important to you. It was important to your dad, and it's important to me."

My eyes widen and so does my mouth.

"I'm shocked, too, at why I hadn't asked you earlier." He chuckles, explaining, "Actually, I know. It's because I can't keep a conversation for more than ten seconds with classy words or remember which fork to use. Plus, my family's business has its clients and supporters, and they don't mix with the ultra-rich part of town. I'm an outcast and don't belong at a ball. But your happiness is more important to me."

I breathe like a choo-choo train—loud and labored. I don't want Theo to feel rejected. I know how much that sucks. "Thank you." Is a start?

If only I could have two escorts. I play with the hair tie around my joystick. How do I come up with the kindest rejection? Theo will hate me for saying I want Hudson to be my escort. Or rather, that I can't force Theo to do something he hates just for my sake, especially when fancy events are in

Hudson's blood. And his lips. Hudson is the one I want to kiss at the ball.

Theo darts to the cabin. "Forgot there's one more surprise. In the kitchen." He trips over a branch but spins around and catches himself on a wooden chair before turning into the cabin. He jogs across the living room, leaving the door open, and thunders with something in the kitchen. The gray sheer window curtains reveal enough and hide enough to give privacy but show someone is inside.

The crackling fire pit echoes in my ears. The ashes are breathing orange and black. The flames have died down and the last flame diminishes.

I've eaten my watermelon balm off my lips by the time I roll to the door. I comb through my hair so rigorously, that I'm pretty sure they're tangled instead.

Theo is actually saying yes to being my escort?

I'm left hovering at the threshold. "Can I come in?" I ask even though I know he wants me to.

The words feel strange. I've never had to ask if I can enter before.

Theo laughs. "You don't have to ask."

Fifteen

I GLANCE at the walls I once drew on. My hand runs along the hard surface and I imagine the smiley face I had scribbled there with chalk. I recall the pictures of Papi and me that once hung there. Theo's mother handed them off to mine and I haven't seen them since.

The floorboards are uneven and still squeak—sharp and high, like a mouse.

There are two bedrooms and a large bathroom with a conjoining laundry room. The living room has wall-mounted bookshelves on two perpendicular sides. One was filled with the wooden toys Papi made. Another was filled with journals and old books. Now they're empty with a few coiled papers, pens, and coins scattered on a few shelves.

I'm missing Papi more than ever. He had a way with words that was gentle and honest. Every sad or hard situation I was in, he saved me.

Papi, give me strength.

The room smells the same: dusty, with the sweet scent of old furniture and cinnamon.

Yet it's not the same. There are no loud footsteps, no scattered journals everywhere, no tools in random places. No Spanish songs and no bear hugs. At my sixteenth birthday party last summer, I asked him not to sing or hug me in front of my friends.

I don't know what was wrong with me or why I acted so bratty as a teen. I must have been trying to figure out how to be my own person, doing so at the expense of Papi's love for me. Was trying to get boys to notice me just so I could have a romantic first kiss worth it?

I wish I could redo my life.

The dust settles around me. A chill travels down my spine. I remember playing in an old wardrobe. The one where Theo and I pretended it was Narnia. It was our safe place—a place where we shared secrets or cried about someone being mean.

I shake off the memories and focus on Theo. The grown-up Theo of today.

He deserves honesty. He planned this whole beautiful moment to tell me he'd be my escort. Now he's motioning me into the kitchen.

"We can practice dancing with our mugs."

"You're so sweet," I say, slowly rolling toward him.

This room has experienced the biggest change. The granite countertops, black stove, and modern refrigerator hold no memories of the past. Only the wooden kitchen table I built with Theo and Papi does. I touch the surface; glitter is embedded in odd places. I realize that it's not the glitter pulling me back into the past—it's the two familiar metal mugs. Old mugs. *The sweetest things in life are not bought.* That's what Papi would tell Astrid and me when we asked for new things.

Theo glances at the two drinks in front of us.

"Hot chocolate." He slides one across the table. It's full of brown cocoa and white marshmallows, topped with cinnamon, a chocolate chip melting in the center. During the holiday season, Papi would add whipped cream on top and a thin slice of butter.

"It's hot," Theo says. "That chocolate chip is meant to be a fancy dancing shoe."

I watch the marshmallows float like boats. The aroma of cinnamon fills the room with more than just warmth. I hate that I didn't have one last sip with Papi. I took every sip for granted; he never did.

The sweet memory is tainted as a hundred-pound weight sits on my chest, filled with the truth of what I did the last time I saw that mug. The past rushes through me no matter how hard I push it away.

Papi slides a hot chocolate drink at me.

"Now?" I ask.

He takes a big sip. I roll my eyes at his mustache from the whipped cream floating inside.

"You have something," I say, and arch a brow as I point to my own upper lip.

"What do you mean, I have something?" he asks in a funny voice. "I know I have a lot of somethings. I have two daughters and books and a bed and a cabin."

"No. On your face. Come on, Papi." I push the mug away. "I'm sixteen now, not a kid anymore. I finished my résumé workshop and don't have time for this. I'm meeting Theo at the lake in fifteen minutes for a special plan. I only stopped by the cabin to drop off the shirt you asked me to bring."

He examines every inch of my face. "But I love our hot chocolate time. Won't you give me five minutes?"

I hand him a napkin from the table so he can wipe his face. "Maybe later."

"One last sip before you outgrow our time together? Can we have that?" he asks.

"I hate it when you do this." My tone is cold. "I have so much to do and that stupid hot chocolate is childish." As I push the mug away, it spills over. "I don't care, Papi."

He sighs deeply.

When I open my mouth to apologize, my phone buzzes. Theo. He's on his way to the dock.

"I'll put you on my schedule," I say. "I need to meet Theo and ask him to be my escort. I've officially been accepted as a deb and need to be the first to announce it."

"You're growing further and further away from me." He grabs at his camera on the table. "Let me take a few pictures of you two."

I squeal. "Stop smothering me. I don't need you anymore."

All Papi wanted was time with me. I yelled at him. I told him I didn't have time for him.

All Theo wants is to be there for me. I want to choose someone else.

None of that feels good. I don't like myself, yet I can't escape myself either.

The pain that pings in my chest circles back. The guilt hits me full on. It bites down on my tears and squeezes my insides.

I've unraveled a buried emotion. I blame everything on bottle smashing.

The steam rises from our mugs and Theo goes for the first sip. "I'd like some more cinnamon." He shoots up and rummages on the kitchen counter before returning with the drink topped with brown goodness. Quickly, he spins around a battered chair and slides into it. "You don't like how I made it?"

My stomach does a weird squeeze. There aren't any words for a safe rejection, no matter how much I hate my silence.

It's too hard to lie and too hard to tell the truth.

I slump in my chair. "I don't want you to feel hurt." I speak so low, I fear he'll ask me to repeat myself.

He shoots up again. "Let me try a new cup."

"No," I say fast. That's as far as I go.

We stare for longer than I want.

Maybe I should reconsider my plans for the ball and think about what would make Papi proud.

"Papi was happy for *you* to go with me." Desperation rips through my every word.

Theo sighs.

"You don't want me," he mutters.

"No," I immediately say again. "It's just a lot. Hudson asked and Astrid knows and she probably told Mrs. D'aureville," I say quickly and then slowly to soften the blow. "I've loved dancing with you over the years." My voice trembles. As hard as it is rejecting Theo, I can't bring myself to let go of Hudson.

Theo's eyes zero in on a nail in the floor. "You chose *Hudson*?" There's hurt to his every syllable. His brows furrow. "Well, I hope he can really be there for you." The hoarseness in his voice is hard and deep.

This is way too complicated. I want to hug Theo, tell him we should go together. I'd do anything to lessen his pain.

"I don't know." My palm covers half of my face. "I don't want to hurt anyone."

Theo paces back and forth, talking to himself more than me. "If you want to have fun with him, then do that."

The way Theo is reacting feels like a break-up. He's been

there for me all these years and now he's upset. The way he stomps and swings his arms, I can just tell.

My eyes fill with tears. I turn away so he can't see me.

"I have to go." I bolt from the kitchen and then the cabin, heart racing as fast as my wheels rotate. I don't want to think or feel or process any of this.

Sixteen

PLANNING FIXES EVERYTHING. Creating a planner for Hudson keeps my mind from thinking about how I rejected Theo. It's an old one I never used. I created some *strengths*, *passions*, and *dreams* pages. I wonder what Hudson's passions are besides knitting.

So far, the last forty-eight hours have been too busy for me to think about Theo—for the most part.

I wonder if he's okay. The last two nights, I stared at my phone wanting to text him. Then again, I left because it was excruciating talking to him. The disappointment in his voice buried me ten feet under the ground.

The ping from the printer says the career quiz finished printing. I reach across my desk and swipe the pages through an automatic three-hole puncher. This is going to be great. We'll go over each page and he'll write in the planner every day. In a month's time, his destined future will open up.

"Abigail!" yells Mother from the foyer. "Limo is ready. Astrid says you'll be late if you don't leave now. Being late is disrespectful."

The first rehearsal has arrived.

"Coming!" I reply and move faster through the motions.

My hands scatter over the pages as I reorganize them.

The minutes drain away, and at the sound of my name again, I let it be.

But I do need my pearls. They sit in the glass container on my nightstand. After the ball next weekend, Astrid will lock them back up in the safe. I am going to enjoy them for as long as I can. They complement my sunflower-themed sundress elegantly.

Technically, it's only a rehearsal, but the pearls make me feel like a true debutante. If the necklace was the only classy thing I wore to the ball, it would be enough. It reminds me how beautiful we'll all look at the ball, not because of what we wear but because of how we share the traditions of what we wear.

After I clip the necklace around my neck, I zoom out and pass Mother. She walks toward her office, focused on the open jewelry sketchbook in one hand and her phone in the other.

"Remember to be classy. Be elegant and smile," she calls to me. "Fight for that crown. Our future . . . I mean, *your* future depends on it."

"Yes, Mother." I pause and turn around. "Are we okay? Is the company okay? You're not getting replaced, are you?"

Our limo disagreement from days ago seems distant now. We aren't a family who talks about our emotions often. We just keep moving onward. Yet, this uncomfortable feeling won't leave me alone because I hate thinking Mother is hiding something painful. If only I could figure out how to ask her to open up to me.

She lowers her phone and sighs. "Don't worry, honey. I have meetings with potential clients set up next week. The biggest client is coming to the ball, so all you have to do is smile and twirl with a crown on your head."

"I'll make you proud," I say. I want to make Mother proud the way I never got a chance to make Papi proud. Even if it means letting her rule my life this month.

Come to think of it, maybe there's something in it for me, not just my family. If I get queen, I can prove to everyone that I can be successful, powerful, and good enough to be heard. Like Astrid, it'll give me a voice and a respect in this town.

Bentley steps through the front door. "I got news for our limo meeting today."

His shaved head is probably as smooth as a stone. The gold-rimmed round glasses sit against his black skin. He's had a wizard obsession for as long as I've known him. Five years ago, he talked in a British accent, twirling a wand, saying how he was going to drive around in fancy spaceships. It was so quirky, I loved it.

My smile grows as I'm suddenly reminded that I had a meeting on my schedule with him planned out for weeks.

"Looking forward to it," I say, and we hurry out to the limo.

On the way to the Grand Royal Hotel, Bentley describes his final design for his future whimsical limo company.

I nod, giving him ideas of what I'd do. He seems to light up with every new idea I share.

Twenty-five minutes later, the limousine stops abruptly.

I lurch forward with a squeal. Astrid is going to kill me for being five minutes late.

"And we're *here*!" Bentley says cheerfully, closing his notebook. "I can't wait to show you the sketches. I'll need your advice on colors for each kind of star. Maybe I'll do a twirling universe gulping a sea galaxy creature?" His pearly whites flash against his skin.

"That idea sounds fun," I reply. "I'd do more of an ocean vibe or a twirling galaxy, but not both."

He gives me a smile and a nod.

After Roosevelt unstraps my wheelchair, Bentley skips out and I follow. The clouds spread thin along the sky, adding texture to the pink and orange hues that scatter the setting sun.

"You look whimsical, by the way," Bentley says and slides his glasses up his nose.

"Why thank you, Mr. Wizardly Wizard of Such Sorcery. Next week, we'll think of slogans," I say, and then turn to Roosevelt. "Great ride. Thank you."

Roosevelt tips his hat and goes to close the limo door.

Hudson, in a nice suit, stands inside the lobby's glass doors. It's been a few days since I saw him, but it feels like months. The butterflies in my stomach stir up and I tell myself he is the best choice.

He's the one I want to kiss at the ball.

Bentley tightens his tie-dye backpack straps over his shoulders. "I've already got ideas. What about, moonlight stars shine only for you?"

"I'd do something more about riding the stardust or catching their sparkle. But I really love that you follow your passions. That planner I found did you wonders."

"You are a magical planning queen. I'm going to grab lunch here and then head out to meet with an investor."

It's amazing to see my planning skills helping someone.

"Congrats. They'll totally invest and you're going to be the best boss ever."

The bellman opens the door to the lavish hotel. Light from the chandeliers festooned with diamond-shaped glass pendants bounces off the icy blue-and-black interior.

"I'll try." Bentley chuckles. "That feels scary. Maybe I'll go back to magic tricks."

"Whatever I can do to help, let me know."

We say bye and go in separate directions.

It's fun helping others plan their futures. Something about it gives me a sense of joy.

Diana's little sister rolls by in her wheelchair—her mother pushing the back handlebars—waving at me.

Layla was in a car accident with a family friend last year that paralyzed her legs. Diana was terrified that she would never wake up from her coma. As time went by and Layla recovered, I taught her a few cool wheelchair tips.

I wave back and smile at the seven-year-old. "Hi, Layla."

Her purple dress is on point with those brown curls. Passing the jade statues, she mutters something.

I don't catch it but yell back, "See you later." Her mom, Mrs. Sevyani, regularly visits Mother. They like to trade jewelry for clothing every so often. That's when I get to tutor little Layla.

This means Diana is here. As much as I want to see my bestie, I can't stop fidgeting with the ends of my hair. It's been a few days since we spoke. Some space should be enough so we can get back to hugging.

I rush toward a group of debs and escorts conversing with each other. The place buzzes with chatter. I smile at two strangers descending the polished staircase on the right.

Hudson joins me, phone in hand. "Hey."

I hug the planner tight to my chest, driving the chair with the other hand. "Hey, I have something for you."

He raises a brow. "A gift for *me*? How did I get so lucky?" As he squeezes my shoulder, I whimper.

The touch feels nice. It awakens something in me. I glance at his hand, wanting to hold it again.

"Abby!" Astrid pops in from a hallway and hurries me along, striding toward the presidential ballroom. "You're late. The last one here."

She's not even paying attention to me. Her phone takes priority. I wonder if she cares about the pain I've experienced these last ten months. Or does she blame me for Papi's death? Her bossiness could be a deflection.

"Being on the debutante planning committee is honorable and respectable," Astrid reminds me. "How do *I* look if my sister is late, which makes *me* late?"

Her high-pitched voice rings in my ears.

"I'm here now. It'll be fine. Don't worry," I assure her quietly. "Mrs. D'aureville isn't watching, so calm down."

She points to her earpiece—the debutante director is listening, though.

"We got this," Hudson says to me. "The videos have been helpful, considering the routine is the same year after year. Plus, I pretend-danced with an empty five-wheeled office chair, so I know when to lower and position myself around you."

Hudson prepared for the ball? A smile breaks across my face. The kind that says check out how straight my teeth are after getting my braces off.

I immediately want to do something as thoughtful for him. I hand him the binder. "I put together a career planner for you." As I say that, I realize the timing seems off.

The guys next to Hudson whisper to each other, chuckling.

I press on and ignore them.

"With a *passions* worksheet and some questions about your strengths. It can get you excited about career options. You can also take a quiz and do a life puzzle game where you follow five different professions."

"Uh." Smirking, he slides the gift onto a nearby table. "This really isn't . . ."

He sweeps his gaze down to me.

"You did this for me?" he says in a high-pitched voice, flipping open the cover. "A whole notebook?" He speeds through the first half. "All my problems are solved." Shutting it, he scratches the back of his head. "Thanks."

Oh.

This was a stupid idea. "If you don't like it, I have five other planner types." I remind myself that he showed up. He actually showed up—fashionably dressed up, despite the other guys being in casual button-up shirts—ready to be my escort.

"It's great," he says politely, but he's clearly just being nice.

"I'll take it back to the limo and meet you in the ballroom." I slide the planner onto my lap. If anyone asks me what it's for, it would be weird to say it's for Hudson. Come to think if it, this is not the best place to talk about Hudson's future.

Guess I can't tutor everyone even though I want to.

A guy with a mohawk gets in front of Hudson.

They fist-bump and another guy joins in. They're a year younger than Hudson, attending the same all-boys private school.

"Told you your dad wasn't going to *really* cut you off," the first guy says. "That suit looks new."

"It's my older brother's." Hudson pops his jaw. "I don't need my dad's money."

This is my cue to leave, and I do. As I look out, I can't spot the limo in the front. Roosevelt must have already left.

I fix a stray hair but it keeps falling out of place. If Diana was next to me, she'd pin it up. I scan the crowd for the polka-dottiest outfit. I need her tight hug and fruity summer splash perfume. She's never not hugged me at a deb event.

"Polka-dot triplets!" Diana cheers. "So glad you let me combine my design with all of ours."

I quickly spin around.

She hugs two other debs—Pyper and Rahki. I hurry, excited to embrace her. Then I immediately realize she might ignore me. If the other debs see Diana turn a cold shoulder, they may do the same.

Still, I try one more time. I text Diana saying we should get lunch tomorrow at the Magenta Diner.

I watch her check her phone and then ignore it.

Astrid parades past me, swinging her arms with a force that could break a brick. "Damn juniors," she mutters to herself, weaving through the crowd. "The Ashleys better not be smoking in the bathroom."

After stuffing the planner into my purse, I regret bringing it.

"Looking good, Abbs," Joey hollers off to my right.

I swerve to face her. As much as fancy events are not her cup of tea, I love that she shows up for Diana and me when we have deb-related activities.

Her motorcycle is probably parked in the front parking spot that's not really a parking spot, where the helmet hangs on a handlebar.

She circles me. "Did Hudson say something dumpstery? What's with the frown?" she asks. "We can throw eggs at the Giordanis' house. Or there's a TP trick with a rake especially designed for mansions." Joey imitates tossing something up into the air.

"No." I shake my head. "Have you been hanging out with Diana? Doing any pedicures with her?" I'm desperate for any news. Any clue about what Diana is thinking and feeling. "Is she still mad at me for not inviting her or did I do something else to upset her? She's ignoring me and it feels mega personal."

"I dunno, I've been skateboarding with Talia this week," Joey mutters through gum chewing. "But we should get friendship tattoos. Facing pain together can bond us."

I laugh a little, imagining Diana getting an ankle tattoo of a dress design or fabric pattern. I really miss her.

Joey blows a bubble just to pop it. "I gotta go pee."

Astrid rushes past me, speaking into her earpiece the entire time and parading to who-knows-where-to next. The wind from her stride washes over me.

She spins around. "It's a packed day. We have to go through the dance, organize father-daughter dances, curtsy, discuss picture etiquette . . ."

I nod and round a corner, letting everyone pass me. The hallway is elegantly decorated with white tulips in black vases.

As I slow my roll toward the ballroom, I spot a little girl twirling around her father. He can't be older than thirty. His combed black hair and clean-shaven face is paired with an expensive watch and a silver wedding ring. In a single sweep, he picks her up. They laugh and giggle, each sound louder than the last. He tosses her up and sits her on his arm, swaying back and forth.

My head pounds, hands going clammy. My insides twist, stomach dropping in on itself. *I need Papi here for the father-daughter dance.*

Suddenly, I can't move. Tears form behind my eyes.

The father's sweet laughter echoes louder and louder in my head, like a train racing full speed ahead, unable to stop. I want to explode, yet scared I won't be able to control the pain that comes with that.

Papi.

Every breath burns like it's my last. I suppress every emotion ripping at the seams.

The ball has been tainted. It's plagued with the pain I've been trying to outrun for months. The ball was the one thing I used to cover the hurt. Now the pain has spread everywhere. Invisible ripples flow in new directions. I feel every one.

"Miss." A member of the hotel's staff waves a hand to get my attention. "We need to shut the door."

Rolling into the ballroom, the tables and chairs sit on each side of the center. The stage is set up as if it's the ball—a ramp rides up to the main spotlight where we curtsy. Everything is in motion. I'm rolling toward the crowd, going through the routine of what I've been programmed to do.

Just focus on the future, not the past.

I suck in a deep breath and rub each pearl around my neck one by one.

The crystal hanging from the ceiling glitters from the lights, creating rainbows under everyone. Hudson's attention is fully on me, a smile playing on his lips. He's classy, with his hands clasped behind his back like that. It makes his shoulders and chest pop.

I don't care if he hates the planner. I hate the planner. The cover didn't need to have cursive handwriting or have pages with stars at the corners. That suddenly seems childish.

His stare falls to the ground before it works back up to my eyes. "You look beautiful." The wink is as flirtatious as his half smile. His leather cologne mixes with my sweet strawberry scent.

The classical strings of "The Blue Danube" add to the sweetness of his words.

When I look at him looking at me in this way, life seems a bit lighter. For a second, I don't want to explode with grief. Hudson keeps me put together, and I hold on to those seams.

"Thank you." A faint smile pops up on my face.

Chatter builds when Mrs. D'aureville instructs everyone to start—for the third time, because no one is quieting their buzzing.

When the first strains of the waltz begin, everyone dances in perfect rhythm as each guy circles their date and the action is mimicked by the girls. I've practiced this dance since I was a little girl. I know it by heart. Yet when it's time to move into two straight lines, I roll in the opposite direction and run over the toes of a debutante. And not just any debutante. *Diana.*

"Hey!" She bends down and rubs her foot. "My shoe. My parents are going to kill me. I have to return these before the fashion show."

I press my hand to her bare shoulder. "I forgot which way to go, sorry."

Gustavo squats down. "There's a small smudge, but I can get it out later."

Mrs. D'aureville marches toward me, her deep huffs growing increasingly louder as she approaches. *Oh no.* My mind works frantically and prays she's heading for the bathroom, but no, she stops in front of me. I can barely catch my breath. If my heart pounds any harder, I might pass out.

"We're a week out. This is no time to mess up. If you can't handle the pressure, you can pull out." Her heavily lined blue eyes scare me. "The whole town will judge you. If you want them to respect you, get your act together. This opportunity is only for the best of the best. Like Diana, who's accumulated more volunteer hours than I've ever seen. The press she's generating is admirable. And you are disrespecting your future queen."

Future queen? So, I don't stand a chance? If Diana is set to be queen, I have to be happy for her. Then again, when she wins, she probably won't want me to share in her celebration. Although, my GPA tops anyone else's, so this title is totally rigged.

I want to say something, but the lump in my throat grows. If I was brave, if I was courageous, I wouldn't stay silent. My confidence has deserted me. I glance at Hudson, begging him to be my voice. But he stands there. Wow. Is even the unflappable Hudson intimidated by Mrs. D'aureville?

The music echoes in my ears. I shake in all the places I can possibly shake, wishing I was home.

But I'm not home. And I'd be more embarrassed by running away than by staying. This is what I've been working toward for years. The ball has been my mission since the first time Papi read *Cinderella* to me.

I take in that memory and straighten up, feeling a bit stronger.

"It was my fault," Hudson finally chimes in. "I didn't pull her in close enough." He sidesteps next to me and squeezes my shoulder.

I sigh in relief that he's chosen to be my voice and shield right now.

Mrs. D'aureville turns back toward the front of the ballroom, and we begin the waltz again.

Hudson spins around and leads. I count each beat. The music mutes in my mind. My thoughts, my movements. My body is at the point of not being able to do anything other than drive my chair.

As comforting as it feels to have Hudson by my side, deep, painful emotions threaten to overpower his touch.

I stop, feeling an avalanche building in my chest.

"We can take a minute," Hudson whispers. He's gentle and calm.

"It's okay. I *can* do this." If I say it out loud, I won't break.

Hudson fixes a hair that's fallen in my face, then traces a finger down to my shoulder. The pressure of his thumb against my sore muscles urges me to fall into his body for a hug.

I stiffen instead. Heavy gasps take over. I shake my head and shiver.

"Everything is too much."

Hudson's brow furrows. "Did I do something?"

If I open my mouth, I should say something. All that comes out is a whimper.

My heart won't stop pounding, and my décolleté is on the verge of being freckled with pink splotches. Hot flashes, Astrid calls them. She says I get them when I get super embarrassed or overwhelmed.

"What is it?" Hudson asks. "Don't listen to Mrs. D-lady. She won't matter after next weekend." He pauses, swaying. "Or did *I* do something? Sorry I didn't take the planner you made me. I like it, promise. It was a bit shocking and I reacted by ignoring it."

His eyes follow my every move—when I fix my purse on my armrest, when I sweep another fallen hair away from my face, when I bite at my lip to the point of discomfort.

A low sigh weaves through my breaths. I pin my lips together to quiet the sound.

"Everyone is watching me and I'm messing up," I whisper. What if I can't do the ball at all? In front of everyone. In front of Mother, Astrid, and the board. I can ruin our entire future. Forget about a perfect first real kiss.

Hudson lifts my chin up. "Then you ignore everyone and pretend it's you and me. Just us."

Focus on Hudson and only Hudson.

I raise my arm and bend my wrist. He smooths his hand over mine, and when the piano note sounds, he disconnects and circles me. He paces to the side with gentle steps. Then he stops behind me. I catch him in the mirror on the wall, scanning me from head to toe.

Circling him, I do the same.

His eyes sweep up to my neck until I turn to meet his gaze. He moves nearer, as if to whisper a secret. I back away and we rotate around each other.

One hand behind his back, he slides to the side until he holds my arm up with his other hand. We're palm to palm. We circle each other until we're back to back. Hudson spins around and raises my arm high. We move a foot ahead. A foot to the left. A foot to the right. We're in sync, like we've done this a hundred times. Hudson knows how to dance with a partner.

He has been practicing.

I spin back, and we swing to the side.

Soft piano notes accompany us as we sweep right and left. Hudson drops to one knee and lifts my hand high. I pivot a hundred and eighty degrees, run my forearm over his shoulder and trace his biceps with my fingers.

After three spins, our hands collide, separate, then collide once more. His hand glides to my arm, those charming hazel eyes holding mine. He threads his fingers through mine, holding me longer than the choreography allows.

My stare works down his nose and to his lips. Moments like

these make me want to kiss him. At the ball, we'll perfectly waltz, then his hands will slide to my face and when the lights shine above, his lips will touch mine with a taste of magic.

I just have to figure out how to communicate that to him without explicitly communicating that to him.

When he squeezes my shoulder, I gasp unexpectedly.

Then it hits me. I like him a lot. More than a container of pistachio ice cream.

Mrs. D'aureville speaks into the microphone. "While we wait for a debutante to change her shoes, we're going to switch it up and do the father-daughter dance."

As Hudson steps away, the cold air rushes in. His warmth evaporates when I need it most.

I meekly smile at Mei-Ling's father coming my way. The shivers shake me harder, my breathing going into overdrive.

Papi, I miss you.

The music plays and everyone takes their place on the floor. My fake smile says everything is great, but my eyes say I'm about to let loose every single tear.

The dancing can't end fast enough.

Emptiness fills me and all I see is Papi's hopeful smile just before I left him with his two cups of hot chocolate. I hear myself dismissing him.

The rehearsal moves along, rushing through the curtsies. But the entire time, I'm seeing myself sinking in the water and Papi pulling me from under my wheelchair.

Seventeen

The comfort of my bedroom can't come fast enough.

The emotions rush in like a flood. I shake my head to prevent tears from raining down my face. "No, no, no," I whisper to soothe myself. "I don't want to feel this pain."

The pressure in my chest thumps out of control. My sorrowful eyes rise to the empty space above my bed. There used to be a picture there once, of Papi and me laughing in a valley. I was holding flowers Theo had picked for me.

I keep staring at the empty space.

I need an escape.

I need Papi.

I need to hold something. The black bag sits on my armchair. I snag it and pull out an old book. The worn, brown corners curl up. The ink stains darken the edges.

It's a journal.

Of course. Papi always wrote about good memories. His shoulders would slouch as he scribbled between the pages—he wasn't a very tall man, but he was built with broad shoulders and the blackest hair. So thick that I used to joke how it could be a bird's nest.

Thump, thump, thump. My heart has never beat this fast.

I stroke the journal's rough exterior—the cover's scars and bumps. A stinging sensation spreads across my hands. Papi gave me this journal on my sixteenth birthday, a couple of months before he passed.

I was too busy to open it, telling him to keep it for me at the cabin. I cared more about visiting with my friends.

A faint scent of old paper and wood transports me back to when I was a little girl holding his hand. I open the journal and find a greeting on the inside of the cover in his cursive hand-writing. I tease the worn-out corner with my thumb, reading his words for the first time.

To my dearest Abigail,

I started this journal before you were born so I could gift it to you on your sweet sixteenth. That way you can remember us through all the memories we shared.

Love you to the depths of the ocean and back, my sweet hot chocolate marshmallow princess. Live for today, not for when today leaves you.

Your Papi

A wave of grief shakes my body. It's not fair he's not here to dry my tears. Or to help me prepare for the ball. I hug the leather journal close enough to feel its rough exterior. I'd give anything to have one more minute with him. One more hug.

My hands tremble. I back my chair up against the door to be extra sure no one can come in. I take a deep breath and flip to the first entry.

Today is the day I'm hopeful, Abigail. That's your name. You're only five months along in your mother's belly, but you're a fighter. The three babies before you didn't make it, and we're blessed your heart still beats. You make us proud and always will. Astrid can't wait to meet you. Your grand-parents love you already. We'll see you soon. We will. No matter what. I will always fight to protect you. We're about to paint your room golden pink. Remember, you are made of love.

My lip quivers. I never realized what it was like being his daughter. He watched me grow up, evolve, and become my own person. Now he's no longer here to do that, and it hurts. I pretend he's beside me, calming me. If only I were a better version of myself. A version Papi could be proud of.

I close my eyes, imagining the Abby I know has disap-peared, but the Abby that Papi saw . . . she's strong and brave. She's happy and carefree.

I wipe the tears off my face and read on. I read until Papi's words mesh into what feels like a foreign language and I can't process any more. I can't tell if a minute passes or an hour.

I linger on an entry twenty pages in.

Dearest Abigail,

You walked for ten seconds today without the help of the wall! They said you'd never be able to sit up, and here you are at four years old, stronger than ever. It surprised your mother so much, she started crying. I've never seen her so happy for you. We're going to your first physical therapy today. Mother has always loved you, even when people disapproved of our decision to keep you. Many people said we're evil to bring a disabled child into this world and that you will be a burden to everyone. They don't understand that life is not theirs to control. Life is meant to be lived out of our control. I told her to never listen to people in this town, to not get caught up in that, but rather to live in love. I want you to remember the same. Life is a gift and we want to give you the best life. I promise to always hold your hand.

Theo just got here. He's helping you stand up. Oops, you fell again. We're going to go pick out some shoes for you and leg braces, per the doctor's instructions.

Your Papi

Tears flow down my cheeks and I don't stop them. Papi loved me so much. I pretend he's sitting next to me.

Reliving and imagining the memories sucks the light out of me. I guess this is why Astrid and Mother don't talk about the pain. All remembering does is bring sorrow to the soul. Still, I want to feel his presence.

I flip to the middle.

You got your first power wheelchair today. Now you can go wherever you want. I didn't realize that meant you'd constantly run all of us down, laughing hysterically. But now you can keep up with the other kids. Like Theo. I hope you'll lean on each other. I pray that as this disease takes away your muscles, you'll fight on as the warrior that you are. SMA is too harsh, but I will be here to fight it with you.

The journal falls onto my lap, and I rest my face in my palms. He gave me everything he had, and I couldn't even deliver his eulogy. Failing as his daughter hurts the most. Everyone was counting on me to have a speech as moving as Astrid's. But I froze. I was the daughter who took everything for granted and who squandered everything her father had done for her and had given her. I selfishly used up everything he'd poured into me. The one time I was asked to give, I had nothing to give back.

He could have failed me a hundred times but never did. I failed him every day.

The laughter of childhood innocence rings in the distance. It's so clear that I lift my head, looking for the source of the sound. I laugh without humor, embarrassed that I'm hearing things, even though no one is here to see me. But I can't stop hearing the sounds from the time when all seemed possible and magical.

Papi coached me how to be an elegant princess. How to be polite and not release farting sounds. At least not on purpose. He said that was only for play dates and close friends. I laugh out loud, remembering Mother's expression when she caught us talking about farts, quite seriously, over popcorn and root beer.

He taught me which kitchen utensil to use for salad and which for dessert. He picked out outfits for me, and I picked out the hairstyles to match.

His Spanish accent rings in my ears, his tone gentle and loving. "*Mija, mi hot chocolate princess, have grace. Trust life's plans for you.*" As much as I want to accept life's plans, there's nothing perfect about his absence.

I grab my phone and text Theo.

I opened the black bag. Inside was Papi's journal for me. Everything hurts. I need you.

In a span of ten minutes, I pull my sundress through one arm, over my shoulder, through my head, and down the other arm. Zaney will arrive in an hour to help me get ready for bed, but I want something comfortable and lounge-y now.

I swipe my makeup off with a quick wipe and let my hair drape over my shoulders.

In my closet, I grab a long purple tee covered in donuts. I push the opening over my head and pull the fabric down my body.

Suddenly, I realize I asked Theo to be there for me when I couldn't be there for him.

Maybe I should let him know he can cry on my shoulder, too. I reread the text and write a new one.

I'm so sorry. I'm emotionally reacting and what I want to say is that I want to be there for you. You can talk to me. You can say how upset you are. I'm here for you even if you're the one I always need. Love you.

Phone in hand, I roll out of my room. It's quiet. The staff have gone home. It'll be a minute before Astrid returns and Mother finishes a late business dinner meeting.

I cross the foyer and turn into the hallway. The ticking of the grandfather clock by the piano reminds me I'm alone. The sound of the dryer rumbles across the mansion—someone left the laundry room door open and the balance of the dryer *still* isn't fixed, making the machine shudder and lurch when the load is uneven.

I roll back and forth in the kitchen, wondering if I should show up at the cabin with matches and twigs in my hands. Campfires solve everything. Ghost stories are Theo's favorite. I need him to see that our friendship isn't over and that I can be there for him.

Although on Friday evenings Theo does inventory at the aquatic center. I slip my phone into my purse and reconsider bothering Theo.

A sharp realization hits me: I left Theo because my emotions grew too much for me. Diana left because the same thing happened to her. It wasn't that she was being rude. She probably felt so hurt and uncomfortable that her only reaction was to leave.

"Hungry?"

I scream and spin around.

Hudson?

"Sorry. Did I scare you?" He bites his lip and squints.

I reach out to the counter next to the fridge, pick up a tangerine, and throw it at him. He catches it one-handed and grins. I throw another.

"Hey!" I yell breathlessly. "You could have given me a heart attack."

He proves he's not afraid of my aim—or tangerines—when he reaches past me and drops the fruit back into the bowl.

I cross my arms over my boobs. If I had another pair of hands, I'd cover my makeup-less face. This is a new level of vulnerability I certainly can't recover from. I can't hide my puffy eyes or damaged lips. Makeup covers up my flaws and insecurities. Now they're all on display for him to see. I'm naked and exposed—not literally, but in some way since I'm in the middle of a breakdown.

"Um . . ." I let my furrowed brows do the rest of the talking. "I didn't hear you enter."

"I called out a few minutes ago, but no one answered. Thought I should check just in case."

That bulky body of his leans on the counter. His hazel eyes get more sensual the longer they linger on mine. It's almost a violation, the way he's staring at me, venturing deep into my torn soul and measuring the damage.

"I brought ice cream. Pistachio." Holding up the bag, he shakes it. "It's still your favorite, yeah?" He opens the freezer and swings it inside. "It's a bit melted, but it should be perfect in a few minutes." The door shuts, shooting air into his face.

"Really?" My voice goes two octaves too high. "I mean . . ." I whip around the counter and park at the kitchen table. "That's very nice, but I'm on my way to see Theo. I'm not okay right now."

Hudson's jaw pops as he struts over. "I can be there for you."

"I'm really . . . emotionally overwhelmed. It's not pretty."

"You can talk to me," he says, dropping into a chair.

Talk. I can talk. Words. I can use words. None come at the moment, because maybe I don't know how to open up on a deep level. In this mansion, I never sat across the table from someone and just *talked*.

"How do I start?" I ask myself more than him. No way am I going to dive into the darkest parts of the ocean right at the start.

"Whatever is on your mind," he whispers. "Start with something small."

Our eyes lock, and the words come easy this time. "Papi would take me to this Spanish café with carnations decorating the walls." The corners of my lips slightly curl up.

"That's amazing. What else?"

"His rich laugh filled a room. He loved drinking hot chocolate around a fire. He got the chocolate from the Roja Clavel Café. He helped construct the building years ago as well as being a donor. It was his favorite place to take me or get a morning coffee, even though we have the best and fanciest coffee machines in the kitchen. He said the aura of the Spanish culture in the yellow-and-red walls gave him a deep feeling of home.

"They have the best hot chocolate there, but I'm too scared

to go. I wish I could have some hot chocolate, but I can't." I choke up. "Something is so wrong with me. It's like I have no idea how to grow up or be better. I can't do anything right and I keep disappointing everyone."

"Hey." Hudson takes my face in his hands. "Nothing is wrong with you. Everyone heals differently. Everyone goes through pain differently. I'll have that hot chocolate with you. We'll make new memories in your dad's honor." His eyes search mine. "Nothing is wrong with that." The firmness in his voice means he's serious. "You are never a disappointment. Tell me something nice you did for your dad."

A pause follows.

Then, "When I was a kid, I'd collect twigs so that I could give Papi a bouquet." My voice is barely audible. "He gave me flowers, and I thought boys got stick bouquets. Then Papi gave *me* twig bouquets. They were extra special. But then I grew up and stopped giving him sticks. I stopped being his baby girl." I should stop before I share something I can't recover from.

Yet, I want to keep going.

"I got sucked into the shiny things of this town and became self-centered. I took him for granted, Hudson. Regret is an ugly thing. I hate myself for putting distance between us because I was growing up. Now he's gone." As much as I want to run in the opposite direction, I like telling Hudson the things weighing heavy on my heart.

"We all suck sometimes. It's not your fault he died," he whispers.

But it is. It's my fault he went into the water.

"What if I chose to spend time with him like he wanted instead of choosing myself? What if I stayed at the . . ."

I can't finish the sentence. The guilt squishes my intestines. I was supposed to spend that afternoon in the cabin with Papi, not ditch him to ask Theo to the ball. I didn't *need* to scout for the perfect spot to take our photo announcement together. I didn't need to be the first deb to share our partnership on social media.

My pulse hammers out the ticking seconds. "I think about what I should have done differently every day," I say as quietly as possible. The quiet will make the ugliness less real. "How I should have treated him better *every day*."

It's not that I hated Papi or meant to be mean and selfish, but I wanted to fit in with kids my age. Making friends in high school is hard. I really wanted a boy to like me. I would do anything to give them my attention just so they'd give me theirs. It doesn't help that I attend an all-girls school, which means I rely on events, school dances, classmate's brothers, and outside of school activities to mingle.

"He loved me, and I never showed him I loved him back," I mutter, choking up. "Papi wanted to share special moments with me; I picked my social status over him."

He was my father and I thought he'd always be there. I thought I'd have plenty of time to spend with him, whereas high school is only a four-year window.

Hudson scoots closer and gently says, "Life is meant to be lived with every emotion involved. Your father understood you had goals and dreams. He knew you loved him and that you were finding yourself. He was pretty smart, your dad."

I shake my head. "I couldn't even deliver his eulogy. I rolled up the ramp and looked at the crowd. My throat clamped up and then I ran away."

Hudson's arm drapes across my chair. His fingers brush the curve of my shoulder, leaving tiny licks of warmth with every contact.

"That day, I realized I'd never had a voice or the ability to be my own person." I turn away, unable to handle Hudson's compassionate expression. "Papi always stood up for me, fought for me. He was my voice. And I couldn't return the favor."

Lips in my hair, Hudson whispers, "Your dad would want you to build your own voice."

I lean into Hudson's hug. His words are perfect, and yet . . .

"If only it were that easy. Whenever I try, it's like a boulder crushes me and I have no place to run to. All I want to do is hide."

"Next time, you run into me."

I sit up on a sigh, and nod.

We fall into a silent meditation, capturing each other's pain in our eyes.

A glassy reflection shines from his eyes as he searches my face further. "I'll always fight for you. Be your voice when you feel you can't fight on your own."

I soak in his every syllable, latching on to him wanting to be my voice. His vow gives me hope, a light at the end of a dark tunnel that I've been trapped in for way too long.

I take him in.

"You make me really vulnerable," I mutter. "In every way."

His lips curl up slightly and I'm about to say it.

In every way that makes me want to kiss you. In every way where I don't need a fancy gown or a cheering crowd.

Eighteen

"Is that a good thing?" Hudson asks. "Feeling vulnerable?"

"It's scary. Nice, but mostly scary."

I think about when he saw me naked. From my naked face to my naked body.

A long second passes. "I scare you?" He looks at me like I'm a girl he *wants*.

It's terrifying.

"A little," I admit. "I feel exposed. Sometimes when you look at me, I think you're picturing my ugly nakedness."

I wish I had a sexy body.

He squeezes my knee and leaves his hand there.

He's touching me. Because he wants to.

"I don't think about that." His hand sweeps up my arm, passes the shoulder, and caresses my neck. Given how slowly he's proceeding, he must want to say something else. Or he's counting each goose bump he's caused on my body.

It's simple and casual, but I try to memorize its pressure, warmth, and gentleness. We're closer than we've ever been. Is this where he leans in further, lifts me up, presses his lips to mine and soothes me with a beautiful kiss? Fireworks and confetti encompassing us? How high would we fly?

I search his eyes for those answers.

"I constantly wonder if I hurt you in any way," he says. "I replay how I lifted you to get the dress off and set you back down. But I don't want you to feel uneasy. I'll get naked and exposed, too." He presses to his feet, giving me a smile that is flirty and a tiny bit shy. Then he tugs his shirt from his waistband and lifts it above his head.

I blink. *This is moving way too fast.* Let's go back to the confetti part. No need to imagine bare skin just yet. I'm not ready. I swallow hard, searching for words because I don't necessarily want him to stop either.

"Being vulnerable is a strength," he says. Then he's quiet. There's something to his silence. Something to his wink.

I can't think of anything other than his abs, as superficial as that is. I've never touched abs on a body before. Heck, I've never had a guy take his shirt off for me.

"Just so we're clear, this will make me *more* awkward and uneasy," I say as he stands there shirtless.

He turns on his heel and slips out of his sneakers. "It's only fair."

My hands get slightly damp, so do my feet. A sweat bead slithers between my boobs. I scan his lean torso again—the six-pack abs—sweeping down to the waistline of his pants and over his hipbones.

There's a burn scar on the side of his hip. It wraps around his lower back and into the depths of his spine.

He watches me stare. I'm completely captured by his body.

"Fire at a summer camp when I was fourteen. Lost half the feeling on my hip." He twists to show me. "Felt embarrassed about it for years. I'd throw fits if anyone saw it. My ex is the only one who's touched it. You can, if you want."

My eyes work to his lower back.

"Still embarrassed, though."

"Don't be," I say breathlessly. "It's part of your history."

Our eyes meet and it's as if we're meeting for the first time. Like that moment during the first day of classes when you spot a cute guy yards away. You stare for a brief second, thinking, *I wish I could know you.* That's this moment right now.

My hands smooth over my armrest.

"We all have vulnerable parts. Things we want to hide. Things we think are ugly. But I don't want *you* to feel embarrassed," he explains in such a smooth way. I repeat his words in my head. "I need help too sometimes. My mistakes and emotions are embarrassing."

There's a calming silence, allowing reality to disappear.

I draw my eyes to his lips. He draws his eyes to mine.

The sky could open up and shower us with cockroaches, and I wouldn't quit staring at him.

His shirt drops to the floor. When he bends down to retrieve it, the burn scar is on full display. I lean forward and do the unexpected.

I kiss it.

It's because I didn't want him to feel alone and scared. Or maybe I kissed his vulnerable part because I wanted someone to be there for him. Or for me. Maybe caring for him is a comfort for myself.

When I straighten up, he turns and slides the shirt onto the table.

My eyes widen. "Sorry. I can't believe . . ." I swallow hard. "It's that I didn't want you to feel embarrassed. Like, to show you that I accept what you're embarrassed about." I can't believe I did that. "See, now I'm more embarrassed than you. I'm gonna get some air."

Moving fast, I round the table and hit the button next to the door. The glass slides across and a blast of breeze hits me. I roll onto the porch and inhale a deep breath while gazing at the stars. They twinkle and sparkle like Hudson's eyes. I bite my lip, wondering what he's thinking.

Soft steps approach, and when I pivot, he's there.

His stare is full-on, his heaving chest glistening.

I glide across the oak porch. "Sorry." Seems appropriate since I don't know what else to say. I almost repeat it a few more times as if it'll solve the awkward silence.

"The only fair thing to do is for me to kiss *you*."

The guy of my dreams did not say he's going to kiss me. I'd never considered that scenario in my plan. The one where he's planning for it, saying he will. I lose all control, hating not knowing when, how, and where the kiss will happen.

He licks his lips, and it's as dirty as whatever he's thinking —something about how he'd sweep his tongue inside my mouth and work his hand down my body. He's probably a fast and passionate kisser. The kind who presses into someone with full force and dances them toward the shower.

"Um." It's not that I *don't* want to kiss Hudson. "Let's plan for it to be special," I mutter, because now that he's here saying those words and they're becoming reality, I'm scared. Scared I won't know what to do. Scared he won't like it. I'm so scared because I like him so much. I hate that I do, because that means I'd never recover if he hates the way I can't kiss.

"*Not* planning is what makes things special." His stare goes intense. He might have picked his moment to lay his lips on me.

He moves closer, one infinitesimal movement at a time. He

could be contemplating where to kiss me. It may not even be my lips at all.

My lungs can't get enough air.

"I wanted to make you feel less embarrassed about your scar," I say to backtrack to the moment before he announced he was going to kiss me. "To feel loved. Because I don't care about scars or how you look." Okay, that's not true. I do care how he looks. He looks pretty good.

Not talking is dangerous. More dangerous than talking nonsense. "And I don't even have any lip gloss on."

He just . . . stares.

My heart pounds in my eardrums.

It's a new level of awkward. "Can you say something?" I whisper.

The heat of embarrassment creeps into my cheeks. The dots on my chest are surely glowing beacons.

I sweep my gaze up his body until I reach his hazel eyes. My mouth goes dry. I whimper, "Hud?"

Say something else.

I can't. My feet go numb, as does the rest of me.

The corner of his mouth twitches up. His cheeks flush as he fights to hold back a smile. In a single move, he drops next to me, one arm around my waist.

Rotating my head with his thumb, our lips are inches away from finishing a connection.

I panic and lunge into his chest, deeply inhaling a faint leather cologne scent. My cheek plasters against his breast. Every particle in me aches to kiss Hudson, but I can't. What if he turns into a frog or bumps his head and passes out? It may be silly to think there's a kissing curse upon me, even though I've never passionately kissed anyone.

Deflection?

145

My eyes shut. I imagine kissing him to manifest how it should go.

I pretend his mouth seals over mine with a lush, soft kiss. Slowly, he licks across my parted lips, slips his tongue inside, and teases me with gentleness. The taste of mint lingers. His tongue pushes deeper as his hand trails down my neck. The touch releases the aches that have built inside me. He breathes me in, strokes his tongue along mine, and turns my body into a shaking mess.

"You okay?" Hudson asks with a chuckle. He definitely wasn't imagining us kissing just now.

I exhale so deeply that I blow some spit on his bare skin. Sitting back up, I use all of my willpower to not press my cool hands against my burning face.

"Just need some air."

He chuckles as I rub my face residue off his chest with a sweaty palm. The mixture spreads over his skin, into his skin. I gasp at how his body consumed my DNA.

"Sorry," I mutter.

I pull away and glance up at the blanket of stars. "You like stars? We can look at those." The North Star blinks fast. "Look there!"

The butterflies in my stomach erupt.

"The view is better from the grass. Can I lift you to the ground?" he asks.

Hudson lifting me? Me touching his body full-on, completely, totally entirely? It's one thing to be lifted for a transfer and another to be in someone's arms like that. My hands go damper. The thumps in my chest speed up.

I nod, picturing being in his arms. Logistical words, that's what I need. "Give me support under my lower back and wrap my arm around your neck." I stretch it toward his neck to signal I'm ready. This is totally and utterly *not* scary, I tell myself. "Wait, I need to catch my breath."

"It's okay if you're scared," he teases.

A blush heats my neck and cheeks, my ears and basically my entire upper half. "I am *not* scared. Just need to inhale and exhale." I take in a large breath and slowly let it out. "Okay, you can lift me."

He leans over and slides his hand under my knees. "We can go as slow as you want."

As we stand, my exhales crash into his neck. Our closeness gives me even weirder feelings in my stomach.

A hint of mint wafts from him. Our bodies are plastered against each other like double-sided tape. My heart's past the point of aflutter. I'm in too deep.

The up and down of his steps almost feels like flying.

I'm so close, the freckles on his nose are pronounced. Hudson's lips are inches from mine. His long lashes capture my attention as he searches my face. His cheeks go red, and I imagine mine are as more than flushed. They're so hot, they're astronomically raining sweat.

He fights a smirk and slowly whispers, "I'm attracted to you, too."

Tingles run up into my throat. I prepare for him to tickle me—not that I want him to or that he will. It's just that every inch of me is tingling enough to give me a tickling sensation.

I refuse to let him see me smile but it pops up anyways. The fear has surpassed—I imagine Hudson kissing me.

"Going down," he says, lowering to the perfectly cut grass next to some carnations.

My butt hits the ground first, followed by my feet, back, and head. My right knee isn't as extended as the left. I stretch during physical therapy twice a week, but I can't fully extend my body without applied pressure.

The grass is soft and prickly underneath us. The fresh scent lingers.

We lie inches apart. He's propped up on his elbow, showing off his bulky appearance.

My chest is on fire along with a strange hollow feeling in the pit of my stomach. My smile grows as a reflection of his.

I release the worries of the world. I'm not thinking about my plans or what anyone would say if they saw us.

His hand glides over my shoulder and down my curved spine, pressing into my back—its dampness penetrates my donut shirt.

"Your lip stuff looks nice."

There must be some remaining makeup residue on them. My stomach twists into knots. "Thanks," I say breathlessly.

I smooth my hands over his shoulders and map out every inch of his arms. "I wish I was more experienced," I say. All I think about is the girls he's kissed and hooked up with—all the things he probably likes a girl to do that I'm clueless about.

He has dated and probably done more things to girls than I could imagine. Me, I'm stuck with planning my first kiss.

"It's all about the journey, isn't it?" he says, giving me a quick peck on the cheek. I laugh into it.

As he holds me, a weird feeling stirs in my chest. It's weird because it's so comfortable. His hand slips under my butt and over my hips with not enough pressure to leave a mark, but enough for me to want more.

I can't believe I'm letting him touch me like this. I can't believe I want him to *keep* touching me like this.

"I love your body," he murmurs, heating my face with his warmth, his gaze searing. A bead of sweat glistens on his forehead, and concern crosses his face. "I'm not hurting you, am I?" He rises an inch.

"No," I whisper. I bite my lip. "It's nice."

"Every part of *you* is nice." His mouth curls up into a sexy smirk. The soft and deep voice weaves through my every nerve ending. His arms fit perfectly around my waist and curved spine.

The fireworks keep exploding in my stomach and I can't stop gawking at his lips.

He fixes the hair stuck at the corner of my mouth.

I'm so in love with this moment.

"Abby?"

A deep voice calls from the shadows, and I startle. Theo. His feet shuffle over the grass. The light from the kitchen porch lamppost illuminates his black work shirt and loose jeans.

Nineteen

HUDSON LIFTS HIS HEAD UP. "What the fuck do you want, *Theo*?" There's an angry tone to his voice as though he either hates him or hates that he ruined our moment. Probably both.

"I'm checking on Abby," Theo replies, lowering to the side where my head is positioned. "Is Hudson doing something he's not supposed to?"

"No," I mumble. "Thanks. I should get back into my chair." I pause and immediately ask, "How are you, Theo?"

Theo's thud plants next to me.

"I gotcha," he says, ignoring my question. Then he slides an arm around my lower back. The other moves under my knees, and I'm swept up into him as he rises. So fast, it causes my stomach to drop and my hair to swing from side to side. His arm muscles flex almost symmetrically. They practically pierce through both our shirts.

I inhale the cedarwood and chlorine scent.

This has to be the actual definition of awkward. I'm so embarrassed Theo caught me with a half-naked Hudson—after being upset I chose Hudson—and now carrying me away from Hudson.

Hudson jumps to his feet before Theo and I get to my chair a few feet away. We're not galloping like horses per se, but Theo's walking sends me up and down.

"We don't need your help." Hudson seems offended Theo stole his thunder.

I'm stuck between a rock and a hard place called Hudson and Theo. Because yes, they're both that close to me. *Four. Three.* I'm counting the feet left until I can be in my seat. Any girl would dream of being in a sandwich with two hulks, but this isn't fun. I'm practically squeezed between solid muscles that keep getting closer.

"I'm not a hotdog," I mutter, hoping to lessen the tension.

They separate and I smile at my chair. The thump that comes when my butt hits my cushion is silent compared to the stare down the two have. "Boys, calm down." I turn to Theo. "Thanks for coming, really. We should talk."

Theo glares at Hudson, who straightens up. The tension makes my stomach churn.

How will I stop them? Theo tops Hudson by a few inches, even standing on the grass. But Hudson is powerful, an athlete.

The wind howls around us. They furrow their brows at each other. Both hold a hard stare. It's like a nature documentary where the male animals are squaring off on my porch.

"You guys. Knock it off." This could get ugly.

The pit of my stomach warns of a possible fight. These two have never seen eye to eye. Theo makes things and Hudson buys things. They hold different values to the point that the town has pitted their families against each other for years— land kings versus the water lords. I don't get the issue, but once a pattern gets set, it's hard to undo it.

"We can all be friends," I say, glancing between the two.

They definitely don't want to be friends.

"Did he *work* to rebuild your trust, Abby?" Theo asks me, scowling at his nemesis. "Have you set him straight for ghosting you all these years? I'll set him straight." There's that protective attitude Theo has been displaying for the last ten months.

"Um." The tables have turned too quickly for me to catch up.

Theo adds, "My father once told me Mr. Giordani stole a new aquatic project for some wine resort aquatic getaway. Hudson will be here and then leave again."

"My relationship with Abby or with my father is none of your damn business," Hudson responds before I do. He's challenging Theo solely to challenge him.

I bite my lip. Words would be great right about now. My racing mind searches for anything to defuse the growing pressure between them.

Theo unglues his stare from Hudson and pivots to me, sympathetic eyes looking down. "Your text sounded urgent. I'm here if you want to talk. Wanna go to the cabin? You can unload anything on me." His concern is written on his face, and though he doesn't come close to smiling, his mouth and brows loosen up.

"I'm okay now." The moment I speak those words, I realize I picked Hudson over my best friend. "But . . ."

"I see. You don't need me anymore." Theo frowns with disgust.

Hudson steps in front of me. "*We* don't need losers like you. Go build something. I'll buy something flashier ten times over."

Theo shakes his head at me. "When he leaves and doesn't

return, don't come crying to me." He spins around and marches off.

"Wait, Theo," I yell, in disbelief at what has unfolded.

Theo ignores my call and jogs off.

I whirl on Hudson. "That *loser* is my best friend who didn't ignore me for years. He's aware of how hurt I was when *you* did. I can't believe you said that to Theo. Being cruel makes me like you less, Hud." That's the second time I've given him a nickname. "Needle!" I add as an insult. It doesn't seem to work, because Hudson chuckles.

When my eyebrows furrow, his mouth folds into a straight line.

He kicks at the grass, hands slithering into his pockets. "Not everyone gets along with everyone."

I stand my ground. "You're not getting away with being mean to Theo."

He shrugs. "I'm sorry. Guess it's easy to pick on him."

"Don't apologize to me. Go apologize to him."

Hudson needs to mean it. As much as I'm sure Theo would not want an apology, the two need to work out their differences. "He's simply protective of me."

Hudson squints into the distance.

"I was a jerk. I'll buy him a boat so he doesn't have to sweat over building one." The lamppost catches him as he leans into it and crosses his ankles. "Okay, I get it, he's the one who'd be able to buy me a boat, which then I'd give him."

I raise my brows. He zeroes in on my face but says nothing smart-alecky.

"Okay, fine. I'll say I was wrong, that I was a loser and a coward, and apologize for being cruel."

"Great."

I stare into the distance. Everything in me is saying to run after Theo. But what would I say? Telling my best friend that I like Hudson will not go over well.

In fact, Theo seems crushed by me being with Hudson. I sigh at the thought of causing Theo more pain. Because facing the people I hurt is unbearable. Last time I couldn't handle it. Why would anything change now?

But his reaction has me wondering why choosing Hudson affects Theo so much. Does it mean he has feelings for me? If only I could talk to Diana and Joey right about now.

In the meantime, ice cream it is.

I spin around and enter the kitchen, heading for the refrigerator. In a swift motion, I grab a spoon from a drawer and the pistachio ice cream from the freezer.

"Bowl for two?" Hudson asks, crossing the kitchen.

I escape into the hallway. "You haven't apologized to Theo yet."

"Really?" he yells from where I left him.

If I let him stay, if we share a kiss, if we feed each other, then that would only hurt Theo more. It's either that or I don't tell Theo anything. But I tell Theo everything. Ice cream is the only fix to this dilemma. Because what if Theo has been in love with me all this time?

We'll find out tomorrow when I volunteer at the aquatic center in the morning. Summer splash sessions are Theo's favorite weekend events and maybe he'll be calmer.

The front door slams and I'm shocked Hudson used *that* door.

The ice cream is a bit much. Gobbling down a whole container, that is. I circle into the kitchen and almost run into Astrid—phone against her ear.

"Oh, hey," I say. "It's you."

She stomps toward the champagne. The heels of her shoes practically make dents in the marble floor.

"Not the car!" she yells, reaching for a glass and a bottle with one hand. There's panic in her voice. "There has to be another way."

Something is wrong. Elijah must have done something wrong.

"Give me until tomorrow. I have a large college fund."

She pockets her phone and shakes her head. "Abby, not now."

I haven't asked her anything until now. "Ice cream?" I hand her my spoon.

A long pause follows and I think she's about to scream, or worse, break the glass in her hand. "I need millions of dollars, not sugar."

We *are* having money troubles. *Serious* money troubles.

"What's wrong? Can't Elijah give you money?" The moment I ask, I want to retract that last question.

She circles the table, walks into the living room, crosses over to the piano, and plops onto the white couch. All with the champagne and glass in one hand.

"What can I sell?"

She drinks out of the bottle, looking small and defeated.

My wheels track closer to her. This is our chance to have an honest conversation about everything. The money, the ball, the jewelry, her wedding . . . Papi. It will hurt at first, but it might also reunite our sisterhood.

"There's an artifact in the basement, a throne, that's probably worth millions," I offer. Then again, it feels wrong to sell a historical piece like that for money. But for my sister, I can part with one treasure.

She sits up and places the champagne on the table. "You're a genius. I actually only need half a million."

Astrid could be trying to fix a problem or prove a point to Elijah. He's given her money before. He bought her the gold convertible for her eighteenth birthday.

I gape at her. "Why are *you* stressing over money? Is your wedding more expensive than you thought or is Elijah not helping?" He would do that just to show his power over her. "Or is the jewelry company going under? Do we have to leave the mansion? I can get a job. Are you giving Mother your money? Should I do that, too?"

How are we broke? Astrid has a large college fund and Mother has been adding new clients for months. But it'd be naïve not to consider the possibility that we are strapped for cash.

I must be missing a piece of the puzzle.

Speculation is only speculation without evidence. So far, nothing adds up. Panashe Jewelry may have dropped in stock price, but they donated a million dollars to VU last month. Mother would never do that if we were in trouble.

What if Astrid got into business with dangerous people? Someone could have a grudge against Elijah and is taking their revenge out on my sister.

Astrid stands up, straightens her dress and parades back into the kitchen, taking the glass and champagne with her. Ever since last summer, she doesn't talk to me the way she did before. It's like Elijah has this leash on her. He's always telling her not to speak to anyone so she can't get sued, but what she's not supposed to talk about, I have no clue. What I have a clue on is she's acting more like Elijah toward me.

Grabbing my phone, I search and find an article about the VU donation. It's interesting how Elijah is the first person quoted saying that him and my mother are honored to support the future of the business and law colleges. Another source quotes how the Panashe Jewelry donated to a charity that was started by the Kippurs' firm.

Something feels very wrong here. Elijah definitely has a hand in our family's business and is probably more excited about marrying into our legacy than marrying my sister.

Circling to Astrid, I feel a sense of urgency to ask if she truly wants to be with Elijah for love. Or if she can make some connection between our money troubles and her fiancé.

She squints at the shirt scrunched up on the table and moves toward it. "Is that Hudson's?"

I'd never had a boy over who leaves his clothes behind. "W-why do you think it's his?" I croak from behind her.

"I don't have time for this right now. Going to the basement." Within seconds, the clacking of her heels fades, and I sneak back to get Hudson's shirt.

The last thing I need is Mother finding his shirt and yelling at me for hanging out alone with a half-naked guy.

If she was mad we broke bottles, then she will be furious about this. I can't imagine what she'd do if she found out. Not let me go to senior homecoming dance or take away my phone privileges?

I'll be smarter about sneaking around with Hudson. Not that I plan to do it often, but the spontaneity is growing on me.

Twenty

THE AQUATIC CENTER'S raindrop-shaped glass looks a lot like a gnome's hat. The silver doors open automatically and the chlorine-heavy air hits me hard. Two teens manage the front desk governing access to the large rock-climbing wall in the middle of the building. You could climb the wall to get to the second floor, but most people ride the elevator or take the side stairs. A small shop sits in the corner selling miniature boats, nature pins, and life jackets.

I unload a second batch of stickers onto the lobby table. The other volunteer left for her break and we were low on supplies. It was busier earlier, so I may have underestimated how many canoe and boat stickers we actually need—definitely less than two hundred.

I've handed out over a hundred stickers to families and helped over thirty kids build miniature kayaks. Two hours have passed and no sign of Theo.

I glance out the window to the faraway lake. Once upon a time, swimming and floating between the seaweed made me feel so free. I ache for that feeling. As I look at the calm waters across the space, I remember asking Papi to watch me tumble in the water like I was a superhero, because I could do and be anything in the water. Then the lake took away that freedom last summer when he gave up his life to save mine. Now, I treat the waves like they're forbidden fruit.

Maybe that's why I chain myself to my planner more than normal these days. I don't allow myself to be free as a way to punish myself.

I smile at a boy skipping alongside his mother. He chirps about how he's going to be a ship captain one day.

Speaking of captains, I wonder where the bold and strong Theo is hiding. Clearly he's keeping his distance.

He might be building something out in the lake shed.

I grab my phone from my purse and check Theo's social media. He's the type to post photos of projects, tools, and the lake from different angles. And trees. He can't go two weeks without posting a tree picture with an Einstein quote about the universe.

His last post was of a sunset three days ago.

At least he hasn't blocked me.

I scroll through the general posts. A flood of debs trying on gowns, finalizing makeup looks, or volunteering at events flash across the screen.

Joey's posts are of motorcycles, boots, and tattoos. Diana has . . . been hanging out with other people? I frown. She would never exclude me from a party invite. When one of us would get invited anywhere, we'd always say we're a package deal. I guess this is worse than I thought. This isn't something that will blow over or work itself out with time.

She spent last night at two birthday parties for the Ashleys. If this is her way of making me feel the way she did when I didn't invite her to see my dress last week, consider me in pain.

Or is this her way of saying we're not friends anymore? If our friendship is so weak as to break after one mistake, then what is our friendship? I refuse to believe that. Phone in hand, I text her saying that I'm here for her if she wants to open up or say she's mad at me.

I miss our fashion parties and tea times. It's been a short span of time, but the distance has grown into five laps around the sun.

A staff member walks past me.

I glance up and ask, "Hi, have you seen Theo?"

She points across the lobby to the outside.

There he is. Fixing the drinking fountain in the far corner. His biceps are the size of my head. I never realized how hard they looked. Everything about him looks hard. The furrowed brows and lips are in a harsh line.

He's tense. Every part of him. Every breath he takes. Every step he makes.

And I made him that way.

As defeated as I feel, I have to fight for a better future than I'm currently setting into place if I do nothing.

I suck in a deep breath and roll over to him.

This is it. Don't run away.

Once the air hits me, he looks up and gives a harsh, "Hey." As he rises to his feet, his wet shirt plasters to his chest. I gawk at his heaving chest. Wet clothes clearly make his body more noticeable.

I scratch the side of my head. "So . . ." I pause. The guilt heightens my empathy for him—this need to retreat and lick his wounds. "Hudson isn't replacing you."

"Yeah, whatever." His saying *whatever* is not whatever.

"Don't close me out."

Theo crosses to the trashcan next to me. He tosses tape and other scraps into it.

"I'm sorry you're hurt," I say. "He's my escort, but you're my best friend no matter what. Can we talk about this?" I reach for his hand. I never reach for his hand.

Theo sidesteps me and stomps toward the entrance.

"Wait," I say on a sigh. "Five seconds, please."

Twisting around, he slides onto the lobby bench.

"I need you, and Hudson is *not* replacing you, okay?" I lead the way because silence gets us nowhere. "Or is it something else?" My hands run down my side ponytail. Do I want it to be something else?

Arms crossed over his chest, he replies, "You didn't go after me last night. You stayed with *him*."

"That doesn't mean I don't care about you."

"People who care do something to make the other feel better. If you knew me at all, you'd know I was upset, but you gave that player your time."

His gaze sweeps past me, leeching uncertainty. He swallows, his Adam's apple bobbing.

"Is it 'cause he's great at everything, including dancing?" There's hurt to his every syllable. "Don't forget that he broke your heart four years ago. He'll probably do it again."

The warning hits me hard. "I'm so grateful for you," I whisper.

Theo leans back into the bench, glaring at me.

"Hudson is perfect. He won prom king." Theo makes fun. "I'm an outcast and don't belong at a ball. Guess I'll never be good enough for you."

I inhale so deeply, I almost choke of my own saliva.

"Theo . . ." My lip-biting habit kicks in. I find the hem of my silk button-up shirt and play with it, hoping to distract myself. I wish he could read my mind and understand the words I can't find.

"I'm sorry." My hands dig under my thighs. "What do you want? You can still be part of next weekend, somehow. We can figure something out. Help me honor Papi's memory at the ball."

My eyes return to Theo's pained expression.

He shakes his head and I wonder if he's breaking off our friendship. "To be frank, I don't want to be a reminder of your father. I'm not him. Just let me be, okay?"

My chest rises and falls harder, and not in a good way. Theo is pushing me away, hurting me in every possible way. A shield slides over his eyes, his expression shifting into an angry one.

The whole world presses down on my chest. Unspoken words hang between us. He wants nothing to do with me anymore?

"I'm sorry." My throat constricts. "Are you upset because you have feelings for me?"

Theo glides his thumb across his lower lip. I imagine he's deep in thought. Or maybe he's moved beyond this moment and is thinking about his next task.

"Don't be sorry," he says, once again ignoring my question. "*I'm* sorry. You should enjoy the ball. Have fun with *Hudson* and forget about me."

He gazes at me sorrowfully. "I've learned that living in the present instead of trying to recreate the past is the best way to move forward. Maybe it's time we live separate adventures."

Searing heat burns my ears. "I don't want to forget about you," I whisper, panicked.

The pause lasts long enough that the silence grows heavy. Ominous even.

Theo shoves a hand through his thick hair. "I have to finish fixing things up around the building." He kneads his neck and adds, "Thanks for helping the kids. You'll surely win over Diana's total volunteer hours."

Then he leaves and doesn't look back.

My best friend has dumped me. He's pushed me away and there's nothing I can do.

A beat passes before I slowly return to the volunteer table. Focus and refocus. We could use a better organization system. If I put the stickers next to the flyers and the flyers next to . . . no, I can't organize anything. My hands shake too much to focus on anything other than Theo.

A towel flies past me and into a gray bin. Joey's dark brown eyes meet mine. The large motorcycle pajamas a size too big, drape her. Her hair is wet, droplets creating spots on the cotton fabric.

"Joey?" I say, pulling myself together.

The last time I saw her with wet hair was after a summer pool party when she got pushed in by a girl she liked.

"Hey. What are you doing here?" she asks.

"Volunteering." My nose crinkles. "Did you go into the lake?" It's not making much sense why she's wet. Pajamas, okay, I get being lazy on a Saturday.

She shrugs. "I like showering here. Fancy showers and baths are a turnoff." Joey has always walked to the beat of her own drum. Once, she ran away when she wanted to live a simple life on the roof of a warehouse building. Obviously, that didn't work out.

"How's Diana?" I immediately ask, feeling the sudden urge to tell someone about last night. And what happened with Theo minutes ago. "It'd be nice to have breakfast soon."

Joey's mouth tugs at the corners. "Yeah, she's okay. I think the stress of the ball is fucking with her head. There's also something about a science fair she seemed super upset about. But her family wants her to win so they can get invited to fancy fashion shows and design outfits for the mayor."

Science fair? That doesn't sound like Diana.

"What if her family did the clothing and mine could style the jewelry?" I miss my friends. "How were the Ashleys' birthday parties last night?"

"So lit," she says with a laugh. "They got so high, they started kissing this guy and then that guy. Then the guy kissed me and Talia, and it was a big kissing party."

I swallow the lump in my throat. Joey talks about kissing so freely. Not that I want to shout it to the world, but I can't hold it in any longer.

"I kissed Hudson last night." That came out wrong. "I mean, I kissed his body." That's even worse. My cheeks burn. "It was only a peck, but then he said he wanted to kiss me and then we almost did, but then Theo caught us and got really mad and now he's ignoring me. What do I do?"

Joey lets out a long whistle. "Wow. Congrats. Diana could help—" A nervous chuckle replaces the words. "You let those lips party."

I sigh and go wide-eyed. "I'm falling for Hudson, but Theo is so hurt." As much as I hate the tension between the guys, Hudson occupies my mind more. "At first, I was scared. Now I can't wait to kiss him and fall into his arms for the rest of my life."

"No! You are not going down that road." She puts her hand to my forehead. "Are you sure you're not sick with a fever or high on syrup? Hmm, I can't seem to diagnose you."

I pull away. "I'm not Diana." We both have seen this many times with her. "This is different, Joey. Hudson and I have basically known each other since grade school. I had a crush on him before."

Joey's hands land on my shoulders and she shakes me. "Snap out of it. You've been talking to him for less than a week! You need a good foundation before you fall for someone."

My smile pops up, and she shakes me harder.

"Okay, okay." I roll back. "So can you help me fix things with Diana?"

Joey steps back. "I've tried. Only you can fix it with her. Do something to *show* her you care more about her than yourself and she'll open up like a flower."

"I'll try," I say, hopeful.

I wave as she salutes me and walks out. I imagine her riding her motorcycle, pajamas billowing around her. That's one way to dry your hair, which she prefers over blow-drying.

Then I think about ways I can show Theo I care more about him than myself.

Twenty-One

HUDSON'S SHIRT smells like strawberry and lavender. It's soft. I sniff it for the hundredth time. Is there a hint of mint toothpaste? Wait, that's all just me.

I told myself that I won't let us hang out until he apologizes to Theo, but it's Monday already and the ball is five days away. It's too bad Diana is mad at me, otherwise we'd have chitchatted over tea this morning. I should have brought over a teapot to her house as a surprise. Something, I must surprise her with something.

"Lunchtime." Astrid enters my bedroom and immediately spots the shirt. "Did you sleep with Hudson's shirt?"

My cheeks burn red with guilt. It's like she has X-ray vision and can see right through me.

"It's nothing." Is the first thing out of my mouth. "So, how are *you*?"

"You like him, don't you?" She gives a small laugh, and it quivers. "Hudson is only an escort. This isn't a dating thing. He said he was going to see you after rehearsal on Friday. Did you two do something together?"

The redness in my face deepens. "We just talked," I croak out. I flap my hand in dismissal and roll out of my room. "You said it's almost lunchtime, right?"

Astrid marches behind me, her heels thundering against the floor. I need to get rid of the evidence. I text "Needle" and ask him to get his shirt.

Can you grab your shirt soon? My bedroom window is unlocked.

I turn my attention back to Astrid. "How's wedding planning going?" If I focus on *her*, she won't question me about liking Hudson. Not that it's any of her business, but she'll probably say he's not into me that way.

She stares at her phone screen. It's obvious she'll pick her phone over me every time.

"Blue or silver centerpieces for the wedding?" Dodging the question only means I've hit a nerve. I wonder if getting married is something she actually wants or if she's simply going along with the motions set in place.

Or worse, Elijah is forcing her to marry him. Say, he's at the root of our money troubles and Astrid found out but is scared to do anything about it. What I need, is get my hands on the wedding plans. The finances can show where money is going and coming from; the guest list can show who is attending and for what purposes, possibly.

I nod. "Both sound lovely. Are any of the investors or board members attending the wedding? How much money is *Elijah* putting into the wedding? Is the jewelry business paying for it all?"

"Silver centerpieces." Astrid's mind was made up before she even asked me. "Elijah will love that, right?"

"Yeah?" I shrug. Elijah is most likely more concerned with the invoice and contracts.

"Gold. I'm going to do gold centerpieces."

"How do you honestly feel about marriage?" I pause. "To Elijah." I say his name as disapprovingly as possible. "Is he causing you money troubles?"

No response. What a shocker.

She crosses the oak floor in her fast, swaying gait. "Diana told me she's hosting a lavish tea party before the voting for Ms. Congeniality closes. You know, the one where the debs vote on how nice and friendly you've been to them. Since you and Diana are neck and neck for the title, you are planning an event for them, right?" She picks up a wedding planner from the hallway table. "If it becomes a tie, which might happen according to the Ashleys, Mrs. D'aureville will break it. You have to give her every reason to pick *you*. Think of the most press-worthy story you can generate and the director will sway in your direction."

This queen business is unwanted stress, but I can't say no to Astrid. Not to mention I basically promised Mother that the crown is important to me. But the twist in my stomach grows.

"Uh. Okay." I agree. Because Astrid will tap one perfect foot, making one perfectly annoying rhythm until I bow down to her instructions.

"I was thinking of doing a decorate-your-own-cake extravaganza." Just came up with that. I smile, proud of myself.

"When, where, what time, which invites, how long, what ingredients . . ." She goes on and on and on.

Taking to my phone, I note the location, date, social media invite, dress code details, cake decorating options . . .

I scroll through cake pictures on Mei-Ling's website. Red velvet is always a favorite. So are cake pops. Or I could have each deb's name decorated on a cupcake. Everyone loves their name on anything in this town—a building, a license plate, a jet plane.

It would be fun to have the girls decorate a huge cake together. The Ashleys would probably draw penises, Pyper a violin, Diana . . . Will she come? Technically, every deb must attend a deb-related event.

Giving her a heads-up seems appropriate. Even better, I'll plan it in her honor. That sounds like something selfless. I shoot her a text so she can be the first invite.

I roll into the living room and park myself at the dining table. The smooth edge touches just over my silk shorts.

Classical music sings from the self-playing piano. Mozart is today's pick. Elijah and his parents have already taken their seats, and the servers have set chicken salad plates for each person. Blueberries and cucumber sandwiches decorate the sides.

Astrid answers a vibrating phone. "Mei-Ling. Yes, brides-maid's dresses . . . . You are a lifesaver . . . . I can take all that I can get . . . . Ah-hmm, bachelorette party at Niagara Falls."

I unfold a napkin on my lap and slightly smile at Elijah. If he's going to be part of the family, I might as well *try* to get along with him. Or at least push his buttons until I get to the truth. My spidery senses are tingling.

"Are you excited about getting married?" I ask. "Or are you using the wedding as some cover up? Didn't you have a gambling problem?" A memory crosses my mind as I remember Astrid crying during her high school graduation when Elijah lost her money to a bet.

Elijah laughs at me. "What?"

I pop a blueberry into my mouth and smile wider. Time to put him in the hot seat right in front of his parents. I pop another one in and chew loudly. "Why exactly were you in my mother's office in December? Is there some sort of money and contract arrangement?"

Elijah snickers. "What a disgrace. I'm *glad* Harry isn't doing the ball with you."

Same here, dude.

Mr. and Mrs. Kippurs whisper among themselves. What if Elijah's parents are forcing their son to dig around or are giving the jewelry company money in exchange for favors? Suddenly this investigation seems over my head. I can't take on the entire Kippurs empire. The stare of the three of them shrinks me into a tiny ant.

Astrid fixes her shorts and slides into a seat next to Elijah. "Mei-Ling was a deb with me, as you know, and agreed to help Abby. She invited us to cake tasting. For the wedding and for Abby's event."

Great, more time with Elijah. I refrain from rolling my eyes.

He fixes his collar. "We'll be signing separate contracts."

Now I roll my eyes. Then again, more time could give me some answers.

"You're not allowed to kiss Hudson," Astrid says out of nowhere. "Or hang out without adult supervision. Clothes included."

I dart my eyes at her. "I . . ." Her accusation trips up my defenses.

Her brows narrow. "The committee has a strong dating and kissing rule, because a lady entering society needs to show a certain image to the people of Verdan. Plus, you are *way* too young to date, especially a Giordani. You should be grateful Diana is looking out for you."

"Um." I try to think of a full sentence. None come. I've never gone against my sister's orders. Anyone's orders, really.

To think Diana told everything to Astrid stings. Secretly, though, I wanted Joey to tell Diana, but not for Diana to pass it on to my sister.

Elijah joins in. "Your escort isn't supposed to be a romantic partner. Do you want to get disqualified? How will that make Astrid look? Your family can't afford to lose the publicity and business deals. You've done enough damage."

He is too invested in my failures.

Astrid rubs his arm. "Babe, don't go there."

"I've done everything Mother and Astrid ask. And why is that even a rule?" My voice goes two octaves too high. "No one even reads the last hundred pages of the two-hundred-page rule book." Okay, I did. But it was my one allowance for breaking a rule. The ball is an event I will remember for the rest of my life. I want to be able to make it a little bit special just for me.

Besides, Astrid went with Elijah three years ago, and they were in a romantic relationship. "Elijah was your escort."

"Mrs. D'aureville is going to look for every excuse not to let you win queen. She plays favorites, and right now it's Diana. She doesn't care if *she* has a full-on boyfriend, but you already got on her bad side when some reporter said you were damaging Giordani property."

I squirm. "This is so unfair! We weren't even doing anything bad."

Elijah's chuckle sounds ugly. "I'm warning you. You mess this up and your family can say goodbye to their precious jewelry company. You want to lose everything that you have?"

I'm silenced, but I'm not afraid of Elijah. It baffles me that once upon a time, we were friends playing dress up. Now we're enemies playing with harsh words. Elijah's stare is full of dark secrets. It's piercing and forceful, yet also unstable. He has no right to put this pressure on me. Yet, at the thought of losing everything, I wilt like a dying flower. How deep are our financial troubles? It's clear he knows something, if not everything.

But what if I have it all wrong and he's saving the jewelry company from going under? And doing so makes him bitter, creating resentment for helping us.

"I won't fail," I mutter. There are other words I want to say, but he's louder, stronger, and more powerful than me. So I stay quiet, but I'm already creating a plan for how *I* can save the company—my family's legacy and future.

The well-polished lawyer-in-training gives Astrid a heated look. She folds her arms over her chest. He's expecting her to back him up. She does, of course.

"Abby, follow everything we say, and you'll be fine." She sounds calm. "Elijah didn't mean to scare you. He wants to protect you, and the publicity from you winning queen will help my wedding get publicity and sponsorship deals. More importantly, this is your chance to prove to everyone you can stand on your own. Especially if you're going to be the business club's president next year and then take on business in college. We're the ones who have to keep our family and company's legacy in good standing."

I nod. It's an automatic response that I can't seem to turn off. As much as I want to be disappointed in Astrid for not sticking up for me, I'm more disappointed that she so easily falls to Elijah's commands. In fact, I feel sorry for her.

"Seriously, Abby." She can see the disappointment, the tears in my eyes. "Don't fall for Hudson. At least not before the ball is over. You don't know what his plans are afterwards and getting emotionally invested is a risk. He's the type to change his mind and want something else. You on the other hand, live in a fantasy land. I don't want you to cry at the ball if his decisions hurt you." Her words echo around me. I don't want to hear them.

My ears heat up. I hate she said all that in front of Elijah and his parents, who are frowning at me.

Astrid straightens her halter top and glances at Elijah. "Sometimes love is dangerous." It's a stern warning.

"I didn't say I was *falling* for him," I mutter and poke at my salad.

But she's right. What are his plans after the ball? He might not even want to date me or have a relationship, and this might be a quick fling for him. Not that I consider myself fling material. We'll mostly kiss. I imagine it will be grand, but I never really thought about the aftermath.

The best romantic kiss can happen to me, and I want that. What do I want after the confetti floats to the floor and the fireworks finish erupting? We could go to being friends again or we could be more. Would I be okay with a one-night kiss?

So many roads, so little room for mutual heartbreaks.

Astrid's eyes narrow on me. She can tell I have feelings for Hudson. "You're a virgin and he's not. He's dated and you haven't." Clearly, we're past the point of personal space. "Focus on the ball. Mrs. D'aureville is coming today and it's your last chance to impress her. I'm looking out for you, Abby. For our family's image."

A cold shiver runs down my spine as I sink further into my seat. My fork stabs into the chicken pieces and I slowly take a bite.

I want to believe my sister is on my side, but sometimes I wonder if she's just covering her own ass.

"I hear you," I say at last. All eyes are going to be on me. That means I can't do what I want. If this is the way I save our reputation and company, I must consider it and prepare to be the perfect debutante. That means no grand romantic, magical, super powerful true love's real first kiss.

Satisfied with my answer, Astrid goes back to planning her honeymoon. I sigh at the thought of losing my dream ball. Not that it's disappearing, but it's no longer my own to have. The last of any happy memories, visions I had for the ball, fade.

Twenty-Two

ASTRID AND ELIJAH continue to loudly bicker at the table well past finishing their meals. If Mother were here and not shopping with Mrs. Giordani, I'd ask her how the company was doing. I'd ask if we could take matching mother-daughter photos at the ball. I'd ask if we can talk about Papi.

I'm so tired of this toxic silence.

Rounding a corner, I ease my stress by scrolling through my favorite online auction pages on my phone. There's a 1920s one closing in sixty seconds. I'm tempted to acquire a hundred-year-old toy train. Those antique lace green curtains also look fun.

When I refresh the website, the "sold" word appears in red and the train is no longer available. There's always someone richer and faster.

Maybe next time. Estate sales are more successful for grabbing fun things. I've found over twenty antique decorations, jewelry, and books at mansion sales.

That reminds me, I need to stop by the Red Antique Store to see how I can volunteer for their summer event. It's the closest I can get to an actual archeology degree since everyone says a business degree will set me up for success. Studying the old layers of history that reveal stories from the past would almost be like living in those times. It's fascinating to think about the secrets every preserved object holds.

I turn into my bedroom and pull up to my desk. On autopilot, I glide some passion fruit gloss over my lips.

A rumble sounds from my window and I turn, dropping the lip gloss onto the glass table.

Hudson's wide smile stares at me.

The windowpane cuts across his chest.

I gasp, my cheeks warming.

He slides the window open with one hand and steps into my room.

"Hey." I scan his collared shirt and sleek black slacks. "Stop doing that. Knock first." I drop my voice to a whisper and glance toward the hallway in case Astrid is nearby. "Grab your shirt. Be quick."

None of what I say fazes him. "Hungry?" He rounds me, slides into the armchair, and lifts up a bag. "I got fast food for lunch."

My mind works frantically to find the best response. As in, grateful-but-hurry-and-get-your-shirt-and-leave. "That's so thoughtful. It's a lovely day. Maybe you can take your shirt and have a picnic outside?"

"The grandmas at the senior center knitted outside today. Then I had an interview at the Verdana's dealership. I'm looking to chillax *indoors*. Don't want to get heatstroke."

"You're job hunting? Where have you applied to?" I'm genuinely curious. There's this interview course I took and I could practice interviewing him.

No, he needs to leave right now.

"Car places. But it's impossible to get anyone to take me seriously when they know I have a full ride to NYU this fall. I don't know what I'm doing."

"Think about your passions," I say and roll by his side. "Find what you really love and want to do and go in that direction." As I say those words, I think about the direction I want to take with Hudson.

"Hungry?" he asks.

Deflection. We are all so good at it.

He opens the bag, pulls out a large milkshake, and plops it on my makeup table along with the bag of French fries.

There has to be another way to get Hudson out of my *bedroom*. Not that I'm not excited to see him. But Astrid and the Kippurs are across the hall. I pivot slightly to hear if they're still bickering.

Total silence. They could either be on their way upstairs or to my room. I circle around and push the door shut with my footrest. I'd lock it, but we don't have locks on the doors. It was a precaution in case I accidentally locked myself in a room as a kid.

The fries do smell good. Imagining the combination of crunchy and warm with cold and chocolaty makes my mouth water.

"Just one," I say and take a fry.

Hudson pops the milkshake lid off and lets me take the first dip. He follows suit and we bite our fries at the same time.

"This is what sharing looks like," he says and winks.

"You're right. Thank you." I find myself smiling just as Astrid's warning bites into me. "When are you free so Demontae can instruct our dance routine? I wasn't stellar at rehearsal, and we need to make it perfect."

The ball is a priority.

Hudson hops up. "Dance with me."

I push back against my seat. "That is the opposite of planning. It makes everything . . . *meh*. Not perfect." It's become clear Hudson has never planned a single thing in his life, not on purpose, that is.

"Come *meh* dance." He bows formally.

I glare. "Don't 'meh' me."

His brow narrows. "I feel *meh* about you."

"So I'm *meh*?" I raise my brows.

He chuckles. "Right now? Kinda."

"Well, I don't want you here if I'm *meh*."

Hudson drops to one knee. "But moments around you are the loveliest of my life." His tone has lost its humor. "You're everything and more. People will worship us together and treat us as royalty. How can you not want *meh* with me?" As he rises, his fingertips trail up my arm. Just as slowly, he lifts my hand to his mouth. The softness of his lips on my skin sends goose bumps shivering through me.

The back of my neck warms and I fight a smile. "Stop. You're totally *meh*."

"Glad we're on the same page. I'm *meh* about the ball, but ecstatic about taking *you*."

I back away so he won't see me blush, forgetting everything Astrid has said. This feels too good to give up.

Heels clack against the floor in the living room. "You have to leave right now." My fear is stronger than my courage. I push him toward the window.

Hudson grabs the bag and drink. "I see. You don't want me." He fake-sighs deeply. But the disappointment in the sigh is real. "Then I'll go."

When he puts one foot in front of the other, I hate parting

ways. Being next to Hudson gives me purpose, a reason to take a risk.

I don't want him to leave. The air is colder without him. The shivers last a little longer. As he slides through the open window, my chest throbs painfully.

"Wait," I whisper. "Stay for a little." If I want to kiss Hudson and he wants to kiss me, then we're going to kiss. Hidden and away from prying eyes, of course. "We can get real close in my closet. I want that if you do."

Getting emotionally attached will make our bond stronger for the ball, despite what Astrid thinks. We'll have such a deep connection, our every move will be in sync and too perfect to ruin anything. Our shine will rule the ballroom, the dancing, the curtsy, the conversation.

The footsteps down the hall fade away.

Hudson doesn't miss a beat. He jumps over, and a clunking tap sounds from his back pocket. The food lands back to the same spot on the makeup table, but I'm focused on more intriguing things.

"Is that what I think it is?" I ask, leaning to see the tools. "Knitting needles?"

"Best of the best." He *was* knitting this morning at the senior center. "We can knit. That's real intimate and close."

"I'd like that," I mutter, looking up at him.

He doesn't wait, and slips his arms up and around me.

I cling tight to Hudson and it's the best feeling.

Moments later, we're in the closet and he lowers down to the ground. We're so in each other's faces that I can't see anything other than his grin and messy hair.

We're hidden by a row of shelves with blouses and tank tops neatly folded on each shelf. My dresses, skirts, and pants hang around the right side. Shoes are stacked next to each other on the left. There's enough room for five people in here. The automatic dimmed light scatters shadows across his face.

He rotates me until I'm nestled between his legs—my support structure. One of mine is bent and the other one straight. I shut my eyes to remember his body against my back.

His chest rises and falls, and pulls out the knitting needles along with the remains of a small lilac-and-pink ball of yarn.

"Knitting is kinda special to me." He twirls the knitting needles between his fingers like drumsticks. "It's a passion I want to explore. You have a worksheet for that?"

I bite my lip and let it uncoil itself. "Possibly." The last thing I want to do is talk about worksheets. "You're enough of a worksheet," I tease. Hmm, maybe I *can* flirt.

I stick my hand between the twirling needles, stopping his play. I grab one and fiddle with it.

"Tell me more about passions," I whisper.

His soft exhale caresses my face. "How 'bout I show you."

The second needle slides into my hand, as does the ball of yarn. One needle moves under my hands. Like an expert, he takes the yarn and knots it onto the needle a couple of times. He's pulling and tying, pulling and tying.

A second wooden needle joins in. He holds one in each hand. Under my fingers, he intertwines them.

"My nonna taught me. When I'd get upset or lonely, I'd knit. Spending time with her made me forget about feeling empty when a girl broke my heart or when my father was an asshole." He weaves the string between my fingers and pulls my hand to tighten the yarn. "This is my way of talking through my emotions. No one knows that's the real reason I knit, besides Nonna. But I like sharing my secrets with you. I trust you."

He's saying all the right words and moving in all the right ways. My heart's aflutter and so are my nerves.

"I love that," I murmur. I love everything about it—the softness of his skin and the words he shares and the body that encompasses me and the story behind the knitting.

"How did you start teaching grandmas how to knit?"

"My nonna brought me to the senior center for knitting events a few times when I was a kid. It felt like home, so I kept going."

"I wanna go," I whisper. "I want to see your world."

"Okay," he replies and kisses my cheek from behind.

His warm breath peppers my shoulder. I let go, sink into him, and listen to the clicking of the needles. They tap and slide fast.

I run my hand down his arm, feeling his muscles jump with every stitch he makes. "Do you knit more when you're happy or heartbroken?"

"It depends. I used to do it a lot when I had to deal with my ex." The needle motions quicken. My pulse falls into rhythm with his movements. "She lies and manipulates to get what she wants. When she slept with my best friend, I told everyone I was going on a run. I was actually knitting by the lake."

His muscles flex faster. I run my free hand up his.

"For the longest time, I thought I loved her, and so I wanted her back every time she did me wrong." Hudson continues to knit faster, harder. "She was never there for me. When my father missed the lacrosse championship, she didn't care." His chest heaves at my back. "I couldn't stop thinking about how she was my first love. But that's not love, and she convinced me love is only for the movies. I had to change who I wanted to become. And that new me wasn't for her."

I rest my hands over his. "I'm glad you're free from her now. She doesn't deserve you, so don't give her any more of your energy." I squeeze his hands. "I'll protect you from her."

He drops the needles and yarn, and wraps me tightly in his arms. "You make me vulnerable, too," he mutters into my ear.

His mouth grazes the side of my neck. I imagine tasting his cologne on my lips.

Rotating my head, his eyes meet my stare. The warmth of his body relaxes me.

Hudson's long lashes waver as he searches my face. "I've always wanted to know more about you." He pauses when his eyelids drop down. "Living next door to you wasn't easy. I was jealous how Theo got to play with you on the hills. Thought you liked him a lot, and I didn't think you liked *me* much." The confession throws me for a loop.

"Seriously?" When I was a kid, I rolled down hills with Theo and Papi. Those moments, where I trusted Papi and lived in the moment, were the ones where I laughed the most. We'd get so loud, Mother had to quiet us. Those were good times, fun times.

Hudson continues, "You'd laugh so hard when you rolled down the hill with Theo. I want you to have that happiness again."

My smile grows. Then I realize a possible source for their feud. "Are you jealous of Theo? Of our friendship?" Not that we have one at the moment, but it would explain their tension. Even if Theo decides he doesn't want to see me anymore, I'll always care about him.

Hudson sighs and turns his head. "If you're asking if I apologized yet, I haven't had a chance. My days have been filled with looking for a job and knitting at the senior center."

Beautiful moment ruined. The rain pours down on my parade. The warmth slowly diminishes.

He squints at the door and keeps quiet. "Can we forget about that right now? Because I just want to kiss you."

I bite my lip. "Then kiss me." This is torture and a kiss will fix everything. It'll lift the world from my shoulders if only for a few seconds. Like a hug when someone is crying—then the crying continues, but somehow it becomes slightly easier.

"With everything you have," I add.

"Mrs. D'aureville is here!" Astrid yells.

"Damn it," Hudson says and grunts.

"We don't have to stop," I mutter. "I need you to kiss me. It'll make me feel whole, stronger." Because everything around me is crashing and Hudson is the only one keeping my seams from ripping apart.

"If we get caught, it could be the end of your debutante life. Astrid's text made that very clear earlier today. No matter how much I want to kiss you, I can't be selfish right now."

I want him to be selfish.

Twenty-Three

I SPREAD MY ARMS OUT, shut my eyes, and practice my curtsy. I've been doing this for almost an hour with Mrs. D'aureville breathing down my neck. She's already spent two hours inspecting my gown, gloves, shoes, and waltz routine. Not to mention Hudson left me unkissed, so my energy is depleted.

I focus on Papi. Thinking of us together is the only reason I can keep myself composed.

"Princessland isn't real," I say to Papi, laughing. "We live in Verdan."

"This ball will feel like anything but Upstate New York. And remember, the curtsy is the most important part." He squats down and lowers his head. "I'll show you, sweet hot chocolate princess."

He circles me and takes my arms. "First, bring your arms up in front of yourself and then pull them apart like you're making a letter T. Then bow down like a swan."

When my stomach meets my thighs, I let out a fart. Papi laughs at my giggle. I immediately sit up. "I won't fart at the ball, promise."

He twirls me in my manual wheelchair. "I can't wait to dance with my future prince, Theo. Then I can dance with you!"

Talking about the ball makes me feel like a princess. It's fun to pretend I can be royalty.

Papi kisses my head and stands up. "I'll be there for you no matter what."

Mrs. D'aureville's breathing outdoes the crackling fake fire.

As I bow, classical music plays in my mind. Piano notes and violin strings blend in a pleasant tune before morphing into a background beat with rock and blues.

My arms go to my sides and I lower my chest to my knees— my curtsy. Blood rushes to my head. I try to pull my torso back up, my cheeks warming. I can't rise without at least one hand pressing into the edge of my seat cushion.

Thought I could do it. I can adjust my technique, but it's disappointing I don't have the strength to do it the way I want to.

"Hmm," Mrs. D'aureville says. "I've seen enough. There is time to fix this. Just remember that I want the best press at this event, and not the bad kind." Considering the ball is her family's legacy and is televised every year, she has a say about every debutante and every aspect of the ball.

"Most definitely," I say and nod once. I want to be seen as someone worthy and strong in this town. I want to build a successful future. I want Papi to be proud of me. I want Mother and Astrid to be proud—they're both watching from the doorway, tall and poised as if they, too, are being evaluated.

Their heels clack on the marble floor.

The director joins them and they converse. One day, I want to be as powerful as the three of them.

"One last examination." Mrs. D'aureville's hands rest at her sides in lace gloves. "Turn, Abigail. Head up," she says in a commanding tone.

I obey.

"Head *up*." Mrs. D'aureville's voice echoes in the living room, reverberating off the walls to attack me once more.

She judges ruthlessly, looking to punish me for having one hair out of place so she can disqualify me because I don't fit perfectly into the lineup of all the girls who've promenaded and curtsied and danced their way through every other debu-tante ball.

Okay, I don't exactly want to be like her, but I admire the authority she has over this town. Not that I want to make people feel small, but having the voice and power to blaze through obstacles—that must be thrilling.

She stands two feet from me, but it feels like two inches. As she searches me for flaws, I see hers. Her unmoving face is unmatched by her sagging neck.

"Be elegant," Mrs. D'aureville instructs.

I straighten my shoulders and push the joystick slowly to the right—pinky out and wrist slightly up. The rose-gold-rimmed wheels squeak on the polished wooden floor.

I exhale slowly, never audibly.

Elijah jogs down the stairs to Astrid as if he owns the place. The kitchen is a clinking circus as Chef Daisy prepares lasagna for later tonight.

Once again, it seems I've attracted a crowd.

I pause in front of Mrs. D'aureville. She fixes me with a piercing stare. Then she delivers a punching statement. "You can be in the running for queen. Your family asked me and I've considered it. Since I'm the director, I can pick the top two girls who will compete for the title. You and Pyper are in. I will call Diana to tell her she is out. Secrecy is my number one rule, and if she can't keep *your* secrets, then she will blab to the press about the tiniest gossip at the ball. Astrid told me what Diana did. I may not want you to win or see you kissing anyone. But if you *happen* to win queen, it will generate great publicity for the town and your family's jewelry company. And of course, the ball, as your mother mentioned. You would be the first wheelchair debutante to win queen."

Did I take my best friend's opportunity to win queen after all the volunteer hours she's put in this year? It should be Diana and me, even though I don't want to compete directly with her. Cutting her out is worse.

Mother steps over and strokes my hair. "We're grateful." She lowers to me. "Right, honey?"

I nod. My smile is taped on, because inside I'm ugly crying. This does not feel elegant or classy.

When Diana and I would pretend to win queen in middle school, it seemed exciting and innocent. Diana and I have never competed against each other. Even when we played chess in middle school, we helped each other win on a turn-by-turn basis.

Mother and Astrid give me a nod of approval. The center of my scalp prickles.

The hairs on my neck stand up. I can't do this.

Mrs. D'aureville taps her phone. "Time to make a call."

"Wait," I say.

Mother ushers our guest toward the door. "Yes, wait one moment." She pulls a gift from her purse—a ruby bracelet—carefully wrapping it around Mrs. D'aureville's wrist. "This bracelet will glorify you at the ball. The way the gold and deep red sits flawlessly on your skin." The marketing tactic of selling anything is all about showing someone how they *need* that one thing. Mother practices it at every corner.

Astrid strides in front of me. "Get ready to win queen!" Her hug basically suffocates me.

"No." I shake my head and grab my phone from my purse. "I'm calling Diana to equip her with reasons why she shouldn't be allowed to be cut like this. This is not me. I care about people."

Elijah snatches the phone out of my hand and shoves it above the mantel. "You are not ruining everything your family has worked for. You're the reason no one wants to work with this family. The reason everything is falling apart."

"How dare you," I say and grab a fork from the table. I use the utensil to slide the phone off of the mantel. My chair has an elevating feature which can raise me fourteen inches, but it's been broken for a few months. Papi used to fix my chair along with Theo, but I'm not ready for anyone other than Papi to meddle with my chair at the moment.

Elijah snags my phone and tosses it on a six-foot-high shelf. "You're the reason your father went into the lake. The reason he gave up his life for yours. Your family has been paying for your mistake and I'm tired of saving this family when *you* can't even pull your own weight."

A pressure builds in my chest. I want to move but I'm frozen. He'll make a great lawyer one day. Intimidation is his best skill. I try to fight his attack.

"It was an accident," I mumble. "Papi's death was an accident. I didn't mean for any of it to happen."

Astrid pulls Elijah to the side. For a moment, she looks at him with pure disgust. Then her features smooth. "Don't do this. Control your anger. So you lost a few hundred. Get it together."

Elijah and I are officially enemies. I've never hated anyone, but I hate him. Being in the same room is not even an option.

How dare he say I'm the reason for my family's financial hardships.

Or am I? Is everyone keeping our financial secrets from me because they don't want me to know I'm the reason behind our demise?

It's my fault Papi is gone. The heaviness of it crushes me.

I shake off the guilt and think about Diana. Circling the couple, I race out, heavy, tan curtains grazing the side of my wheelchair.

Before I even realize it, I'm out the back door and on my way to Hudson's.

I pass the fountain at the side of the fence that connects our properties.

As I approach, the mansion backyard door swings open and Hudson steps out. Drink in hand, he skips three steps at a time as if he's in a rush, yet his stride is suave and he's confident enough to do it without looking down.

He descends the dozen steps in seconds. His loose sweatpants look cozy on him. They hang loosely over his hips. While a black muscle tee molds to his sculpted form.

The way the hem of his tee brushes the pants' waistline is a tease. So are his biceps and his eyes and . . . everything else about him.

Something is different. The pit in my stomach grows. My hands tingle.

I realize I'm crushing really, really hard.

Not why I am here.

I wave and motion him to come over. "Hey!"

He sets down a glass of what appears to be champagne on a table and jogs over. "You want a drink?"

"Sure, but first, your phone." I extend my hand and he gives it over.

Logging into my email account and finding Diana's number, I try to stop my hands from shaking.

She picks up on the first ring. I talk fast, "Hey, it's Abby. Listen, do not talk to—"

"I hate you!" She screams and hangs up.

My best friend did not just say she hated me. Tears burn behind my eyes.

Hudson stares at me. "You okay?"

"Um." I hand the phone back. "Thanks."

He wipes a fallen tear. "Your mother just showed up, but we can go elsewhere. I'm gonna grab you that drink and we can go talk." He jogs off.

I drive through the vineyards, trying to unwind my mind. Our mothers converse, complimenting each other on their looks.

I turn toward the tables and suck in a deep breath.

"Oh, I love it!" Mrs. Giordani yells from the front of the vineyards. "That sapphire is lovely on my wrist, Sylvia. It will pair perfectly with my outfit for the ball."

Mother claps once. "Your favors never fall short, Margaret. You have truly saved my family. I had to tell you that Abby will win queen."

Listening to her be proud of me makes me feel fake. I won't "win" queen on good, hard-working merit. It will be on a deal. Everything is like a big fat business transaction. There are many accomplishments in my life but in this moment they all feel like a huge façade.

It'd be great to have one thing I can control, instead of following the plans others want me to follow.

Maybe I don't even want to go to college. Maybe I want to open my own museum or major in archeology. What is my life if it's not mine to live?

The seconds tick on and I realize Verdan is suffocating me. The ball is supposed to be an experience of a lifetime. Yet all I do is fall in line with what everyone else tells me to do.

I don't even know if I'm a deb because I want to be or because I've been told to be one my entire life.

When I imagined dancing in a beautiful dress and laughing, it included happy moments, not devastating ones. Can I go back to when my biggest heartbreak included not being able to find an escort?

Mrs. Giordani sips loudly. "I am happy to do any favor for you." She takes another loud sip. "I am proud of Hudson, despite his past decisions. Abby needs someone to save her. To be her hero." The words have an undertone of pity. "He needed this to be inspired about his life again. Soon he'll move to Manhattan and his girlfriend will follow along. It'll be picture perfect for the most prestigious magazine covers."

My chest rises and lowers. I take in as much cool air as possible. Every part of me deflates. My heart feels like it might tear in half.

I eye the mailbox in the distance. The flag is hanging at the bottom.

I speed over and pull on the cold metal knob. The letter I originally wrote sits inside. He never read it.

Being with me was just a favor? Did my mother ask Hudson to save me? It can't be true. Then again, he's never made plans with me for *after* the ball. Astrid must have known and that was where her warning came from.

How could I think he actually liked me? He kisses girls for fun, at parties; whenever he wants to. I'm nothing special. And his girlfriend is clearly not an ex!

He played me. I hate how good he was at it. I fell for it because I wanted it to be true so bad.

My shoulders cave in, eyes watering.

This whole time, was I nothing but a game to him? I hope his girlfriend knows what a player he really is. It's time to face the facts: I should have chosen Theo and listened to him. He's always right. Now I don't have him to dry my tears. I did this to myself.

I snatch the letter and rip it into pieces. Little by little, the bits feather down to the dark ground. The white roses complement the white paper, and I want to rip the petals up, too.

I slide a hand over my chest and place the other over my mouth so no one hears me scream. The shock settles in so deep, I can barely move. My stomach goes hollow and chills run down my arms. A wave of cold sweeps over my entire body.

The softness of my fingers against my hair soothes me. I cover my face with the long strands so that I can't see anything. All I am is part of everyone else's plan. I want to sob and throw up at the same time. Neither release comes.

There should be a rage churning inside me. An attack building. Yet, none of that happens. I can't feel my arms or legs. The numbness takes hold of my brain.

Everything is too much and nothing is going according to plan.

I glance at the only place that can give me peace. I'm taking a page out of Papi's diary and taking to the lake. I'm going to float my worries away.

Twenty-Four

I SPEED off toward the lake shed for a canoe. Every dip nearly bounces me out of my seat. Papi used to ask me if I wanted a canoe ride after a hard day. Today was an especially hard day.

Papi and I would float on the water and the world would just disappear. All the piano lessons and French classes would fade away.

The sounds of the world would fade away, and all my worries with them.

The June rays ripple gently on the surface of the lake, hiding the rumble of death that lies beneath—the weeds ready to grab at my ankles, the snakes ready to suffocate me, the water that could dissolve me until I'm nothing.

On the surface, I'm calm, but underneath, something else is going on. It's been a long time since I floated on the water. On this lake that took Papi's life ten months ago, all because of me.

I don't care if the door is locked or that the canoe weighs fifty pounds. I'll find a way to get one out. My footrest rams into the door with zero effect.

I may have lost the words to argue, but I haven't lost the will to fight.

Heavy steps jog up to the shed.

"What are you doing?" asks Theo.

"Canoeing!" I yell and pull on the doorknob. It doesn't budge.

My tear-filled eyes meet his stony stare. Then his soften.

"Okay, okay. I hear you." He unlocks the door and struts inside the shed. Sounds dance with each other. I inhale a deep breath and calm myself.

Within seconds, Theo drags the canoe across the ground. It splashes halfway into the water with a thud. He runs back into the shed and rumbles inside. Moments later, he returns with a blanket tossed over his shoulder and a large wooden board slung under his arm like some superhero geared up for action.

Papi used to do that—set a blanket down on the custom-made rectangular wooden platform that locks into the rims of the canoe. Theo and I would lie on top like it was a bed while Papi paddled to the middle of the lake. He'd join us and we'd look up at the sky, counting either clouds or stars. One time we slept the entire night under the stars just floating.

Striding toward me, Theo seems fearless. "What's wrong?"

"You were right. Hudson played me. Mrs. Giordani said he's moving to Manhattan with his *girlfriend* to take magazine photos." There. I said it. Now the emotion can pass and leave me alone.

Ha! If only it were that easy.

"That jerk. If I ever see him again . . ." Theo pounds his fist into his hand. "I'm talking to *Hudson*." There's a new sense of confidence in his tone. "He isn't getting away with making you cry now or back then."

I throw my head back against my headrest to stop the tears

from coming. "And Diana hates me." A tear escapes. Theo's fingertip sweeps it away.

If I had my own power, I'd march over to Hudson and tell him what a jerk he is for playing me. I'd tell Mrs. D'aureville I don't need to be micromanaged. I'd tell Diana we'll find a way for both of us to win queen. Then, I'd run over Elijah's ass.

But I'm not strong like Papi. I can't control a single thing. If he were here now, he'd defend me against everyone's betrayal.

"I'm sorry I hurt you, Theo." I lean my head into his waist and wrap my thin, frail arms around him. "I wish Papi were here to make us feel better."

Theo sighs heavily, his voice pained when he says, "I miss him, too. I miss you being with him the most. But he's up there, watching us now." The words sink into me.

Accepting the idea that Papi is no longer here stings. That I'll never see him again. Never tell him how much he meant to me. How much I loved him. How sorry I am.

Theo curls his shoulders inward, bends, and squeezes me tight. I don't care that I can barely breathe. He rubs my lower back before moving his hand up to massage the nape of my neck.

The touch opens me up. "I don't want us to fight. I need you no matter what, Theo. Please know I never want you to feel like I don't need you anymore. Ever."

He blows out a steady breath. "Let's go float."

I nod and extend my arm. He picks up on my cue, raises my armrest, and swings my arm around his neck.

When he lifts me into his arms, I gain three feet. I like it— height—the ability to see the world from a standing position. For a person with muscular dystrophy, it's a silly thing to complain about, but sometimes I wish I could tower over *something*.

I brush off the thought and return my attention to the present. The thudding footsteps remind me of how Papi would carry me through the woods when the terrain wasn't smooth enough for my wheelchair.

I hate to admit that Theo's the one I always run back to. I'm so dependent on him, so desperate for him.

When he places me on the platform, I stare up at the sparkling stars.

The canoe wobbles when Theo maneuvers to the center, kneeling down.

He paddles to the middle of the lake where nothing but nature surrounds us. He drops down next to me, settling one arm under his head. The canoe rocks slightly, a soothing movement that keeps my tears at bay.

I sigh. To grieve or not to grieve, that is the question. "Everything is so hard," I admit.

Theo softly kisses the top of my head. "You're stronger than you think." His voice is gentle. "You have to let yourself feel your emotions." His expression wavers from inscrutable to pleasant. "I was mad when your father passed. I was hurt and broken, too."

"I don't want to feel things," I whisper. Especially angry feelings. Anger at myself, at Elijah, at Hudson.

I wish I had Papi's strength, his voice. If I did, I wouldn't be hiding. Elijah is so right and I hate that. I am the reason Papi is gone, creating a path of damage. The business tanked when he died. It's no surprise Mother and Astrid take heat for what I've caused. They work hard, but it never seems to be enough.

It got so bad, that Elijah probably had to help us survive, and he's bitter at me for that. Thinking he stole money from the company or is using Astrid for personal gain sounds ridiculous.

I am a failure.

I turn away and sweep my hand over the water. It's ice cold, but the sensation is familiar, which is satisfying. Ripples spread across the surface before disappearing.

The tips of my fingers play over the top once more. The surface ripples again. The lake is so peaceful. No worries; no pressure.

The frogs croak in the distance.

I lean toward the edge of the canoe. I can swim—or lie there like a synchronized swimmer, using a support scull.

"Don't roll any farther. You might fall in." Theo rubs my shoulder. "Seriously."

He balances out the canoe, but I push further. Because I want to roll further. I want the water to crash into me. I want to feel the cold, the numbness. I want to be free from the chains that tie me to the words of others.

I pivot to the edge and shift my body weight close to the water. I rotate my knee to the side and roll my shoulder toward the center of myself. Gravity takes over, and I hold my breath, anticipating a subtle splash.

Suddenly, Theo slides me to the other side of the canoe.

"What's really going on?" he asks. "Talk to me."

We have a staring contest and then I spit it out. "I just want to feel close to Papi, hear his words of encouragement. I don't know how to do life. Sometimes I wish I could trade places with him because he could make the world better and I can't. I'm so weak. Everything is my fault."

Theo's gaze zones in on me. "Don't ever think that. Never ever in the entire world and universe's black hole. No." He's firm in his stance, but the truth is, if I had stayed with Papi and had chosen him over my image, he'd still be here. And my family wouldn't be financially struggling.

"I'm sorry," I mumble.

A hug comes quick, his torso resting against my ear as we wobble on the water.

"*I'm* sorry," he says. "I should have yelled your name when I saw you get on the broken dock. I should have known your chair would break the wood. I should have run faster to warn you instead of admiring how beautiful you looked posing for the perfect picture."

I take a deep breath. Almost as big as the one that brought me back to life that day. A humming sound rings in my ears.

"How have *you* been doing with the aftermath?" I ask. "If you want to talk about it . . . ."

He stays silent until, "You can blame me."

"Never," I say, choking on the word as my chest tightens.

"Do *you* want to talk about it?"

I stare at him. The simple question begs a simple answer. It's not that I don't want to talk, but neither do I *want* to talk about it. The fact is, I need to talk about that day, every detail and emotion included. "Maybe."

A long moment passes, and I prepare to be hit with a metaphorical rainstorm. This is going to be really hard.

"I loved the rawhide and pink petals on the dock." I slide an arm under my head and exhale. "The water looked beautiful, too." The sun was perfect over my head. The butterflies more so.

I'm stalling. This is the part where I want to run away from the storm that's about to thunder down on me. But I have nowhere to run. I have to face this head-on. "I saw the caution sign, but I didn't care. It seemed like the perfect place to take my deb announcement pictures." My eyes shut and I'm there again, on the dock.

"I took pictures on my phone to plan for later." A beat

passes. "When the dock gave way and I fell into the lake, I'd already broken Papi's number one safety rule. He always told me not to wear a seat belt around the lake or the pool, because it would trap me under the water. And it did. Face against the ground, knees digging into the sand, my arms were no match for my 300-pound wheelchair."

"That's why you never wear the chair's seat belt anymore." Theo speaks my thought out loud. "Nothing was your fault."

I tug at his hand and he lets me hold it, returning Theo's penetrating gaze.

I have no memory of drowning. The next thing I remember was Theo looking down at me, kneeled over me. Cold air hit me immediately. I rolled over and coughed up water on the shore. I caught a glimpse of Papi's camera inches away. He must have been taking photos of me after all, after following me from the cabin, leaving behind our cups of hot chocolate.

"I wish I hadn't passed out after that," I say. Tears roll down my face and I'm burning everywhere, my breaths heavy.

Theo squeezes my hand. His eyes close before he opens them to again focus on me. "It was a tragedy." He gives me a sympathetic smile, but his eyes are pained. "How can I help you?"

"Talking to you is helping enough."

The sparkle in his eye is lovely. His gentle soul has me accepting everything that has happened—finding peace in the torture. I finish the story. "I woke up alone and disoriented in the hospital. Then I heard a nurse telling the doctor how her heart broke for me, having lost her father as well. She said she knew Santiago Verez-Panashe and wished his family peace. For weeks on end, I thought it was a dream." My gaze shifts to the swaying trees. "I'm still trying to wake up from it."

Theo explained in the hospital that Papi was the first to dive into the water, but when he got the chair off of me, his foot became lodged between rocks. Theo pulled me out of the water and then he called 9-1-1. Suddenly he realized Papi was taking too long, and he dove back into the water to retrieve him, but in the end, even the paramedics couldn't save him.

Theo and I lay in silence.

My eyes soften as the burn of tears strikes them once again. "I'm so grateful to have you in my life."

Theo's nod is enough to warrant a faint smile. I want to live through it, learn from it, and let it go.

"The reason I wanted us to meet there was to ask you to the ball." I confess to him for the first time. "Ever since what happened, I'd been terrified to ask or talk about you as my escort. Terrified to feel the guilt and pain of that day."

He sits up. "You were? All these months, I thought you didn't see me as good enough to be your escort."

"And yet . . ." I run my fingers up his arm and stop at the elbow. "You've always been there for me, no matter what."

Theo does whatever I need. He always does and I clearly have taken advantage of it.

"Sorry I show up when I'm broken. It's time to break that habit. I need to find comfort and strength in myself some-times." I'm forever relying on others to be my strength. "I should go. Can you sit me up?"

No more running away or hiding in Theo. The new me needs to figure life out on my own.

He sits me up and one of my legs dangles over the edge, barely touching the water. My arms extend behind me for support, both shoulders rising up to my ears.

"Abby." Theo's voice is strong.

I glance up.

He runs his hand through his hair. "Being there for you is everything to me. I don't want you to leave upset."

"I'm too much." My words are barely audible.

"You're never too much," he says, reaching for my shoulder. He squeezes a little too hard. I manage not to squeal.

A minute passes. Two.

"You know, I overheard you girls talking that day. I don't think it would be weird if we kissed," he says, taking me back to the morning I said that to Joey and Diana.

A smile plays on my lips and I can't believe he's held on to that for days.

"You think?" I tease, eyeing his mouth.

He scoots close enough for me to rub against his leg. Suddenly, he lifts me, rotating my legs to bend over his, and I straddle him. He smooths his hand over my thighs before securing an arm around my waist to pull my hips toward him. His hand presses against my curves and bolsters me up. My chest presses against his. A calm hum races through the ripples of the lake.

His focus on me leaves me almost breathless, his slow exhale crashing against my warm one. A wave of silence covers us. My back heats and the roof of my mouth tingles.

Are we about to have our first romantic kiss?

My heart pounds.

The tip of his nose grazes mine. When I let out a barely audible sigh, he takes a deep breath.

Our eyes close. His lips meet mine as gently as his hand cups the side of my head. The softness of his tongue strokes the seam of my mouth; the taste of mint and cocoa lingers on him. His touch is warm. I need him to keep going.

He does. And it feels so good.

His lips are so velvety soft, his tongue moving ever so

smoothly. It's as if I can almost feel his every muscle against me, hugging me.

I moan against his lips. Happiness fills me. The kind that turns my stomach into a war zone.

His thumb grazes the side of my jaw and his body blankets me into a tighter hug. A fire brews between us.

When our lips part, I rest my head on his chest, smiling into him. We hold each other, both our chests heaving.

His lips touched mine. Tasted me. And I tasted him back.

This is what happiness should feel like. Hope and joy and excitement lift me up, and . . . I'm flying—flying in the dreams of Theo. Before I realize it, I'm inching forward for another kiss.

This one's a quick peck. Theo smiles against my lips.

"Abby." His smooth and calm tone drags the warmest feelings from me. "You feel better?"

"Mm-hmm." My hands map out his chest, exploring its curves and valleys. He's even bulkier than I thought. His biceps are bigger than both my hands. I feel safe in his arms. *He's* safe.

I'm still flying.

"*You* feel better?" Maybe I should have feelings for him. I'm willing to give it a try.

"Better than ever," he whispers. His head drops, but his grin grows. A dark blush creeps into his cheeks. "I want to make you feel better, happy. Always."

As I trace his chest, an electric shock bolts through my body. When he pulls me close once more, I fall into him, reveling in the closeness.

He's the one who fits into my plans. With him, there's no change in direction or spontaneity. There are no surprises or unexpected detours.

He's my perfect match.

Is this destiny? We've never been this intimate before. Of course, we might not have wanted to or didn't think we could be since we've been friends for so long.

I bump into his inner thigh by accident, sending his knee toward the edge of the canoe.

We outweigh gravity and slip into the water with a loud splash.

Twenty-Five

FIELDS OF SEAWEED brush the soles of my feet. As I sink, my clothes buffet around me. The water is silent. The cold bites me to my core. My hair dances around my head.

The freedom of being in an almost no-gravity space . . . . Oh, the peace. Gravity is a fascinating thing. It attracts everything to its center, yet in space there is zero gravity. Water is the state between gravity and no gravity. I can move my body to the right and the left. My hips open up and I rotate my ankles. The blouse and shorts sway side to side. It's amazing not having the pressure of the world suffocating me.

Or death pushing down on me.

Happy memories flash before me. Papi is near. I let go of everything. The moment I do, I see him. I see his light.

Papi waves to me from above.

"I've missed you, daughter. Oh how you've grown up. Let's have that last cup of hot chocolate together."

An eerie feeling expands my heart. I nod.

"I miss you," I say. "I'm sorry I took you for granted. I love you. I wish I had your strength and selflessness."

"I'm always here," he whispers, tapping my chest, over my heart. "All you have to do is look deep within your heart and you'll find your own strength."

"How do we live without you?" I ask.

"You sing and dance. And do everything in love."

He slowly twirls me to the classical *Blue Danube*. I want to hang on to his embrace, his hands.

"Tell me the right path I should take, Papi."

Our fingertips disconnect as he suddenly pulls my soul with him, taking the hand of a little girl and leading her out of my heart. The light draws away from me.

I'll forever be his little girl and his daughter. I'll never forget him.

A shiver passes through me. I hear his voice echoing in the distance. "Be true to who you are. Never get lost in the world of others. Live for today, not for when today leaves you. Trust life's plans for you."

The emptiness fills with comfort.

An arm wraps around my waist and pulls me up. The wrist pushes into my stomach and ribs, and that weightless feeling slowly transforms to crushing pressure as I rise to the surface. When air hits me, I take in a massive breath. I'm covered in goose bumps like it's zero degrees. The breeze that was pleasant a few moments ago now chills me to the bone. My teeth chatter. I'm officially a popsicle.

My wet clothes hug me in Theo's arms. I lock onto his neck as he emerges out of the water, a rush of waves following his every stride forward.

Shoulders broad, he feels stronger than I last remember, not that he carries me all the time. His warmth brushes away my shivers even as water streams down from his hair.

As we pass my chair, I glance back at it.

"I'll come back for it," he reassures me.

Theo's body is a comfort. Being in his arms warms me up just enough.

I glance over to the lake. It's time to walk away from everything weighing down on me. Living in what I can't change helps no one.

I wonder if this is how Theo carried me out the last time I fell into the water. There's a hardness in his eyes as the sunrays hit right above his forehead.

"You okay?" I ask.

"I am, are you?" He looks down with a fiery glance. "Can you breathe?"

I nod. "Thank you" doesn't seem adequate enough of a sentence.

"We'll live on," I whisper. "I'm here for you, too. Just lean on me." The moment I say that, I know it's the opposite of what is happening. I'm the one in his arms. "Emotionally or whatever," I add.

The open cabin door wavers side to side from the slight wind.

When we enter, the water drips on the floor with a *tap, tap, tap*. If I wasn't so cold, I'd stop clinging onto him so tightly or thinking about finding a really big blow-dryer to dry us off in one massive whoosh.

He crosses the living room until we're in his bedroom. His bed, shelves mounted to the wall, and desk are the only furniture in the room. The $E=MC^2$ poster is the only decoration on the walls. Not even a clock or a nice bedspread spice up the space. My drawings used to be pinned to the walls and art supplies once lined the floors.

We're headed toward that hard bed of his. The one he made for himself last year. I land on the firm mattress and exhale. I don't sink in like with most mattresses, which I appreciate, because it lets me move around more freely.

We don't make eye contact, even when he wraps my hair into a fresh T-shirt. But I do make contact with his drenched clothes. He must be freezing, too, but doesn't show it. His concern is all for me.

He tugs a bedsheet from a shelf and wraps it tightly around me like a sushi roll. I'm pretty sure my insides are squishing together into soy sauce.

"I can't move," I say with a slight laugh. My cheeks burn from the shock of cold to hot. Not that the cabin is hot. It's Theo's gaze on me.

"Sorry," he says, just above a whisper. He pulls the sheet away fast enough for me to bounce up.

I squirm a little.

"I'll get your chair."

"Thanks," I mutter. "Feel free to change first."

Theo jumps up and jogs across the cabin, his steps loud across the wooden floor. He's the only person I trust driving my chair. We taught each other when I got my first one years ago. Whenever something got damaged, like a joystick or a caster, he was the first to try to fix it.

For both of us, it was like a first car.

I'm reminded how, if I had only talked to Theo about being my escort instead of being scared, so much heartache would have been avoided.

Theo has always been there for me. I wonder if we're meant to be more than just friends.

A thump sounds from the doorway. It's the wheelchair going over the threshold. Theo walks next to it, controlling the joystick, until finally, he parks the wheels inches from me.

When he lifts me, I feel like a feather. He swings me over and lowers me into my chair.

I lean forward and press my hands into the cushioned armrests, scooting myself back into the seat.

When I sit up, the room is silent. A shiver runs through me and I'm desperate to get out of these wet clothes. I rub my hands against my thighs.

"I have a T-shirt, but it's an extra-large," Theo says.

"That's fine. And for you?" I want him to put himself first, not me.

He pulls a black T-shirt out of a hidden closet. His eyes shift up and down a couple of times.

"I can do it," I say.

The tension in his face eases as he nods.

"I—" He clears his throat. "If you need . . ." He scratches the back of his head. "Okay, cool."

He cracks his knuckles, struts to the doorway, and shuts the door.

We don't talk; we just love. We don't push conversation; we just act.

I unbutton my blouse and wiggle out of the shirt. Letting loose his shirt from my hair, I hang both items on the bedframe.

This is weird, getting naked in Theo's bedroom. The window isn't covered, but I doubt there's anyone there. I face a corner just in case and pull the extra-large shirt over my head. The thick fabric drops down to my thighs.

My wet bra leaves circle boob imprints in the shirt. Slipping my arms out of the bra straps, I unclip the front and it drops around me.

My shorts are a different story. I definitely need help slipping those off, although it may be weird asking Theo to do so.

I feel a bit exposed even though the shirt covers me completely.

When I pull at the doorknob, the hinges squeak.

My wheels thread across the floor, slowly, very slowly. "Are you dressed?" I ask even though I doubt he'd take over fifteen minutes, like me.

He materializes from around a corner, black hoodie and tie-dye pajama pants mismatching his whole look.

He scans his T-shirt on me, cheeks flushing. "I'll throw your w-wet clothes in the dryer. You should wait for them. I want you to wait . . . for them." His teeth dig into his lower lip, eyeing the two wet boob spots.

"I've never seen you in my clothes before. I need more time to look at you." There's a sureness to his words. His cheeks grow redder.

Theo is asking me to stay, not the other way around.

"Okay," I say and let him pass into his bedroom. Neither of us make eye contact.

Are we being weird?

He stops inches from me and we still for a few seconds. "Everything good?"

"Uh." I pause. "Can you take my shorts off? If you have an extra towel, you can put it under me," I say so quietly, I'm not sure he hears me.

He nods once and dashes past me into the bathroom. Reaching at the top shelf, the hem of his hoodie rises to expose that V that draws my eyes to inappropriate places.

Circling back to me with a white towel in his hands, I nod. Pressing into the short's elastic waistband, I push the fabric down my hips.

Theo cups my butt and slips them off with such a force, my entire body comes sliding into him.

We laugh into each other until he scoots me back into my seat. My arms wrap around his neck as he lifts me enough to glide the towel over the seat before setting me back down.

In a swift movement, he tugs the silk fabric down my legs and off my feet. The commotion is fast yet slow.

"Thanks," I whisper and fix a hair from my face.

There's nothing but a smile on his face. "Anytime."

We exchange a quick glance and move to opposite parts of the cabin.

I stay quiet in the middle of the living room.

As he manages the laundry, I run my fingers over my lips. I had my first real kiss with tongues and hands included, and I can't believe it was with Theo.

We kissed. I liked it. A lot. The next time I look at him, will he tell me he liked it, too?

"Theo?" My stomach is aflutter.

"Yeah?" he yells back. "Be right there."

"We kissed, right?" I holler. "That was real, right? We kissed and it wasn't weird, right?" I say louder.

I relive the moment right before we fell into the water. A smile plays on my lips.

It was weirdly magical.

The moment I look up, I'm taken aback by Hudson standing in the doorway. There's a twig bouquet in his hand.

"You kissed Theo?" he asks me through gritted teeth.

Twenty-Six

A MUSCLE in Hudson's jaw pops. "Well played, Abby." He tosses the twigs at the trees and shakes his head.

Theo strides into the space and moves around me. He gets in Hudson's face. "You listen, *loser*. Abby hates you and never wants to see you again. If I catch you so much as looking at her, you'll regret it. You're an ass for hurting her four years ago, and now you did it again. Your fake apology this afternoon was a fucking joke. Volunteering to knit blankets for events is the stupidest thing I've ever heard. And don't you dare think I believed you needed a job following your *passions*."

I can't bring myself to see the pained look that must be on Hudson's face. Theo did not just do that. For one, crushing anyone's dreams is wrong. Secondly, I wanted to stand up for myself to Hudson, not have Theo rescue me. As much as the weight gets lifted off my shoulders, I can't keep living on others' strengths.

Hudson yells and I can't bear to listen to his anger. "I can sink your little aquatic business in a single clap. And *you*, Abby, running off to Theo as always. Don't you dare talk to me. I wanted to check on why you left when you were on the verge of tears. It was a hunch you went to see Theo."

"Abby and I don't care about you. Go be with your girl-friend in Manhattan so your mother can take pictures." Theo pushes Hudson, who catches himself on a tree. How the tables have turned. Once again, I'm speechless, mad at Theo and sympathizing with Hudson.

Seeing someone else in pain is heart-wrenching. If I apologize to Hudson for Theo, who knows how the two will react. If I scorn Hudson, I won't forgive myself for kicking someone when they're down.

Hudson shakes his head. "Only fools move in with an *ex* and *only* if they planned to move somewhere. My mother lies about everything to sell a certain image. My parents are getting a divorce, but I bet you'll never hear about that until after it's done." A hurt look fills his eyes. "I really liked you, Abby. Actually wanted to take you to the ball when we ran into each other on the path. I could tell you were upset that the other guys quit." His jaw pops and I ache to soothe him. "The night you opened up and kissed my scar, I wanted more than just going to the ball with you." He runs a steady hand down his face. "I wanted to fall for you."

With that, he turns on his heel and jogs away.

His confession is so real, I have to believe it. This whole time, our connection was more real than I could have ever imagined. But now everything feels worse.

"I don't like this," I mutter.

My gaze shifts between Theo and the empty spot where Hudson had stood.

I never thought my heart could be torn between two guys. Feelings are complicated. I have no idea how to process or understand what is happening.

I inhale the pine tree scent, feeling the warm breeze whispering against my cheeks. The sun is starting to touch the peak of the tallest hill far in the distance.

Theo swings an arm around me. "I'll hate Hudson for the both of us. He just wants sympathy and is playing the victim card. *Forget* about him and let's pick out my suit for the ball."

There's no rule in the rulebook that says an escort can't change. This is how it's supposed to be anyway. Theo was the first person I wanted to be my prince charming when we were kids. It takes me back to that dream.

As long as Theo knows the routine—which he does—no one will care. Except maybe a few people. I can hear Elijah laughing at me from a mile away with some slick comment about how another escort quit. Meanwhile, Astrid will take another sip of champagne. Mother and Mrs. D'aureville will preside over me with their judgmental stares and perfectly straight shoulders.

Whatever, they can all suck it.

Then again. "Wait." I can't believe that word came out of my mouth. "I mean, of course I want you as my escort. Everything is moving so fast. I need a minute to breathe." My thoughts are jumbled up between what I truly want and what I should do for others.

Theo grabs a battered old, wooden chair he made himself, spins it, and sits down, the backrest between us. "I was thinking, *not* fast enough."

I swerve back and forth. "I don't know." The best friend who is there no matter what; the crush who I can't stop thinking about.

The downside of having everything planned out: you fail when life gives you the unexpected—when there's no agenda telling you what to do next.

"Was it the kiss?" Theo asks. "You felt it, right?"

I run my hands through the ends of my wet hair in distress. "Yeah, I felt it." My lips curl upwards. "It was amazing."

Theo and I kissed.

"You wanna get out of here? I'll grab dinner," he says. "Change of scenery helps me clear my head."

"I don't know," I say once more, panicked this time, because . . . Hudson.

Was kissing Theo a mistake? If not, then I should be shouting from the rooftops that I had the best first real kiss. If it was a mistake, then I'll never get my first romantic kiss back. My emotions are tangled in a web I can't free myself from.

He's my first real, passionate, full-on kiss. The shock of that is still sinking in. That and being in the lake again where Papi's spirit visited me.

Theo takes my hand and presses his lips to it. He's being flirty toward me. Not that he's never teased me before or touched me. This is different. He's being romantic.

I definitely need to clear my head. "Okay," I say.

Jumping to his feet, he spins and trips on the ground but makes it into an acrobatic move. "Be right back. Don't go anywhere."

With that, I'm left to myself.

After twenty minutes, the silence isn't as daunting as are my thoughts. Hudson and I had so many lovely moments together. I cover my face with my hands. Favor or no favor, I think Hudson genuinely cares about me. And I care about him.

It's possible I could be deflecting my feelings onto Hudson because I'm scared to fall for Theo. The idea weirds me out.

We've been friends for over a decade. Theo being romantic toward me is so new, I have no idea how to process the affection. Because maybe I've secretly been in love with him this entire time.

I need a drink and a distraction. I need to feel Papi here guiding my next move forward.

Rolling to the kitchen, I grab Papi's favorite mugs. Then I grab cocoa and cinnamon. It's time I make my own hot chocolate.

My mind races through how Papi would warm the water. The laughter and joy floods through me. Every happy hot chocolate moment flashes before me.

I face Papi at the kitchen table taking a big sip of his hot chocolate.

I giggle at the mustache created by the whipped cream floating inside.

"You have something," I say. Then I scoop some whipped cream from my mug with my finger. I make sure my mustache matches his.

"What do you mean, I have something?" he asks in a funny voice. "I know I have a lot of somethings. I have two daughters and books and a bed and a cabin."

"No." I laugh harder. "On your face. Like me. Look." Eyes wide open, I point at my lips and lean forward in my wheelchair.

He examines every inch of my face. "I see. Like you, I have eyes and a nose and a mouth on my face."

"No! You have a white mustache." I point to his face.

"Oh, well, where did that come from?" His eyes cross like he's trying to look at his nose. He takes a long sip before setting the drink down to reveal an even bigger white mustache.

My eyes shut as I guffaw. "It's bigger now." I cover my mouth from laughing too much.

As I come back from the memories, I stare at two mugs of hot chocolate topped with marshmallows and whipped cream on the table. My hands automatically wrap around one of them. The guilt of rejecting Papi's last sip of hot chocolate surfaces, but I pretend he's got his hands around the other mug.

There's a sense of wholeness I can't explain. I'm about to take my first sip. I pick up my mug and watch the marshmallows twirl on the chocolaty surface. As the warm, rich drink crosses my lips, my soul fills with comfort and sweet moments. The kind that can be enjoyed in full silence. I swallow a tiny marshmallow.

The hot chocolate is creamier than I last remember. And darker. It tastes sweeter than it ever has. I sip again. Then I sip for Papi from his mug.

Serenity envelopes me. Images of Papi don't flash in my mind, and neither does the pain of missing him or the weight of guilt for what happened.

I'll cherish this moment as the biggest turning point in my history book. Little by little, I will bring Papi back into our home.

Another minute passes and when I finish both drinks, I set everything back in its place with a new sense of happiness.

This is how Papi would have wanted me to live—enjoying every moment of life without the pain of not having had that one last sip with him along with all the moments that never came after that. He'd want me to be spontaneous and make mistakes. He'd want me to have life experiences.

Being in the cabin by myself is comforting more than I thought it'd be without Papi. On my way back into the living room, I touch the chair, table, lamp. There's a sense of peace and tranquility in the air.

Papi's favorite pen rests on the bookshelf. I roll over and grab it.

He wrote in his journals with its ink. I want to write with it.

I spot a lone notebook under some papers in the corner of the bookshelf and grab it. This whole time, closure is what I needed most, and it was pages away from me. I begin to write.

Dearest Papi,

You were the greatest father. I was the daughter who got caught up in a fake town and ignored the most down-to-earth man. You gave me everything. I gave you hurt. I took your love for granted. Now you're gone. A day doesn't go by wishing you were here. I never got to say my goodbye to you and, therefore, never started healing.

The eulogy that never was spoken finally finds its perfect time.

You gave away the greatest gift every day, sharing it again and again: sweet, precious time with those you loved. Every chance you had to love your daughters, you did it. You helped me navigate a world that forever put obstacles in my way, always searching for snares that would trip me up, even when they wouldn't have been snares in your world. But I took you for granted, and the regret has eaten me alive.

Life is full of mistakes. I can own them because I understand them. Most people don't intentionally try to hurt the other person; we just need to work on empathy. We're complex, and that's why one mistake can't be the weakness that breaks us. It should build our character. Life is about exploring and living, not doing the routine habits we think are right. That's wrong.

I want to kiss your forehead and tell you I love you. I always have, even though I rarely said it to you those last few years. My saving grace is you're at peace. Every day, I will live in your strength. In your honor.

You'd never want me to keep silent. You would want me to live the happiest life moving forward. You'd want me to fight on, no matter how that may scare me and those around me. I don't need anyone's authority or approval to make change happen.

Thank you for being the greatest Papi a child could have.

Love,

Your Abby

I rest the pen next to the journal. Anytime I miss him, I'll fill more of the pages.

I need to live for me, not be haunted by something I can't change. I need to make new memories, not relive the old ones simply because I miss Papi. He'd want me to enjoy life, not cry because he's not here.

My eyes shut and I smile at our laughter ringing in my ears. At all the moments we had together—not the moments we'll miss. "I love you, Papi," I whisper as if he's nearby. "I'll forever have hot chocolate in your honor."

A grunt sounds from the outside.

I jolt in my seat and peek out the window.

A go-kart swerves in front of the cabin. My wheels track against the wooden floor until I'm outside.

"Hey!" My tone is playful. A feeling of lightness lifts me up.

Theo stands up and straightens out his work polo. He must have changed clothes at the aquatic center.

"Wanna go see nature?"

I nod and park next to the vehicle.

His arm wraps around me and I basically strangle his neck. As he lifts me, my hair falls loose until my butt hits the white leather seat. I can sit up with proper back support as long as the surface is not too soft.

Theo jogs to the opposite side and jumps in, tilting the cart with his weight.

Just like we've done this before, he presses the pedal and we're off.

We both take the steering wheel in the same way as when we were kids. Then we scream at our terrible driving. Although, Theo has gotten a lot better.

One time when I was eight and Theo was nine, I convinced him I was a pro driver who knew how to speed. Let's just say that wheelchair racing and go-kart racing with the Giordanis proved to be very different sports.

Throughout the fifteen-minute trip, Theo stops and picks a flower here and there. When Papi took us out in nature, Theo would gather a bouquet for me.

I have no idea where we're going, but it becomes to look familiar as the larger trees and colorful flowers pepper our path.

We soon arrive under an oak tree—our childhood spot. The colorful flowers and butterflies dancing in the field capture my attention. The clouds are painted purple and pink across the sky. A perfect sunset.

The peaceful, aromatic vibe of the woods keep my worries at bay. Being able to turn my brain off and be in the moment of tranquility is refreshing.

The houses at the bottom of the hills and the surrounding

valley look beautiful as the lights start to flicker on. The breeze ruffles the leaves on the trees above us and the blossoms float through the air with ease. They land in my semi-dry hair and lap.

This was our favorite spot years ago. It's open and free.

Theo hands me the flowers and I press them to my chest. "Thank you." The bouquet of white, yellow, and pink over-power my senses: sweet daisies, wild geranium, and clover. "Perfect as always."

He's so quiet, I'm spooked. All he does is watch me with wide eyes like I'm a prized brownie—his favorite dessert.

The wind whisks between us. My gaze sweeps down the lush green hills. "Remember the butterflies you'd catch in the field and then we'd let them go?" I ask.

Theo leans toward me. The beams of sunlight filter through the gaps in the overarching branches behind him. His grin is warm and appealing.

"Yeah, I do. I remember everything about us."

The casual attitude is suddenly replaced by a more assertive manner. "When can we have a round two with our lips?"

His hand glides down my shoulder.

I've become a deer in headlights, listening to my best friend flirt with me. The thought is stranger than I'd expected.

I want him close. To touch me. Kiss me. Tell me I'm beautiful.

That's what I want from him—I have to tell myself that, because Hudson's face keeps popping up in my mind. It's probably his ancestors haunting me for not apologizing to him.

My stomach drops as I play with the petals in the bouquet.

"Um," I say and sigh. Why am I not excited about kissing Theo? We shared our first kiss—my first romantic kiss—but the aftermath is not as glowing. I want to be giddy and start planning our next date.

In a quick shift of topic, he asks, "Want food? I got tuna sandwiches."

I nod and once again his hands are on my body. His breath on my neck tickles. The way he holds my body makes me feel attractive, sexy. Or maybe it's because I'm in his shirt, totally braless. Yes, I must find every way to give us a romantic chance.

Within seconds, we settle down at the top of the hill under the large tree. I rest my back against the trunk.

Uncut strands of grass between my toes occupy me. I love the feeling of being shoeless.

"Shoeless girl! Come and put your shoes on!" Papi would say and chase after me.

Handing me a sandwich, Theo sighs deeply. "Damn, that says chicken, not tuna. I wish I got the fries and fish instead."

The paper wrap slips off easily and almost floats away into the wind.

Fries in a milkshake.

Hudson's piercing stare and crooked smile flashes in front of me like an unexpected ink stain on a page.

My stomach drops further as I take the first bite. And the second one.

Theo chews a large bite like it's the best thing he's ever tasted.

This is wrong. No matter how perfect life looks like with Theo, it's wrong. My heart knows I can't plan out love. Because when my eyes travel up to Theo's smile, I see him as a best friend.

I'm using Theo as a shield to not face Hudson, refusing to understand my real feelings.

The ones I have for Hudson.

"What's wrong?" Theo asks. He's downed the sandwich in record time. "Bread too soggy?"

Sighing, I shake my head and set my food back into the wrapper. I'm doing what I always do—run to Theo. He's my past, and maybe there's a chance we could be a couple. But I want us to be a couple because we want to be, not because a traumatic event has us uniting for comfort.

I work my pained eyes to his. "I can't forget about Hudson." There's a pause as I find the words to reject Theo again. "My feelings are too strong for him." The freedom of the unknown releases a tension in my chest.

Theo swallows hard and runs a hand through his long locks. "Really? After everything?"

"I love you, Theo," I drawl. "But I'm not *in love* with you." My emotions were just running high from Hudson and spilling over into Theo. I feel shame at this realization, at the pain I'm causing my best friend. Again, I'm choosing Hudson over Theo. Is it a mistake? Possibly, but I have to follow my heart.

"We grew up together. We were each other's comfort these last several months." This next part is too hard to say. "But I see us as friends, being there for each other, without the kissing part. I don't regret my first kiss with you. It was perfect. The way it was supposed to be. Almost like a release that freed me. But I want to move forward to new experiences. Ones that scare me." And Hudson scares me a lot.

It's the best way I can explain it. "I wouldn't want to give our first kiss to anyone else, but part of growing up is moving onward. You haven't dated anyone all year." I wipe the side of my mouth and gaze at him. "We need to go outside of our comfort zone, otherwise we're not really living, are we?"

Theo searches my face. "Maybe." There's a panicked glare

in his eyes. A long pause passes while he rubs his hands down his face. "Maybe," he says softer.

My best friend caught me and kept me from crashing to my own demise. I choose to cherish us instead of regretting what happened. Being attracted to him in a time of need is part of being sixteen and curious about guys.

Theo runs his hand through his hair and grips his neck. "Yeah." He nods, his smile guilty looking. "Maybe always needing to be there for you was my problem. I liked it when you needed me. It made me feel important." He zones in on me with a serious stare. "I've known you since forever, Abbs. I hate the thought of someone hurting you, but you're strong and you have your own voice. I just want to protect you, and maybe that's wrong."

We share a moment and a sigh. Then I reply, "There's nothing wrong with that. You're being the best friend you can to me because you love me."

Theo cleans his hands of any crumbs.

"What are you feeling?" I ask.

He leans back and stares at the grass. "I've always wanted to know what it'd be like to kiss my best friend. But forcing something can—" He clears his throat. "—ruin a friendship." Smoothing the grass, he continues, "If I'm being honest, it was the best kiss and I'm happy we shared it. But maybe we have too much history and childhood memories to cross that line. When I think of you, I think about being there for you. When I wonder if I want to kiss you again, I guess, it does feel . . . weird."

"Then it's settled, friends forever, lovers never," I say.

He grins and I release the breath I didn't know I was holding.

"We'll be friends no matter what," he replies.

He throws me a high-five; I find his pinky with mine. He lifts my hand, and we slide our palms together. Our index fingers hook, we lace our fingers into a butterfly, and then our palms, then the backs of our hands clap against each other. I pull an air trigger, and Theo snaps his fingers.

We still remember our secret handshake.

"Don't be afraid to be honest with me, even if the truth might be painful," I whisper. "Promise me you'll put yourself first and let *me* be there for you as your best friend."

"I promise," he says with a chuckle, then squints into the distance. "If you truly like Hudson." He pauses. "I'll . . . try to mend our differences with him." Another beat passes. "But you have to tell me why him."

I push my arms behind me for better support. The calmness of the flower field fills me with life—the possibility of a full life.

What are your passions? I ask myself. *Who can pull you out of your comfort zone?*

"He's a risk. He's spontaneous. He's the unknown. Which is the total opposite of me. He scares me, yet I want to be vulnerable with him. He fires me up and at the same time makes me emotional. He makes me live."

Theo leans his back against the tree trunk.

"It's not that I don't want you as my escort," I'm quick to explain. "I want to start making new memories and not be controlled by the old ones."

"I'll come cheer you on at the ball."

"Thanks," I reply.

This is good. Now I have to get Hudson on the same page. Whether or not that includes a first kiss with him.

Twenty-Seven

"I CAN'T WAIT to meet everyone at the senior center this Sunday, too," I say into my phone, gazing at the carnation garden through my bedroom window. "It can be a scarf-knitting party."

"This will be a nice surprise for Hudson," Darby, the Verdan senior center assistant director, replies. "He has been low on supplies lately and our next budget meeting isn't until next month."

"I have more than enough in my savings to cover everything for this month."

Yesterday was too much. There's more to our connection, and I won't give him up. I've been thinking all day and night of the perfect plan to win Hudson back. This feels like the perfect one.

Darby shares her appreciation, and we hang up.

I hope he can forgive me.

Cutting each other off seems silly—something we'd do four years ago. We're older now, so facing the pain we caused each other is the mature thing to do. At least that's what I'm telling myself. I have to believe this will work.

Either way, I won't sit and wait for things to fix themselves.

Giving my window one last glance, I turn my joystick on and wheel out of my room.

Maneuvering through the mansion, into the garden, and through the Giordani's backyard, I'm ready to fight for us.

I have no clue how he's taking the me-kissing-Theo situation. Not to mention how I let Theo yell at him.

"Hudson!" I holler. This is totally a Romeo and Juliet scene—roles reversed, though.

It's a new day, so I hope the emotions have died down a bit from the last twenty-four hours.

"Hud!" I yell louder. I'm seconds away from texting him, but that ruins being spontaneous.

I'll beg him to be my escort. When I dance at the ball, I want Hudson to hold my hand and spin me. I want to see him and remember how beautiful we are together. I want *us* back.

Footsteps sound behind me.

"No one's home." The voice thunders. So angry.

Hudson walks up, backpack in hand. It's packed to the top like he's going on a hike. A piece of yarn pops from a small, zipped opening.

He stomps up the first two steps.

I feel an irrational stab of disappointment and rejection.

"I'm sorry I kissed Theo. Sorry that he was cruel." I pause, wait for him to turn around. He doesn't. "But I want *you*. I was upset hearing you had future plans with your ex. Hated to believe I was a favor and that you played me. My heart hurt. *Hudson . . .*" There's a strange knot in my stomach like I've swallowed an octopus whole and it's sucking on my insides.

He takes one step at a time up the stairs. "I don't do fucking favors, Abby."

Joey told me to show I care about someone more than about myself. Instead of apologizing, I should *show* him that I want to be there for him like he's been there for me.

"I'm helping the senior center plan an event for your knitting group. I want to support your dreams and passions. Little by little, you can build onto it and then turn your hobby into a career."

He spins around to face me. The sun casts shadows on him as if for a dramatic effect.

Up there, he's so tall and mighty.

"What are *your* hobbies? What are *your* dreams?" he asks in a heated tone. "*Planning* isn't a dream or a hobby."

There is truth to that, as much as I don't want to admit to it. It may look as though planning well means I have everything figured out, but the truth is the opposite. I plan because I have *nothing* figured out.

"I don't want your help. Forget this career crap. If you haven't figured it out, *planning* is not for me," he says harshly, ascending a few more steps. "It's time to do what is guaranteed instead of something risky. I'm going to Manhattan and signing my contract. I'll party how I want and won't have to worry about money. Almost done packing."

"You're what?" I ask, my voice shaking. This isn't what he wants. "Are you sure?"

"I don't have to explain my life decisions to you. A Giordani is who I was born to be." He stomps to the door. "Trying to be anything else is foolish. Why would I give up moving into a swank, furnished apartment this weekend or refuse to bond with the lacrosse team?"

"You're mad and I get it. But it means we care so much that

it makes us *this* emotional." My heart softens even though he's angry with me—it proves how deep his feelings are for me.

"I'm fucking mad and I can't wait to forget about you," he sneers.

The hurt is written all over him.

My breaths become shallow as I search for powerful words.

"Don't do this. I care about you."

He ignores me, pushing the door open. "I'm done with you."

Betrayal doesn't come close to describing how my heart hurts. But I'm not running away or giving up. I find the strength in my own voice.

"No!" I yell. "Face me."

I'm trying so hard, giving it my all here, fighting for us.

He slowly turns. The backpack in his hand drops with a thud.

My stomach gives an anxious lurch, but I push on. "Am I nothing to you? Because you're everything to me," I say, choking up. "I had opened up to you and it *hurt* to think I was only a favor. I liked you so much that the possibility of you wanting someone else was painful. If you deeply care, you won't give up at the first sign of tension."

Our eyes meet and he shakes his head. "I've been nothing but all-in with you. And you go kiss *Theo* at the first sign of hurt? You should have run to me." He closes his eyes but opens them again right away, as if he can't bear to see the images playing in his head.

"I've wanted to kiss you since I was thirteen. Yeah, I liked other girls, but I liked you more. My brothers wanted me to kiss older girls, so I followed them. I'll take the blame for that."

The confession catches me off guard. Hudson Giordani has

wanted to kiss me since forever? While that may be true, his face seems to have forgotten. He's not looking too happy.

"I'm sorry. I haven't experienced any of this before," is all I can express.

Processing his confession has me dumbfounded. I'm split between cheering in excitement and crying in failure.

"No matter how hard I try to be there for you," he pauses, eyes becoming glassy, "you'll never care about me the way you care about him. Never want me the way you want *him*. Need him."

Hudson's hopeless stare crumples me with guilt.

Hurt can do a lot to a person, make them react in a raw way without any filter. I press my palms into the hem of my sundress. He's disappointed in me and the guilt chokes me up.

Silence weaves itself between us. My mind is tangled up like a ball of yarn.

"Just say you don't care about me." He descends three steps, never breaking eye contact. "Trying to kiss a girl several times and then not being able to do so is frustrating. But what hurts *me* the most is Theo being able to kiss you without any trouble at all, it seems."

There's more to the story than just Theo and me kissing. "Theo and I had a moment, but we're just friends." My voice goes high and my throat aches. "I wasn't rejecting you by kissing him. Yesterday we had an emotional conversation, and it just happened. We wanted to make each other feel better."

Hudson drops to a squat and looks down at me from the middle of the stairs. "Abby. You can't blame *me* for not being able to make your own decisions."

"I'm used to having Theo save me. Always part of my plan. But I realize that's not living," I say, tears threatening to fall. "I want *you*." No matter how many times I say it, he won't believe me.

The knot in my stomach tightens. My fingers lace through the ends of my pigtail. Everything is ruined.

"I'm gonna go," he says and rises high. "Because you can't handle this, and I can't stop being mad." He gazes at me but stays put.

"Whatever you think I can't handle is not your decision to make." As confident as I sound, I turn and shut my eyes.

I'm not giving in to tears.

Don't cry.

Tears rush out.

Don't sob.

My nose turns into a river.

Don't weep.

The convulsive gasps make me lightheaded. A throbbing pain begins above my right eye.

"I'm sorry!" I yell, turning around. "Okay? Can't we move forward?"

He stands where he was a minute ago. It's a bold and heavy stance. I'm both impressed that he can carry off the bold look along with the ticked off one.

We both stare. We both breathe hard. We both wait.

He moves first, descending one measured step at a time.

I want to cut our twelve feet of distance to two. Speaking through the tightness in my throat, lungs, and my entire body, I say, "Don't leave like last time. You said you hated not being in my life for these last four years." My voice grows quiet at the end.

He reaches the first step. Automatically, I reach for his hand but he drops his arms by his sides. Affection, we both need it; I can see it in his pained look.

A pause follows and then Hudson passes me. The heaviness of disappointment—his and mine—presses down on me.

His gaze sweeps to his car at the side of the mansion, to the ground, me, and then to his clean white sneakers. Then he shakes his head in disbelief. "I'm trying hard to let last night go, but I can't get the image of you kissing Theo out of my head. Of you choosing him over and over again."

He pivots and the air from his movement hits me. Seeing him low sends shock waves through me.

"Wait." I choke on the word. This is not over. I refuse to lose him over one mistake. "I'll do anything for you to come to the ball with me. For a long time, I was stuck in the past and now I want the present with you. Dance with me?"

His chuckle isn't nice-sounding. In fact, he's laughing at me. All hope is lost and this is the end of us.

"You only want me so I can be your perfect escort." He spins on his heel and walks backwards toward the side exit. "The only reason you're here now is because you have this grand plan worked out of how you want me to fit into the ball with you."

"I'll quit the ball," I blurt. "I honestly don't even want to do it anymore if everyone else controls every part of it." As preposterous as that sounds, I'm desperate. But it's true, I'll do anything for Hudson. Not to mention, if I pull out, Diana will most likely win queen over Pyper, and she won't hate me any longer.

Hudson tilts his head. "Oh yeah?" Confidence oozes out of his question. "Go tell Astrid you quit and have her text me to confirm it." He pauses and a smirk escapes. "Because I want to make up and finally fucking kiss you."

I refrain from smiling, my heart beating faster. "You do?"
He wants to kiss me after everything?

Hudson pivots on his heel for the millionth time. "Yeah," he yells over his shoulder. "It'll be the best damn first kiss you've ever had." I can't tell if he's angry and wants to one-up Theo or if he likes me enough to look past my mistakes.

Either way, I can only move forward. "Really?" I whisper to myself, but I'm sure he hears me. A moment passes and he's gone. I'm still stuck gathering all of my emotions.

I want our first kiss. Our second and third. He's my firework—the one who can get me flying and keep me there. There's a new confidence about our future.

Wiping away any evidence of tears, I hurry back home. The smile on my face is in disbelief that Hudson and I can finally be together.

I plan to tell Astrid that I don't care about the ball anymore. Papi made sacrifices and I can do the same for the people most important to me.

If we need money, I'll apply for jobs and start a tutoring business. If we need a strong image, we'll build cabins and coffee shops. The ball shouldn't hold so much power over our lives.

The only thing on my mind is running back to Hudson and telling him my future is with him. That my lips belong to him.

"Ugh!" A scream echoes through the backyard.

I race faster toward the commotion coming from our driveway.

"Let me at least get my phone charger," Astrid yells.

A scene of an imploding Astrid unfolds. Her golden convertible clicks to a tow truck. "Sorry, lady. Contracts are contracts." The guy tips his trucker's hat toward her.

Astrid squeals and spins.

I rush around her. "Why is he taking your car?"

She shakes her head. "Elijah can't wait until Monday!"

"What's going on?"

"I should marry Elijah next month and then he can't do this. I can totally move up the wedding date." She paces, her breaths heavy. "I'll have access to *his* bank account. I can be sneaky, too. I'll see what he spends money on and transfer back everything he took. I'll pay off the debt and save the company and we won't have to sell things."

"Astrid!" I roll in front of her. "Talk to me. What's going on?"

"After Daddy died, Mom couldn't attend a single meeting and I had to pretend to be her. She tries to act invincible, but she's only been to one board meeting these past ten months. I've had to answer half of her phone calls and learn how to do her job." Astrid tears up. "When the door shuts, she falls to the floor. She has her brilliant days and meetings with clients where they reminisce about the old days. I should have never let Elijah interfere, telling her he'd save us. Now he's drowning us instead." She glances to the mansion and then back to me. "I'm not supposed to tell you any of this."

"Wait." I pull her to a bench and she reluctantly sits down. "Are you only marrying Elijah for the money? Are you planning to steal his money and give it to us? Is he the reason the company is struggling?" She is throwing too many truth bombs at me to understand everything.

Leaning on the wooden armrest, she whispers, "Of course not. That would be selfish."

"So, you're honestly happy with him?" I ask the one question I'd been wanting to ask for months. Maybe even years.

A tear rolls down her cheek. "He's all I've ever known. Our love is special. We always go back to each other even when he breaks up with me over little things like me being late or not wearing the right shoes. But I feel safe with him. Physically, financially, social status-wise." The defense sounds rehearsed. A bit of memorized generic nonsense that she can whip out when she doubts their future together.

"But is the inside of your soul happy? Could you . . . could you laugh over milkshakes and fries together or connect over knitting in a closet?"

"We're not kids anymore," she mutters, eyes down and hidden from me. "We're happy."

"The hell you are! When you're happy for cake, you jump and clap your hands. When you're happy because you arranged flowers perfectly, you do a twirl and giggle. You haven't giggled over Elijah since you got engaged last year. And *you don't sing anymore*, Astrid." She isn't a great singer, but she loves to sing. It's been forever since I've had to tease her about her choice of songs. "I haven't seen you smile when Elijah's been around for over a year. Why are you in such a hurry to tie the knot?"

"He's . . . familiar. We grew up keeping each other's secrets. Who else would I marry? I've been planning this for years. You remember playing wedding stuff as kids."

She must be the least romantic woman in the world. "Does he take you to break bottles to get your frustrations out? Do you only see *him* when he dances with you in a group of others?"

I swallow hard. At this rate, Astrid and I are both going to end up in a pool of regret.

"I can't break Elijah's heart. When you love someone, you work through the small and big bumps in the road. He's careful because his image impacts his career. I have to respect that."

She turns away from me, hiding her face once more.

"If I ran away every time someone wronged me, I'd be at

the North Pole by now," she says and sighs. "Yes, I haven't laughed in years, but he has my back when I need it the most. Plus, I've already ordered my dress." She looks out at the cars passing by the main road.

I don't mean to attack her. Her history with Elijah has merit, but I won't quit asking about her happiness every single day. "Do what you want. Just remember that happiness is more important than a perfect plan."

She gets up and glances down. "Life isn't that simple. When you and Hudson do the ball this Saturday, we'll be back on top. I've made sure the best press attends and interviews *you*, Miss Future Queen. Everyone will see how strong and classy we are, and the board won't have any other choice than to keep our family in power. Just win congeniality, which you are already rocking at. Pyper can't plan a single thing in her life and hasn't reached out to anyone. Votes are due by midnight the night before the ball. You've helped her, so she might even campaign for you to win. Why do you think Mrs. D'aureville picked Pyper as your competition?"

"Hudson isn't escorting me anymore," I say and watch her face transform into a frown. "He would if I quit the ball, but then that doesn't make any sense. I can't force him to do it. We're too emotionally invested."

"I warned you." She drops into the bench again, tears in her eyes. "All that work Mom and I have put into you winning. You're our last hope. Everyone thinks we're broken after Papi's death, and you *have to* show that our family is stronger than ever. That Mom doesn't need a man or marriage to be success-ful. We're about to lose everything. Already basically have lost it."

Is that why Astrid is desperate to get married, fearing a breakup would ruin her chances of success? Or will the company tank further without a man tied to our legacy? Elijah could be manipulating Mother to hand over the company. The more I unravel these strings, the more tangled up everything seems. There is no simple solution to it all.

My soul sinks to the depths of the ocean. Mother and Astrid *have* worked for my success. I hold back my own tears as I offer the solution that kills me. "Ask Elijah to escort me," I mutter.

The base of my head pounds, a headache forming. "It'll guarantee perfect publicity for everyone." I can't make Hudson or Theo escort me. That's selfish and I want to rebuild our relationship, not use it for any personal gain.

If Elijah is the evil man in this equation, I have to stop him and prove to everyone I command him, not the other way around. That my family is doing better than ever and that we don't need his family's money.

I turn and wipe a fallen tear. Elijah is going to ruin me. He'll make the ball hell for me, but I have to fight with everything I've got. With Papi's strength, I will get through this. Or at least try.

"That is the best plan. You're a genius!" Astrid hops up and hugs me, squealing.

I crumble. There's no way I can face Hudson now.

I'm never going to plan or think about kissing anyone ever again.

Twenty-Eight

IN THE STUDY ROOM, I rub a pencil between my palm and the desk. My other hand props my chin up. The last twenty-four hours have been such a blur. I sigh. Hudson is gone. Or at least that's what the picture he posted of Manhattan must mean. When anyone uses the caption "new beginnings" it means they're leaving behind the past.

I am *not* looking forward to dance practice with Elijah. He claims he's a pro and still remembers the routine from three years ago, so one lesson will be enough. There are a few parts where it's different because of my wheelchair moves, but I don't even care if we mess up. If we do, he'll probably play sly and say we didn't make any mistakes. Besides, the perfect curtsy is what everyone will be observing the most.

"Is this pen purple or blue?" a high-pitched voice asks.

Layla.

Mrs. Sevyani dropped her off half an hour ago, as per my tutoring schedule this summer. I wanted to ask about Diana, but Joey and I are setting up a secret mission to confront her, and we can't give away any clues about it.

I sigh again.

Layla's little hand tugs at my cardigan sleeve on the table. A giggle follows. "Are you in outer space?"

I glance at her brown curls and sparkling green eyes.

"Um . . ." I straighten up and nod. "A little bit."

She writes her name on the paper at the bottom and on the sides, and any other place she can squeeze it into.

"My dad made me a wheelchair spaceship one time." She spreads her arms out. "I was flying."

I smile at the seven-year-old. "That sounds like fun, but let's focus back on . . ." I pause. "You went *flying*?"

Her face glows as she shows me. She rolls backwards in the manual wheelchair.

I smile genuinely, my teeth on full display. "Wow, tell me everything you did with your dad in that spaceship." I truly want to know. I want her to hold on to every memory she has with her father.

My phone vibrates in my purse and Layla giggles. "It's the aliens from the gold planet calling you."

Joey isn't a gold alien, but I do reply to her question.

Yes, Bentley is still helping me with the gown. Now get Diana home alone and I'll see you soon.

Last night, I recruited Joey and Bentley to be part of an intervention for Diana. Not an intervention per se, but the only way to her heart is by sharing clothes. That means getting dressed up in our debutante gowns together.

Layla makes babble sounds and we have transformed into gold aliens. We spend more time playing than sticking to our schedule, but it's worth it. Not to mention, I'll take any good distraction I can get. The thought of Hudson being far away in a brand new life without me sucks balls crawling on walls. Or at least that's how Joey tells me it must be.

Layla's face lights up as she talks about building a planetarium with her dad. She's even invited me to the birthday party she'll have there next year.

I agree and promise to dress up as an astronaut.

"That's fun, but what's funner is the ball," she says. "You're going to be so pretty in your dress." Her squeal is loud and fast like a mouse's.

"Thank you," I say as her mother parades the hall with mine. "You go enjoy some ice cream at the park." It's their ritual after every tutoring session.

We see them to the door.

After they leave, Mother turns to me. "Why did Hudson quit? Astrid said you wanted Elijah to escort you?"

The hairs on the back of my neck stand up. The unexpected questions take me a minute to catch my breath, along with finding a proper response. "He's super busy with moving," I mutter. "The timing was off."

Where is he now? If he left for Manhattan yesterday, he's probably already signed the NYU lacrosse contract, met with the teammates, and is moving into a luxury apartment. He's probably bought himself a million things now that his finances, which are tied to his father, are unfrozen.

I can't hold back my own questions. "Are *we* okay? Are we going to move out? Are *you* okay?" A terrible thought occurs to me. Maybe Papi's things have been disappearing because she's secretly packing up the house.

Mother fiddles with her phone. "We'll be just fine. You don't worry about a thing. My parents took care of the mansion's finances a long time ago and the business is simply having a small . . . rearrangement."

I wish I could believe her, but thanks to Astrid, I know better.

"If only Papi were here," I whisper.

Mother rubs my shoulder and sighs. "He would have loved seeing you at the ball." Her words fade at the end.

"Yes, he would have," I say and try to think of a deflection. It doesn't come, and instead, I take Mother's hand. "Do you miss him? Does it hurt? Why did you get rid of his things? I don't want you to hide your pain and act perfect."

The tears in her eyes build, and she pivots, walking quickly toward her office.

I glance around the polished tables and large vases. It's so quiet, it's eerie. A low whisper haunts the halls—it might be curtains rustling from the air conditioner or the ghosts who are asking me to visit the antiques room. I strain my ears, but the sound has subsided.

One day, we'll get to a place where we can talk about our pain.

Then again, how long will I let us be silent about Papi? No more excuses and deflections.

I drift past the fireplace just as a piercing cry erupts from Mother's office.

I've never been inside her office for more than a minute because she insists on privacy. But when I find the door ajar, I take in the view. Empty. She's nowhere. I quietly roll further in.

The office is large enough for a party of twelve. An elegant crystal chandelier, too big for the room, hangs from the ceiling. The black couch in the corner has an engraved painting of a carnation above it. I round the table, inhaling the carnation scent that lingers.

The papers on the desk are piled on top of each other in three perfect sections: budget numbers, jewelry designs, contracts. Golden pens and letter openers are scattered over them. The walls are covered in awards and diplomas. I draw my eye to the walnut cabinets. Full of more files and contracts, no doubt.

"Santiago!" A muffled cry breaks the stillness. Light reveals a narrow opening to another room—her office closet. The voice continues through a sob on the other side of the wall. "I'm failing the girls. They're not the same as they were before you left. I don't know how to help them. I can't do what you did."

It's Mother. She's crying.

I suck in a steady breath and pull on the closet door. The sight of a living-room-sized space floods me with emotions. Not a closet at all.

Mother is on her knees, surrounded by Papi's old possessions. I cover my mouth to hide a gasp; it stays open as I shake my head in disbelief.

She never threw anything out? His pictures, pens, berry-picking baskets, canoes, clothes, books, journals, tools, and chairs fill the space. I'm in awe at how much she's hidden.

If I could move, I'd spin around in amazement, but the sight of Mother, in obvious anguish on the floor, has me frozen.

Still unaware of my presence, she continues, "You always knew how to make the right decisions." She wipes away a tear. "You were so good at building strong relationships. It's been impossible this past year. So hard to keep everything afloat like it was before you passed away. How do I give the girls strength when I don't have any to give to myself?" She sinks deeper to the floor and covers her face with her palms. "I'm a terrible mother."

"You're not a terrible mother."

She startles and turns to me, her makeup smeared on her cheeks. I give her a sympathetic look.

"You're doing the best you can in a life you never expected."

She's quiet for a moment, cleaning up her appearance.

I take her hand. "Why didn't you tell us you had all of this?"

She stands up and brushes the hair where it has fallen out of place. "I didn't want you to miss him. I wanted you both to move on and live a happy life. The kind he'd want you to live." Her words seem real and genuine.

"Listen, Mom," I say. "Avoiding the topic of death doesn't make the reality go away. Let's put his things back and remember him every day."

She clears her throat and straightens her shoulders. "I can't." Her voice shakes. "I can't control my emotions if he's all around us."

I suddenly realize that a crown won't fix our problems. There are deeper issues past fixing our image. There's damage within.

There is a remedy for this, though. "We smash bottles."

She glances at me and lets out a short laugh. "I don't break things," she says less forcefully than she seems to want to.

"Then we start a new tradition."

She lunges forward unexpectedly and gives me a hug. "I love you," she whispers in a shaking tone.

My voice is just as wobbly. "I love you too, Mom. It'll hurt to talk, but that's how we move on. By remembering him."

Both our phones buzz and she grabs at hers first.

"Thank you, honey," she says to me while focusing on her screen. "I'm late to a meeting but . . ." She walks around and I follow her out into the main hallway. "Well," she pauses. "It'd be nice to craft some flower crowns with you and Astrid."

"I'd love that," I say, ready to repair our relationship.

She nods once and answers the phone call.

I fish for mine out of my purse. It shows a new text message from Bentley.

Here! Brought an extra wand for you just in case you want it!

Time to fix my friendship with Diana. Not having her in my life has been torturous.

Twenty-Nine

TWENTY MINUTES LATER, Bentley steps out of the limo, humming as he walks, my gown draping over his shoulder. For the first time, I didn't critique or offer business suggestions. When he realized my only reactions would be nodding and smiling, he talked about what he wanted. Not interjecting with how I thought his plans should go let me listen to *his* plans.

Part of me feels guilty for planning other people's lives because I've been scared of my own plans going awry. Like the one several feet away.

We take in the sparkling driveway decorated with rainbow stones. Every imaginable kind of flower grows here. Along the path to the mansion's main doors are colorful lights looping up the trees. They add a mystical vibe to the pearly tan mansion.

I love coming here. Diana's home has always been my second home with the most polka-dottiest little ramp over the threshold.

"Thanks for the help. You're awesome," I say, facing Bentley. "I love the small wand. It fits perfectly into my purse."

"You're awesomer!" He pulls out a card from behind my

ear with his free hand. "Three of hearts. You are generous and compassionate."

"Thank you, gracious sir. Where is Roosevelt taking you next?" I ask.

"Signing a contract with the investor. Mr. Bijan seems on board since Joey's dad owns luxury cars."

I nod. "I'll throw you a wizardly-themed party to celebrate." Planning others' futures is not my responsibility, but I can celebrate others' plans and accomplishments. "You can hang the gown over my shoulder and ring the doorbell."

He does just that, and then we wave farewell.

Then I wait.

How will Diana react to my showing up?

When the door opens, she stands before me, popping a mint into her mouth. Joey is right behind her, giving me a thumbs-up.

Dresses come and go. Friendships should last forever.

"I hope you're happy." Her voice is so loud. "Mrs. D'aureville told me off. Was stealing my chance at winning queen your plan all along? I hope it was worth it."

Her words sting. "Hurt people hurt people, huh?" I've heard it before.

There's a pause.

"I miss you," I finally say. "I wish you told me how much you wanted to be queen."

"I'm not hurt," Diana says defensively. "You were threatened because I had eight debs voting for me to be Miss Congeniality, weren't you? Astrid has been on my tail for weeks, saying how *you* would win."

Her eyes give me a haughty stare. Then they soften as she scans the gown draping down my shoulder to my wheels.

"I'm sorry, okay?" My footrest hits the shimmering door.

"For everything. This is an event we both wanted since forever. I want us to enjoy the ball together."

She reaches for the fabric but quickly retracts. "You ruined my ball, so I owe you nothing." When she stomps into her living room, Joey holds the door open for me.

I mouth a *thanks* and briefly wonder what fashion show Diana's family is preparing for. Sheets of red fabric and yellow dresses hang on display all over the room. There's a dining table in the middle of the room and a couch, but the table is covered with sewing machines and spools.

"Mrs. D'aureville can't change the rules by picking the top two girls eligible to win queen," I say, offering an olive branch. "In the rulebook, the committee has to approve it and then redistribute the rulebook. So the old rules still stand: top two debs are ones with the highest GPA and volunteer hours."

Diana leans into my chair's armrest. "So, we're officially the top two?"

I nod.

She fixes one of my stray hairs behind my ear and says, "The truth is, my family is pressuring me to win. But I don't even care about the crown. I just want to dance with my date, take pictures, and celebrate our hard work together." Diana doesn't meet my eyes. Instead, she tosses the glitter threads off the sofa and pulls a necklace from under a dress.

I'm overcome with relief at her admission. "I'm sorry, too. Now tell me what has been going on with you. If it's about me or something deeper, you can tell me."

Diana deflates on a pile of silk fabric. "It was petty of me to be so mad. I overreacted because when you didn't include me in trying on your gown but invited Joey, it reminded me of last year's science fair. I was trying to be friends with the science department and I thought they liked me, but they thought my submission for the fair was a joke and didn't include me in it. It's so hard to tell people I want to be a biochemist. They look at me as if I said a hilarious joke. It's not that I hate fashion, but it's just not . . . *all* of who I want to be."

There's a pause, and then I smile. This is news, the good kind, because I can't wait to hear about what she has planned for her future. "I can totally see you as a scientist. We'll help you with every one of your science fair projects and they'll have no choice but to accept each one." As much as I associate Diana with clothes and fashion, I realize I never let her be more than that. "You should explore *all* your different passions."

"Thank you." Diana claps her hands and eats a mint she finds on the table. "Now tell me about Hudson. Do you like him? Like, like him like him, or like him like him, *like him*? Or like, hate like him?" Diana's eyes go wide and sparkly. "Can I set you two up on a cute date? I had one on a hill overlooking the city on a night lit with fireworks and it was so romantic. What a fun way to start off senior year. With a boyfriend. Then you and I, and Joey, can triple date." The hopeless romantic.

Diana twirls two yellow markers on the table as if they're dancing together.

"Well," I say and sit up, "I kissed Theo and Hudson found out."

Diana and Joey stare at me for so long they look like gawking statues.

"I messed up," I whisper, sweeping the back of my hand over my forehead. "I hurt Hudson. I really, *really* hurt him. His eyes had this awful, pained look. He was so upset." Every consonant chokes me up. "He was so angry. He yelled at me." My lip quivers. "Then we were supposed to have our fairy tale kiss, but Astrid was crying. And . . ."

Diana has written an entire romance novel with her face.

"Take a breath and give him some time." She rubs my hand and leans in. "It'll be okay. We can plan a fashion show party for him or take him shopping."

I giggle a little, imagining Hudson strutting down a catwalk. Diana smirks at her own joke.

Then I tell them everything they've missed, minus the Elijah part. He's irrelevant in my world and I won't give him any more of my energy.

Joey smirks. "Theo's a fun dancer even if he can't dance. You two go bust some party moves." She waves her arms in the air and shimmies her shoulders.

I spin a thread through my fingers. "Neither Theo nor Hudson will be escorting me. It doesn't feel right."

The girls sigh with me.

Diana sits up. "Josh and Khalid are still available."

"How about it's a surprise," I say and then quickly switch topics. "The dresses are calling our names."

Joey laughs like a wild woman and strikes a Superman pose. "Let's get you two into those damn dresses."

Diana smiles so wide her mint pops out of her mouth. Let the laughing games begin.

In a flash, Diana changes into her gown and twirls into the living room. The heart-shaped white satin rests beautifully on her body. The A-line skirt falls flawlessly down to her ankles.

"You look so beautiful." I fix one of Diana's red curls. "Truly glowing."

She spins around me. "I'm so happy you're here."

Joey points at me. "Your turn."

They both squeeze me into my dress and it's perfect.

"Say 'motorcycles.'" Joey holds her phone out and we smile for a photo.

"Take another one," I say and take Diana's hand. "Let's do

a heart shape with our hands." I curl my fingers and extend my thumb.

Diana leans in. "I love you both so much, I could kiss you!"

Joey kisses each of our cheeks and we all laugh.

Diana and I chatter, scheming of ways to get Joey into a ballgown, too.

After a few minutes of protesting, she agrees to a purple fluffy one.

"So . . ." Joey twirls the fabric between her fingers. "Is this what I'll look like for homecoming in a few months? Senior year is going to rock!"

"I can't wait!" I say.

This feels normal. The normal that was before Papi died. Not that everything could ever be as beautiful as it was once upon a time. But I feel lighter, freer. I realize Papi only encouraged me to do the ball because it was *ours*. It was something I loved, and he did too, because he wanted me to be happy. For him, the deb scene was never about the fancy people. It was about the experience we could have together.

It's time to live in his spirit. Everything about him was freedom—not about fitting into the mold. That includes making the best memories with those I care about.

"Let's visit Mei-Ling's cake shop for tomorrow's event," I say. There are still decorations, party favors, and photo booths to pick out. "We can tell the debs to vote for every girl, and then we'll all win queen."

Planning anything is more fun with friends. Especially in fluffy gowns.

Joey's nose crinkles. "Sometimes I question your planning skills." She fixes an invisible pair of glasses and continues, "You have the highest GPA and Diana has the highest volunteer hours, and if you each get one vote, then Mrs. D has to break the tie."

She has a point, so I come up with a new idea. "Then we tell everyone to vote for Pyper and she'll win congeniality. The rulebook has nothing about top three debs. Mrs. D'aureville won't have any other option than to crown us three as queens."

"Eh, that could work," she says, pushing her pretend glasses up her nose.

Diana and I giggle, no longer concerned if either of us wins queen, if that even happens.

We do agree to make it our own ball and compete to impress the most spectators at the ball. Whoever gets the most mentions by the press wins a slumber party.

Thirty

THE MORNING of the ball is hectic, but for me it feels like the world has ceased spinning. The hours don't seem to exist. I should be dancing, singing, and taking selfies. Diana has already sent me her documented morning. All seventy-five photos, while leaving five for the social media circles. The other debs have posted about their day as well. I'm dreading seeing Elijah at the hotel. I pretend he's got a pizza hat and eyeliner on his face just to make every interaction with him bearable.

The gown had a small tear in the back from when I had first tried it on. While the seamster, Tommy, fixed up the stitches, Mackenzie finished my hair and makeup. We didn't discover the mishap until after I put the dress on, so leaning forward for twenty minutes wasn't the most comfortable.

Tommy cuts the thread and I sit up, thanking him.

Mother hollers my name.

"Abigail," she says in a panicked tone. "My day is packed. Your day is packed. Astrid is at the hotel, which is packed." Anytime we go on vacation or have an important event,

Mother gets frazzled on the day of departure. Being low-key has never been her forte.

She's on her way to the airport to pick up Grandpa, who is flying in from Spain. They will then arrive at the hotel for the ball.

In an hour, I'll be posing for pictures and shaking hands with powerful people. In two, I'll curtsy. In two and a half, I'll see Grandpa and dance with him. In five, it will all be over and I'll be back home.

"I won't be late, don't worry," I assure Mother.

When I arrive early, I'll get an interview with the Verdan magazine editor and tell them the history and legacy of the jewelry company, how Astrid and Mother are boss babes who don't need a man to be strong and powerful, and that many spectators are wearing fabulous one-of-a-kind designs. Buzz, that's what the business needs.

"You can go," I add. "I'm so happy you're actually going to pick up Grandpa yourself and not sending someone else to get him."

She nods and faintly smiles. We may have a long way to go in becoming a wholesome family again, but I'm hopeful about the future.

"Tommy," Mother says to the seamster, "I can drop you off home, but I'm leaving right now."

Tommy swiftly collects his sewing supplies from the table and dumps them into a gray backpack.

Valerie, my nurse, accompanies Mother to the door. Both discuss this summer's schedule.

Mackenzie jogs into the living room with the last accessory for my hair. "Your pearl headband." Her steps are soft as she approaches me.

I bow my head like Papi taught me, slowly and amicably, without moving my shoulders.

She slides the accessory into my half-up, half-down black hair.

"Thank you," I say.

As Mackenzie holds up a mirror, I smile. It's the perfect smile, but not my happiest.

I look and feel pretty, but something is off. Something is missing. The princess I once imagined has an emptiness inside her. The shine that's supposed to illuminate her, to give her light to the world, is nowhere to be seen.

Mackenzie darts at her vibrating phone. It's her six-year-old calling—a picture of a petite, red-haired girl blowing out birthday candles pops up.

"Sorry." Mackenzie puts the device away. "She's nervous for her first dance recital."

"That's amazing. Please, go home," I say.

"Your mother has instructed me to go to the ball with you and—"

"Go be with your daughter. It's Saturday." Time is precious. I'd give anything to be a kid with Papi again, for a chance to share one more dance with him.

She whispers, "Who's going to do all your touchups?"

I grab her hand. "There are more important things." It's the kind of thing Papi would have done. Mackenzie cherishes family time, and I don't want her to sacrifice that for this job.

Mackenzie nods and speedily packs up her things. "Thank you for this favor."

"It's not a favor."

Her phone rings. I gesture for her to answer it.

"Hi, sweetie! Guess what? I'm coming home. We can make

that sign with Daddy for the dance recital." Her joyful voice echoes down the hall when she leaves, almost running.

I enjoy the moment and breathe in silently, calm and deep, sitting in my beautiful gown with just myself.

Maybe I can still be a princess even if I don't have a prince to kiss at the end of the night. Because maybe being a princess is not about how I look or who I have next to me. I don't need a title, a platform, or an audience to have power and influence. It's my inner self that has to grow stronger and the rest will follow.

With a few minutes to spare, I'm inspired to show my ancestors how the pearl necklace matches my entire look.

I whip around the hall and rush into the antiques room. The wind on my face throws my hair up. I smile at the anticipation of seeing something familiar. My footrest presses into the door as I turn the knob and push forward.

I gasp, grasping at my chest, unable to breathe. The dust settles around the empty spaces. The throne is gone. So is the cabinet and the lamp and the . . . "No!"

Half of the things in the room have vanished. Things that Papi collected and books that he loved. Astrid sold more than she should have.

I shake my head. Everything is disturbed. The dust is in the wrong places and the chairs have been pushed to the wrong side. Nothing is as it once was. It's as if Astrid didn't care about anything but selling things. My collection of firsts are tossed to the ground. A wooden chair is tipped over and the candle stands are piled haphazardly on top of the glass jewelry boxes.

This can't be real. The peace, the sacredness, of this place has been disturbed. I pull a napkin from my purse and wipe away the dark dirt on a Worcester pedestal vase.

A voice sounds from the hallway. "Abby, your mother

wants me to tell you Roosevelt is ready for you." Valerie is peering at me from the doorway.

I squeal, spinning around. "Just give me a minute. This needs to be fixed. Can you bring some cleaning supplies?"

"Absolutely," she replies. "I stayed an extra hour, so I must leave after that."

"Thank you."

Valerie jogs down the hall, her steps fast like the quick taps of raindrops.

I push my footrest against a wooden nightstand and pull it back into its place. My collection of firsts could use a better spot, I'd admit to that. I lean over my armrest and grasp a handful of items from the floor.

After two minutes, my lap is covered with old treasures. Each object has a special memory, and I can't let them go. A secret spot would be wise. I open a drawer and lower the items inside.

I look at my dust-covered hands and then at my pristine gown. Better be careful.

On the floor, I see an old copy of *Don Quixote*. The brick-red spine with gold engraved letters is stained but it's blemishes only add to its character. The book's as thick as a textbook and definitely heavier than a pound. The rounded pages are glazed with some sort of gold ink, which is one reason we keep it under glass. I shake my head in disbelief at Astrid's disregard for the fragility of these treasures.

Steps echo down the hallway. It must be Valerie, returning with the cleaning wipes before bidding me goodbye.

I lean down to pick up another old book, dusting it off so I can read the title.

"What happened here?" a voice says from behind. A deep voice.

Definitely not Valerie. I turn around, and for a second time, I can't breathe.

Hudson's eyes meet mine. I do a double take. He's calm, dressed in a fine suit that fits him like a glove. He's wearing the same shocked expression I had when I first saw the ransacked room, but when his eyes meet mine, that wicked half smile flickers on his lips.

He came back?

He sets the cleaning wipes on the table without speaking. I can't seem to find any words either. The hopeful romantic in me imagines he came back to be there for me on my special day. But before I can fly into his arms and kiss him, I need to be self-less with him, and put my wants aside.

Leaning his bulky stance against a table, he tucks his hands behind him. The wooden legs wobble and he immediately straightens.

My heart bounces around in my chest. I look down, real-izing I'm holding the dusty book on my lap. It has left a faint smudge on my gown. I grab a cleaning wipe and carefully rub at the stain, avoiding Hudson's gaze.

He slides over and takes the book from me, setting it at its correct place on the bookshelf.

I'm not sure what else to say other than, "Why are you here?" I'm obviously happy to see him, but his coming back gives me that naked and vulnerable feeling again. Especially that this place is all naked and vulnerable.

The way he gawks at my dress sends hot flashes over my face. That half smile is something else. It's louder than his voice. More potent.

"To take you to the ball."

I need him to say that again, because it's everything I want to hear. I want this with him.

Then I take a few inches back. Hudson is only doing this for me because he knows I want it, not because he wants it. This is the moment I put others first and take responsibility for my mistakes.

"That's really nice, but Elijah is doing it." The words taste disgusting in my mouth. If my hands weren't dirty, I would cover my face and run them through my hair.

Instead, I grab a wipe and clean the dusty surfaces in quick, circular motions.

"Astrid told me yesterday," he says, moving toward me. "I won't let you do that to yourself."

"That's not your decision to make." My voice comes out harsh because I mean it. Forcing him to do this—save me—is selfish of me. I am my own savior and I'm not scared of Elijah. Despite how this looks: me hiding away in the antiques room.

Showing up today proves Hudson cares about me. If *I* care about him, I can't let him do this. Not to mention that he's going to New York after this. It does neither of us any good to go down a detour. I've accepted not having him in my life and watching him leave again when the ball ends will only hurt more.

He should forget about me and go. I hurt him and the guilt is unbearable. I can't accept him coming back for me after what I did. I ghosted him when he said he wanted to make up and kiss me. That must have stung. Twice. Once for when he found out I kissed Theo and a second time when I didn't come back to let him kiss me after our fight.

I've hurt him and he should be mad, not selfless.

Yet, he stands there, looking confused and lost. "I'm sorry about what happened the other day." His eyes meet mine for a moment, then he looks down. "I hated thinking you liked someone else or wanted to kiss someone else. But I made peace with Theo and he invited me to a wave-boarding event next weekend. Maybe we *can* be friends."

"Good." I keep dusting the surfaces I can reach on the tables, cabinets, counters, glass containers, candlesticks, little gadgets, big gadgets. This is my space, my moment to be with myself. I wipe a little faster. A little harder. *Focus on the task.* I need a minute to process and dust and . . . figure out how to react. How Papi would want me to react.

Hudson and I exchange glances. I want to hug him and say I care so much and that I want him to be happy and that I hate being standoffish.

Quickly grabbing a cleaning wipe, he whispers, "Here, let me help."

He rubs the high counter where the precious stones sit behind glass.

I attack a new area, unsure how to react to his kindness.

The longer we clean, the more the area takes on the luster of a well-cared-for museum.

If I stay here a little bit longer, I can fix this and restore what was lost. To some degree, at least—in spirit, that is.

We continue to dance around each other. He wipes the top shelves. I tackle the lower ones. It's a routine that works. I hate that it works.

I hate that when his hand grazes mine, I struggle not to gasp at the subtle contact. His touch. It's enough for me to warrant a full stop to this nonsense and grab his hand.

He parades to an armchair and dusts each tiny crack in the leather at the very top. I follow and take care of the armrests.

I should open up. But I *can't*. It's as if I'm driving a boat in the middle of the ocean, lost at sea but need to keep moving yet unable to ask for directions.

Hudson tosses the dirty wipe onto the pile we got going by the door.

"You know, maybe ghosts are real," he says. From the corner of my eye, his mouth twitches a bit.

"Maybe," I mutter. I still can't meet his eyes. I'm too scared of the cries bubbling up inside, ready to spill out.

I realize he's stopped moving.

"Don't you wanna talk?" His voice is calm.

He came back for me. The thought keeps me motionless. We *should* talk. My hands press into the edge of a cabinet. I stare at them, my head bowed.

Overwhelming gasps take over and I can't push away how badly I want him.

Hudson exhales. "I'm sorry."

The silence grows. I imagine those intense hazel eyes staring right into my soul.

Okay, yes, I'm done giving myself this headache. Let's do this together and remember tonight even if it's only for a moment in time. He may want to make the ball special for me, but I'm going to make it more special for him. Milkshakes and fries included.

When I look up, he's gone.

Grabbing at my purse, I fish my phone out. My fingers fly across the screen.

Needle.

I text as I roll toward the door, apologizing and asking him to wait.

Suddenly, a tug tightens at the base of my neck. The necklace pulls, being caught on something, then the pressure releases. Little taps echo throughout the room as a few pearls hit my lap and bounce to the polished black cement floor. Part of the necklace lands softly on my lap. My heart lurches and it's like someone has undressed me. I feel stripped of everything I have.

My free hand grazes my neck, then drops to the partial necklace coiled over the white fabric on my lap. Another portion of the necklace slides down my back and around the side of my chair. Little white pearls continue to scatter over the floor.

I pat my naked neck again. The pearl necklace has shattered, the unity of the original creation is now lost.

My eyes fill with tears, shaky hands grab at the remains and try to piece them back together. My fingers tremor harder the longer I try, seeing that it's an impossible feat. Bringing the broken pearl necklace pieces to my chest, I shake my head. A high-pitched squeal leaves me. I've broken the most precious treasure. The necklace will never be the same again.

The air tightens around my neck the longer I stare at the damage.

The pearls of yesterday are gone. The past that once lived in this necklace is no more.

Whatever pearls I can salvage, I slide them into a white glove inside my purse, along with my phone. I scan the floor for other scattered parts. But it's like I can't see anything except for a cracked floor swallowing me up.

I focus on a single white dot at a time. There's one against the wall and another next to the chair and another under the table. I collect them and sit back up, lips quivering. The rest are sprinkled in places I can't reach. Even if I could, I can't put the necklace back together the way it was.

There I sit, motionless.

Yesterday's world is gone. No matter how hard I want to hold on to what once was, it belongs to memory now. My breathing escalates, and then levels.

Little by little, I calm down and remember the moments I had with the necklace.

Grandpa told me at Papi's funeral: "Don't be sad something is lost. Be grateful you had a chance to know what is now gone." I meditate with that thought.

A minute passes. Maybe two.

When I check my phone, somehow an hour has passed by. Astrid has called and texted. Mother as well. There's a flurry of messages from Diana and Joey and Theo asking where I'm at.

I'm so late.

Thirty-One

ROOSEVELT UNCOILS the limo ramp and I wheel down it, holding tight to my armrests. The hotel is bustling with people.

Astrid sits on a black bench next to the main doors. Her knees are tilted toward each other like she's in middle school.

"Hey, what's wrong?" I ask, moving closer. She sniffs, wiping the corner of her eyes. They're puffy as if she's been crying. *Crap.*

Her eyes narrow, taking in my dirty dress. "Everything," she says in the most melancholic way.

I roll next to her. "I realize I'm super late. But it's okay, I don't even care about the group photo. I'll impress those billionaires and get our business some good publicity in another way."

Who am I?

Her hand runs down her face. "Why isn't Daddy here? He should be here for you. For us."

"Oh, Astrid." This is new. Then again, grief can hit at any moment. Especially when you least expect it.

She smiles gently and then she's not smiling at all. "I yell when no one's home." Her words are a whisper. Then they heat up. "I envy you for the memories you two made. For the memories you'll always have. Memories I will never have. He loved you more, so I moved on a long, long time ago." She stares at me, then adds, "You had him in your past, and you get to carry him into your future. I'll never have any of that."

I'm stunned. I don't know how to answer that. "Papi loved you so much," I say with conviction. "Remember when he danced with you at the ball three years ago?" As much as it stings that she has that memory and I won't, I want us to celebrate the time we had with him. In each of our own special ways.

I feel guilty she thinks Papi loved me more. Astrid was the good child, the easy one, and he probably did give her less attention. I grew up selfish, wanting him to stop smothering me with his love. The harder he tried with me, the more I pushed him away.

"Every place important to him is foreign to me. Why didn't he take me to the cabin or the lake?" She covers her face with her hands. "I like swimming, just not wearing a bathing suit in front of others. So much judgment in this town."

Guilt hits me again. I've dismissed Astrid, losing her, too. She may have never asked me how I was feeling, but I never asked her either.

I stroke her shoulder. "I'm so sorry. Let's remember him together, starting today."

She nods half-heartedly, which means she's not convinced.

"I can teach you how to make his hot chocolate," I offer.

She watches me. I don't think she knows she's nodding again.

"We can paint," I add. Papi and I used to laugh at the messy brush strokes on the murals. "We can build things."

"That would be nice." She looks at me with distressed green eyes. "Tell me about the life you had with him." Slouching, agony fills her face. "I want to enjoy his memories, not be stuck in the one where I treated him the way I did. The last thing I said was that I didn't want him to walk me down the aisle if he was going to wear those worn-out brown shoes. His favorite."

Another wow. I hadn't been the only one to be so mean to him.

"I'm a bad person," Astrid says, her voice gravelly, each syllable cracking. "No matter how busy I get, I can't out-busy the pain."

She's also been living in the past. Neither of us has found happiness in that. We have to move forward. I understand wanting the fantasy of the past to be real in the future. We've been going through the same grief without realizing it.

We sigh at the same time.

She holds my hand. For the first time in forever, I feel less lonely. The one person I needed for comfort over Papi's death; the person who could make me feel whole the last ten months, has been right next to me.

"Are you okay?" Her soft mutter is barely audible. "Why were you *so* late?"

"I had to clean the antiques room." I pause and tread carefully. "I didn't realize you'd sell so much." Some items had been there for decades. Others were treasures Papi had found. "What did you do with the money?" My voice is level, but at any moment, it might heat up thinking about the wreck she left behind.

She straightens up and sighs. "I only sold the throne to pay back Elijah for covering my car insurance and other expenses for the last ten months." She grimaces. "It wasn't worth anywhere close to half a million. It was actually a facsimile."

Oops, news to me. Note to self: do better research.

"Elijah must have taken the rest," she says and sighs. "He said he gave Mom loans and this was his way of taking the money back since he doesn't think our business will recover. And don't get me started on the money he lost over the years with his gambling habit."

Elijah! I should have known. Astrid would never treat Papi's things with such blatant disrespect. My brow narrows at the thought of interacting with Elijah. He does not get to bull-doze over our life in any way he pleases.

The next time I see him, it will be war. How that will happen, I have yet to decide.

As I glance down, I spot a lone pearl resting on my lap. I squeeze it in my hand. My strength grows a little bigger. "*We* will help the business recover. You don't need him, Astrid. Think about what *you* want, not about what others want you to want."

Her phone buzzes in her pocket and she checks it.

"I'm going to clean up and get to Pyper. She's been blowing up my phone." Astrid rises and hugs me. "Thank you for—"

Thumps sound behind us.

"Have you lost your mind?" Elijah screeches at me. "Here I am greeting everyone and saying you have a good reason you missed debutante photos and the receiving line! I'm fucking tired of your failures."

He pinches the bridge of his nose. "Your family's future depends on this ball and you're out here dillydallying? Both of you? Astrid." He gives her a look that says they're going to talk about this later.

Astrid slouches, sliding back onto the bench. I won't let him control us. My strength grows, my voice coming into fruition.

"No." I won't run from my fears, hardships, or embarrassments. Nor will they crumble me.

I'm always messing up and doing everything wrong in everyone's eyes, even when I try to be a version of perfect for this town. Especially Elijah, who's slowly turning this family into something else.

I fix him with a confident stare. "I've been so scared of disappointing people. But I will not live for others or let them control me anymore." My gaze wanders to the cars entering and exiting. The event I've dreamed of for so long is playing out around me, and I'm not a participant. Yet I've never felt more in control.

Elijah huffs. "The mayor could be watching you through the hotel's windows." He scans my body from head to toe. "Maybe everyone expected too much of you. Your behavior is out of place and you need help. Better yet, I should let you fail and make a fool of yourself. I'm not escorting you." His hand waves me off.

"I don't need you," I say, suddenly relieved he's cutting our ties.

"Once I control the jewelry company, you're not getting an allowance. After tonight, the board will see I'll be the best co-CEO. Since I've been helping my father rewrite the Panashe Jewelry contracts, your mother will work for me and so will Astrid."

"No!" I yell back. He's trying to overpower me. To hold me down. Shock me with his plans of taking my family's legacy away from us. He can't just take the company, right? "*You* listen to *me*." I sit up straighter, taller. My voice rings with confidence. I *feel* it. "I'm going to have a purpose and a reason others can look up to me even when I fall. I don't want any crown because I will make my own. My life will be mine. You can either support me or torture me for that, but I won't live life according to someone else's plan. And I will make *your* life hell." I've wanted to put him in his place for so long.

He squeezes his phone to the point that veins pop out of his neck on one side.

I stand my ground. This town has taught me the importance of fitting in and doing everything to obey what everyone else says. But there are more important things than an image. Papi valued real, genuine relationships.

That includes protecting my family.

Elijah glances at a tearful Astrid and then back at me.

"This is your opportunity to fix your reputation. I'll give you one last chance for Astrid's sake." Then he whispers harshly, "People say you are a depressed girl who can't get over the accident and who's not ready to step into society. Someone who will fail at everything else if she fails as a debutante. Even if you win queen, you'll never truly have any power, so give up."

"No. I'll never fail. I'll fall, but never fail." I pretend I'm on a throne. "I have no idea what the real world, what life, really is. But I'll find out in my own way. On my terms. You will have to bow down to me. And I'm doing this ball on my terms," I declare in a voice that is clear and unwavering.

The window of a limo passing by catches my reflection. I'm beautiful and strong.

Then I smile. It's a happy, genuine smile full of excitement for the unknown.

I pull Astrid's hand, and we dash into the lobby.

"You're so brave," she whispers. "How did you take on Elijah like that?"

I spin around and roll in backwards. "You start with a 'no.'"

"Hmmm." Astrid glances at her vibrating phone. "No, Elijah."

She doesn't actually answer the call but replies with a text. A long one. This looks like progress.

"I wish I were more like you."

I laugh at her statement. "I wish I were more like *you*." We share a silent glance and then both smile.

She sighs. "Elijah lost the money he embezzled from our company and forced me to cover it up when I asked for his help with Mother. He threatened to go public with our financial problems if I didn't go along with his plans. He is so manipulative, I want to pull my hair out."

"What?" I ask in shock, although I'm not surprised. "I knew he was the reason for our money problems. We're totally suing him."

"No." She pauses. "Okay, yes, but I'm not allowed to tell or sue anyone. He made me sign a contract. And the last few months, the board has been unsure if Mother is fit to run the company as CEO and I can't do it on my own. Definitely not when Elijah takes over."

"I can do it," I say.

She snickers and then quiets when I don't laugh with her. "You're still in high school."

"Fine," I say. "Then we come up with a plan, but I want to be included in family discussions."

Her mouth curls up and she scans my face. "You are no longer my baby sister. I guess it's time I let you grow up."

Thirty-Two

I THUNDER through the crowds of people rushing in every direction. Astrid barely keeps up as we turn into the ballroom. The lights flash down at the center while the debs are scrunched up along the wall.

"I'm doing this my way."

"Okay," she whispers. "I'll do whatever you need me to."

"Thank you. You can go find Pyper, she must be anxious."

The echo of music hangs in the background.

Astrid nods and strides to the fidgety deb in the middle of the lineup. I take the last place in the line of debs who are minutes away from performing their curtsies. They're across from their escorts, awaiting for their names to be called for when they walk down the center of the room. I spot Diana toward the front. She looks nervous, biting at her nails.

My stomach twists and I second guess my choice in breaking tradition and escorting myself.

Then I imagine Papi telling me how beautiful my inner self shines.

"I only get one ball, and this is for you, Papi," I whisper.

He wouldn't want me to give up. I will make this day count.

The crowd claps when each name is announced on the speakers.

The spotlight beams down on each girl elegantly strolling down the center. Each one smiles and waves, then turns to bow. Shoulders straight, posture impeccable. The debs have all polished their skills to a fine sheen.

I take a deep breath and take on the world.

Here goes nothing.

As I pull up to the bright lights, the crowd buzzes with chatter. They'll judge, scrutinize, and make sly comments. But I don't care. I am not doing this for them. I'm doing this for Papi.

My name is announced into the microphone. "Our next debutante . . ." The announcer's deep voice echoes through the room. ". . . is Abigail Maria Panashe. She is accompanied by . . ."

I spin in a circle like I'm on a runway, feeling my own element and rhythm. The crowd murmurs, but I continue on my path to the curtsy. Someone says something I don't catch. What others think of me is none of my business.

My wheels trail along the carpet to the top of the stage. The large lilies in vases and the white backdrop surround me. I scan the dumbfounded crowd. Then, a familiar voice breaks the stiff silence.

"Go, Abby!" Joey yells.

As I curtsy, Diana cheers, clapping.

I've never felt happier to be here, living in this moment. This freedom.

When I finish and roll back down, a hand grabs mine. It's warm and strong.

I gasp, glancing to the right. Then I melt into sweetness. My heart skips a beat and I'm full-on smiling. This time, I don't push away.

Hudson stands before me in his elegant black suit. The way he watches me watching him sends a shiver down to my toes.

He asks me something. I'm in such a trance, I barely catch it.

"Can you?" he asks. "Can you forgive me? I want you so bad, it hurts," he says, circling around me. "You're the girl I need. You challenge and push me."

I can only nod because his eyes render me speechless.

He's here.

He could have walked away like he had in the past, but chose to fight for me—twice in one day.

"I care about you, and I'm sorry I was scared to tell you the truth. I'm sorry for feeling threatened about Theo. I'm sorry for all of it."

His confession is everything a girl wants to hear. His words vibrate in my mind, and with every movement of his lips, I nod. Over and over and over again.

"I was angry you kissed Theo." He pauses. "Because I wanted to be the one to do that, and that anger scared me. I've always been scared to have feelings for you."

As the debs and escorts come together to form a circle for the waltz, we fall into rhythm.

"You've changed me," Hudson whispers just loud enough for me to hear and no one else.

We part ways and I twirl before he grasps my hands again. My breathing picks up, and so does my heart rate. I can't believe this is even real.

Hudson slowly leans down and places a gentle kiss on my shoulder, tender and warm. "You've shown me real and raw emotions, and I wouldn't change a thing about our past." His fingers leave mine and then reconnect again within seconds.

I forgive him for everything in the past, in the future and to infinity. He's melted every part of me into him. If only I could come up with a confession to equal his.

"I'm sorry, too. I got caught up in trying to plan everything and please everyone around me, and I made a huge mess when every plan came crashing down." I can start with that. Then I let myself get lost in every one of my emotions. "Having feelings is scary and I was trying to protect myself from you. In the end, though, I hurt us more. But you make me want to fight. You make me want to face things that scare me. You make me want to stay rather than run," I say a bit louder. "Can you forgive *me*?"

He nods, brow narrowed, concentrating his full attention on every word I said. "Yeah, gorgeous, I forgive you."

Our eyes meet and his closeness gives me butterflies that won't stop fluttering in my stomach. Whatever he wants me to do, I'll do it. "I care, but sometimes I show it in the wrong ways. I'm so sorry about the mistakes I've made with you," I say, squeezing his hand tighter. "I don't ever want to let you go or push you away."

We're still for a moment, stopping our part of the routine.

The couples swirl around us as if we're the center of the universe.

"I was in Manhattan about to sign the contract but then realized you were right," he confesses. "I'd be happier doing something I'm passionate about. And even happier with you as part of that plan. At the moment, I'm taking a gap year to decide what *I* want to do. It's not that I don't want a career path or goals for my life; it's that I honestly don't know who I am yet. But I'm figuring it out. That's good enough for now and my father finally came around." He drops to one knee and we're at eye level. Smoothly, his hand wraps around my waist. "You are the reason my life is better, fuller. One worth living."

It's dangerous how close those words pull me into him.

The chandelier lights fall on Hudson's face, illuminating his clear complexion and half smile. He's beautiful. He shines from the inside out. I want all that goodness to rub off on me. My feelings grow as though I'm about to burst.

There has to be magic in the air, because suddenly I hear clapping. In the corner of my eye, I spot Astrid holding a crown and a microphone.

Hudson traces his hand down my shoulder and I lean in. Our breaths collide, peppering our faces with waves of warmth.

I'm so lost in his eyes that I barely notice my name being called. In the distance, the debs and their escorts are clapping all around us.

Hudson inches closer and glides a hand up my neck. His radiating heat connects with mine, twisting into its own.

The side of his thumb rubs my cheek ever so gently, his eyes watching my mouth. I drag my stare to his lips as he inhales my exhale.

Cupping my face, he brushes his lips across mine, his forceful breaths grazing my cheek. His mouth is soft and gentle, warm and desperate. I never knew his lips could suck like that or that his tongue could waltz like that.

He tastes like a pepperminty milkshake.

My hand slides up his biceps.

The longer we let our lips dance, the deeper I sink into him. That electric tingling feeling runs through me where his hands touch me. When his tongue is intertwined with mine, when our hearts pound in sync through our clothes.

Hudson presses against me, his tongue gently tracing the

inside of my mouth. When he kisses me harder, his nose rubs my skin ever so slightly. I draw in the burst of his exhale before diving in deeper. His tongue runs up the roof of my mouth, and I moan unexpectedly. Time is fixed on his lips, and I'm flying in the ticking sounds of destiny.

My dress is dirty, I'm missing my necklace, and I don't have any lip gloss on. But those things don't dictate the magic of a perfect kiss.

Instead, I'm lost in the good times: how he pushes me beyond my comfort zone and challenges me; how he makes me feel important and teaches me things; how he dances the waltz even when he hates fancy events.

I want everything with him. All of life's pains and joys. All of life's plans and detours.

If I had to tell my younger self how to plan for my first kiss, I'd say, "Your first kiss is the one that's wrapped up in the feelings of true love, not lips." Because love can't be planned, neither can the kisses that come along the way. There's the first kiss, then there's the first kiss *kiss*, then the real first kiss, and finally, a true love's first kiss that's the first true kiss every time you kiss the person you can't get enough of.

We pull back slowly and I can still feel his soft breath on my face.

The smell of lilies and roses suddenly overpowers me. Confetti pours down and Diana's giggle thunders into my dreamland as if she's an inch away.

I turn and laugh, meeting her gaze. She practically *is* an inch away.

Astrid steps next to us and sets a crown on my head.

Diana's squeal rings in my ears. "You won queen." She hands me a bouquet. The flowers rest against my chest. They are light enough for me to hold, yet not light enough for my wrists to keep straight.

My eyes widen. "What?" Now this definitely has to be a dream.

"I told everyone to vote for you," Diana explains. "I also signed in as you and introduced myself as Abby to strangers."

"You did what?" No way she gave up her position for me.

She hugs me. "I wanted this to be *your* night."

A photographer snaps a picture of me. I barely throw him a smile. Hudson stands up and then we're waving to two, three more photographers. The flashing lights overwhelm my senses.

Astrid says how proud she is of me for winning queen and then makes an announcement that dinner will be served twenty minutes after the father-daughter dance.

The bouquet wobbles, and she takes it from me, straightening the crown on my head. She nods in approval and lets us be.

I smile at Hudson, who isn't done surprising me. He hands me a small, folded paper and suddenly I'm a middle schooler, giddy to read a note from the cutest guy in class.

I open and read it.

You're the yarn to my needle.

Before I can squeal with happiness, the call of my name sends shockwaves down my shoulders.

"Abigail!"

We eye Mrs. D'aureville marching in our direction. Even from across the room, I can see her thick, black eyeliner around her angry blue eyes.

"We should run," I say, feeling spontaneous. I hand the crown to Diana. "You take my place until I get back."

If I get back.

Joey stomps to the thunderous Mrs. D'aureville and puts her hand up in front of her. "Chill your tits, lady."

Hudson and I race out of the ballroom, laughing. I catch a few congrats from people I've never met by the door. A photographer positions a camera in my face but I point him to Diana, and he bulldozes forward.

Astrid's voice interrupts our reverie from the opposite corner of the hall.

"No, Elijah!" she yells, stomping into the center of the hallway. "Money is *not* everything." She pivots quickly on her heel and confronts Elijah as he stops shortly behind her.

He has several inches on her, but she stands straight and confident before him.

He sneers. "*You* love money. I give you status. We fucking rock this town because I know how to. You won prom queen and debutante queen because of me. I even booked your favorite singer for our wedding. I loaned your mother a fortune until I realized being *her* husband was not my role."

Astrid's eyes fall and so do her shoulders. "You've done a lot for me over the years. You helped us. But I can't do this anymore."

He grabs her arm and whispers harshly, "Get your head on straight."

She pulls back from his grasp so hard she almost topples over. Then she straightens herself and looks him in the eyes. "My soul is not happy. I want to sing in the shower."

Elijah's brows narrow. "*Happy?* No one here is together for happiness."

She steps out of her six-inch heels and spins around. "*I* want to be happy." There's a new sense of strength in her face.

Elijah interrupts her twirl and towers over her five-feet, two-inch stance. "Get your shit together or don't marry me."

"I'm not marrying you," she says through gritted teeth. "If I have to lose wealth and status to be happy, then so be it. I'm going to petition the board for *me* to be the co-CEO with my mother. This time will be different. I won't be stressed with wedding planning or the ball. Plus, I'm going to let Abby share her ideas for the business, too. If you say she's too young to know about our business, then you missed the memo of how the board is eating up the social buzz she created by escorting herself. Bravery is saving our family, not manipulation."

Elijah's laugh roars. "You don't break up with me. *I* break up with you!"

She grabs her shoes and prances back into the ballroom, not looking back. My mouth falls open. My sister found her voice. I always thought she had it, but this whole time, her voice wasn't hers until now.

Elijah stomps toward the lobby, cursing at a passerby.

I clap and cheer on the inside.

"We should go check on Astrid," I say to Hudson.

He nods and gives me a wink. "Lead the way, Your Highness."

Thirty-Three

On the dance floor, Grandpa's old, tired eyes find mine. A long, soft hug follows. His skin is warm against mine. He leans further, so much so, I almost topple over. With the help of my armrest, he stands up, smiling the way Papi used to.

He arrived a few minutes ago with Mother.

The father-daughter dance, a waltz with occasional hugging, is going lovely. Grandpa is the perfect partner. He murmurs sweet words in Spanish and his eyes sparkle like Papi's. I'm choked up for an entire minute.

When Hudson helps him back to the table, Grandpa insists he forgot something in the car. He hurries into the hall and Mother rushes after him.

Thankfully, she wasn't as furious as I thought she'd be seeing my expensive gown a little dusty.

Diana looks fabulous in the crown, twirling with Gustavo.

A lady in a fur coat and fabulously large diamond earrings wobbles toward us. Her breathing is louder than the surrounding chatter. Her sagging skin gives away her age, but the sharp taps from her gold cane keep a lively pace on the wooden floor.

"Hudson, is this your exquisite young lady?" Her Italian accent bounces between words. "Hudson has told me much about you."

I glance at him, blushing at the thought that he talks about me.

Hudson beams. "This is my nonna. I wanted her to meet you."

He helps her out of her coat and we gather at our table. Mr. Giordani nods, but doesn't offer any further greeting. Mrs. Giordani sits between the empty seats for Astrid and Mother.

Nonna gives me two kisses on each cheek.

"Hi," I say. "It's so nice to finally meet you."

"Hudson told me he wanted to do the ball for you and that I *must* meet you," she says, shaking my hand with both of hers.

"Really?" I ask with a laugh, suddenly feeling shy.

Hudson's wink sends shivers down my spine. Goose bumps run across my skin.

"He asked for my help to knit you something special."

My cheeks burn, wondering if he's crafting me another scarf.

Nonna leans close. "You like him, too?" she says in a loud non-whisper.

My nod is quick.

"Good. Now you kiss." She claps her hands together as if to instruct us how to do it. As if we should get to it right in front of everyone this very second.

Hudson doesn't waste a moment and plants a big one on me.

Nonna cheers us on until we're all laughing. Including Astrid, who has finally sat down with us.

When Grandpa returns, I make him a promise Papi would have wanted. "We're going to visit Spain this summer."

We haven't been back there in years, although Papi kept us updated on how our family there had been doing. I plan to pick up right where he left off.

Astrid swings over and wraps Grandpa in a big hug.

He pats the seat next to him and she sits. Slowly, he pulls out a journal from his jacket. It resembles the one Papi gave me.

"Your papi left this in Spain. You were supposed to find it —hunting a treasure, is that the saying?—on your next visit. When you couldn't come, he said leave it for the next time, you would have fun searching for it." Grandpa strokes her face. "But another visit never came. And your papi, he hid it well. Abuelita found it only this month."

Astrid practically falls to her knees. As she opens it, there's a scripture on the inside of the cover that's similar to mine.

Hudson pulls his hand out of mine, and only then do I realize I've been squeezing the life out of it.

Astrid looks at Mother and then at me. I mouth the words, "I *told* you he loved you." But she doesn't need my confirmation. She knows how much Papi loved her. If he could keep a gift secret for years just so she could go on a treasure hunt through Grandma and Grandpa's home, the one with zillions of nooks and crannies, well, she knows that really means something. Astrid loves treasure hunts. Or at least she used to.

Theo robot dances into our view. "You rocked, Abby."

"Thanks," I say and ask for a picture with him.

We pose on the dance floor for a selfie just as Hudson rounds our space.

The two keep silent until Hudson says, "Good job." He runs a hand through his hair, nodding.

Theo nods in rhythm with Hudson. "Yeah, you too, man."

Whether or not they're past their feud, there is only up from here.

Hudson leans over to me and whispers, "I should ask my father to work at his company while he's in a good mood. I'll come visit you at your after-party." A wink accompanies that statement.

I'm not having an after-party. "Okay." I giggle and think about what is running through his mind.

I watch him go, excited for the next time I see him.

Joey snaps lots of pictures of the crowd and the decorations. Including selfies, but mostly of herself even though Talia is here, who too, is busy on her phone. Their families had bought a table together, along with Diana's family.

"Joey!" I holler. "Take a picture with me."

She jogs over. "Yeah!"

Theo does the honors and takes a few close-up shots.

Joey stands up and glides into his personal space. "Theo! Are you into threesomes?"

He chuckles, blushing, and takes a step back. "What?"

In a flash, she leans into his ear and whispers something.

"You want to date me?" Theo says so loud, Joey's face reddens.

"Talia and I broke up yesterday. I heard you're a great shoulder to cry on." She soft punches right above his bicep. "Why do you think I shower at the aquatic center? To see you regularly."

Theo blushes harder and throws me a glance. I nod in approval.

He swallows hard and shrugs a shoulder. "Okay, Joey."

She throws her arm around him and they walk off.

I'd say they'll be kissing in a day or two. I can't wait to see where it goes.

Diana skips by me. "Come here."

I roll around, letting her take my hand.

Diana's younger sister, Layla, rolls by in her wheelchair. We wave and do a silly dance.

"I can't wait to be a debutante," Layla says with a huge smile.

Her mom leans down. "Sweetie, you're in a wheelchair and that's hard for a debutante."

Layla sighs and slouches in her chair.

"Mrs. Sevyani?"

She meets my gaze.

"We need queens in wheelchairs, so let Layla fight for what she wants. Change paves the way for great futures," I say.

Layla spins in a bigger circle. "Thank you, Queen Abby. I can't wait!"

The giggling Layla twirls side to side with her father.

As I snap a picture of them, Diana dances into my path and places her crown on me. "Your turn to be queen."

"Thank you." It slides toward my ear and I straighten it. "How about we give it to Pyper and she can snap some pictures and then pass it on to the next girl?"

Diana claps and goes to do just that.

Pyper hugs Diana and they take several selfies together.

I close my eyes for a moment, taking it all in. This was the perfect night. The most unexpectedly magical night.

I glance through a window and watch a flickering star in the sky. Papi was here, undoubtedly making that magic happen.

Thirty-Four

WHEN WE ARRIVE BACK HOME, I make sure Grandpa gets help from Zaney, my night nurse, with whatever he needs. I give him a soft kiss on the cheek and vow to spend every second I can with him this weekend.

"Sweet dreams." I wave him off and sigh.

"*Buenas noches, princesa*," he says with a smile.

I turn to Zaney. "Just change me out of my dress in thirty?" That should give her enough time to help Grandpa.

Astrid will arrive later, after she makes sure all the debutantes and escorts are safely on their way home. Mother wants to make sure the board members are safely on their way home as well. Along with convincing them that Elijah was irresponsible and emotionally unstable for storming out of the ball.

A tap sounds below me. The loose pearl rolls on the wooden floor. I lean over my armrest and squeeze it between my fingers.

I can't toss it into my purse. It belongs around my neck. I spot a white spool Tommy must have forgotten on the dining table. It's only fitting for me to craft myself a new jewelry piece.

After I weave the thread through the pearl, I roll into the main bathroom where I first tried on the dress. I loop the string around my neck and tie it.

I rub the one pearl, wanting to gift the same necklace to everyone: Mother, Astrid, Joey, Diana, Layla, Theo, Hudson, Bentley, Pyper . . .

To give new life to the memories of yesterday so others can make their own traditions and new histories.

The smudges and gray spots on my gown glow under the bright light. I'm sure my chest and neck have traces of dust as well. Somehow, this imperfection turned out to be just perfect.

"Knock, knock."

I dart my eyes to Hudson.

"Need help taking that off?" he asks in a harsh but warm whisper.

I'm more than comfortable, empowered even, to have him do so. To have him look at my nakedness.

"I do, but what will I change into?"

"Well." Hudson slips his backpack off his shoulders and swings it around. "How about this? I thought about you every day ever since we ran into each other in the woods. When I couldn't get you out of my head, I put needle to yarn." He pulls out a knitted white and blue dress.

A note accompanies it.

Made to fit your every insecurity and vulnerability, which shines with a beauty of its own.

The soft garment rests on my lap. I trace the bumps under my fingers.

"Ready?" He sweeps my hair over my shoulder and unbuttons the first pearl button in the back.

"Yes," I say in a sexual way even though I don't mean anything by it. "I'm not scared of you seeing me naked." Not anymore.

As I hold my hair to the side, he works his fingers down as quickly as a running treadmill. His hands draw over my curved spine. His touch, his hands on me, unlock every vulnerability in me. And I can't wait for him to see all sides of me.

The front of the gown opens up like a flower, uncovering my beige, strapless bra.

Hudson pushes the dress further down my waist and then his fingers dig around my buttocks. I grip onto his neck and he lifts me enough to slide the dress down my legs. Goose bumps cover my uneven hips. I shiver ever so slightly.

He sets me back in my seat and for a two-second stare, I let him gawk at me. He maps out every inch with those hazel eyes. When he can't look away, I feel so sexy.

He blushes and I smile, handing him the knitted outfit so he can dress me in it.

"It'll keep you warm," he says and clears his throat. Then he slips the soft fabric over my head, down my shoulders, and around my hips. The sleeveless dress rounds under my armpits and falls to my legs enough to cover the knees.

I admire each detail of the design. "It fits my every curve perfectly," I say. "Thank you." One day, I'm going to knit him something. It won't be an outfit, but maybe a mitten. Or better yet: a holey scarf.

"Because *you're* perfect," he says, biting his lip. He kneels and wraps his arms tight around my waist.

I grab his shirt and pull him in for a kiss.

Our mouths move quickly. His tongue is warm and enticing when it meets mine. My skin feels softer when he touches me. My heart feels fuller when he holds me.

His tongue caresses mine, leaving me begging for more.

Then the kiss is hot and heavy, laced with spice. Electricity runs through me. It's so passionate and strong, I laugh into him.

Whatever lies ahead for us, I'm ready for it. With Hudson, I will live every day ready to take on anything.

When we part ways, he places a soft kiss on my forehead.

"Got plans for tomorrow?" I ask.

"Nope. But I have a feeling you do," he says and gives me that Hudson wink.

There's a sparkle in his eye, and I want to say the ultimate words of affection. But it scares me. He still scares me.

Leaning into me, he glides a hair behind my ear. "I don't want to make a single plan without you." There's a warmth to his words, his touch. Searching my eyes deeper, he whispers, "Because . . . I'm falling for you."

My mouth opens to say the same. "I'm falling for *you*."

Rubbing the single pearl around my neck, I exhale the past and inhale the present. There are no endings or beginnings, just moments strung together. Sometimes that string breaks and sometimes those pearls scatter. Sometimes the string breaks you and the pearls make you scatter. But when everything is tied back up and put in its place, you grow stronger. Life grows stronger inside of you as you become your own pearl moving down the string of life.

Epilogue

Dearest Papi,

It's been two months since the ball, and a year since you passed away. You wouldn't believe what happened with Hudson. He and Theo took a canoeing trip last month without killing each other. I've been volunteering at the senior center with Hudson. I even knitted a full scarf for him. Now we have matching holey scarfs. We're planning to visit Spain this weekend as a last vacation before I start senior year. I'm going to explore all of my career options this year and apply to work at the antiques store.

Diana is already planning to run for the science club secretary position. She broke up with Gustavo, said she needed to fully find herself and that meant being single. But he's taking her to homecoming as a friend. You should see my teal homecoming dress. Actually, you should see Joey's black and purple leather dress. She's started a tattoo business and Bentley has been helping her with branding, since he wants temporary whimsical tattoos for his big limo business launch. Theo is dating Joey and I'm happy they keep each other adventurous.

By the way, I asked Theo to fix my chair elevating bolt and exchange the battery.

Astrid just went on her first date since the Elijah breakup. Guess who got sued for forging the mayor's signature on a document? Elijah definitely won't be ruining our lives ever again. Mother has slowly put your things back in place at the mansion. The cabin has been a fun place for slumber parties with Astrid when Theo goes on trips with Joey. Next week, we're making Mother join in our campfire fun. I can't wait to make flower crowns and not talk about jewelry designs. It's overwhelming but at least we aren't losing money anymore.

I should get to my cup of hot chocolate. I miss you every day and think of how your love now lives on through me, Astrid, and Mother. We love and miss you!

Your Abby

Thank you!

ACKNOWLEDGEMENTS

Thank you to the INCLUDAS team, the editors, beta readers, and social media influencers who believed in this story.

ABOUT THE AUTHOR

L.S. Rydde is an author of YA contemporary romance who believes in true love and true love's first kisses. Writing this book gave Rydde the strength to fight for her freedom when using her own voice felt terrifying.

www.ingramcontent.com/pod-product-compliance
Lightning Source LLC
Chambersburg PA
CBHW020602260626
47157CB00003B/823